BOOMTOWN

A SOUTHSIDE HOOKER NOVEL — BOOK 4

BAER CHARLTON

Rogena Mitchell-Jones, Editor, www.rogenamitchell.com
Cover Artist: Nina Golemi
Cover Design: David L'Bearz
Laura Reynolds, Illustrator

ISBN-13:978-0-9849666-9-1 (paperback)
Published by Mordant Media, Portland, Oregon
10 9 8 7 6 5 4 3 — 2019 Edition

ALSO BY BAER CHARLTON

<u>NOVELS</u>

The Very Littlest Dragon: NEW 2019 Editions
(Newly edited editions available: an all-new full-color ebook, a paperback with coloring
pages, and a full-color Collector's Edition hardback)

Stoneheart
(Pulitzer Nominee 2015)

Angel Flights
What About Marsha?
Pirate's Patch
Dry Bridge of Vengeance

—

<u>SOUTHSIDE HOOKER SERIES</u>

Death on a Dime – Book One
Night Vision – Book Two
Unbidden Garden – Book Three
Boomtown – Book Four
One Day Under the Grass – Book Five

Southside Hooker Series: Books 1–5 Box Set
(Collector's Edition hardback & ebook available)

—

<u>THORNY WALLACE SERIES</u>

Death in the Valley – Book One
Light to Light – Book Two

CONTENTS

Box   vii

1. Boomtown   1
2. Drunks and Ice Cream   7
3. Breakfast at the Hacienda   15
4. Another Bomb   27
5. Blood Alley   31
6. Breakfast at Sweets   43
7. Frontier Village   49
8. Milpitas Regrets   63
9. Going North   69
10. Quiet on the Home Front   75
11. Another Envelope   87
12. Bits and Pieces on the Mudflats   93
13. Slop in the Streets   105
14. Dolly's Table and a Colorado Plate   113
15. Helmut's Son   125
16. Can You Tow A Train?   133
17. Cog in a Larger Crime   139
18. Pulling Railcars   145
19. Coffee Run   155
20. They Took Her   167
21. Revenge   175
22. Word from Colorado   183
23. The Delivery Van   195
24. Wake Up the Neighbors   203
25. New Developments   213
26. Paint and Deception   219
27. Where Did He Go?   225
28. Rigging   249

29. What to do with a 3-day Weekend   257
30. Dirt and Bombs   265
31. Boom   269
32. End of the Line   279
33. What to do about Mae   285

SNEAK PEEK

One Day Under the Grass   289

Baer Charlton   300
About the Author   301

BOX

No man knows what Hell drives another to do what he does until he toils in the bowels of the same mountain beside the other.

ANONYMOUS WELCH COAL MINER

BOOMTOWN

Milpitas was a thug town. The reputation didn't bother Felix. In fact, he liked it. Felix knew he was a thug, and so he fit in—disappeared. Felix hadn't always been a thug, and he hadn't grown up in Milpitas. He found Milpitas because of its reputation, and he had worked hard to fit into the reputation.

His left hand held a winding of solder as the tip of the small soldering iron in his right hand turned the wire into a tiny bead of liquid silver. The solder melted and flowed around the connected wires to form a solid electrical bond. It became an almost indestructible joining, which only three ounces of custom cooked explosives could, and would tear apart... which was the idea. The formed wires would become so many three-inch pieces of thin metal wire... easily missed in the rubble of what used to be a building.

The cool evening was turned colder by the low mist from the San Francisco Bay. The chilly mist was pushed down the bay by the inflow of sea air squeezed between the Marin County hills to the north and the hills of the city of

San Francisco, south of the Golden Gate. This natural squeeze gave the gentle breezes more power as they moved the colder air south over the late winter bay. Milpitas was aligned to receive more than its fair share of the bone-numbing chill, but Felix knew from experience the real cold weather was soon to come. Summer on the San Francisco Bay could rival the cold of many winters elsewhere.

As the light breeze blew into the screened sleeping porch where Felix worked, it drew out a rare smile from the man's face. It reminded him of the shoulder seasons in his childhood home of Colorado. He slid his bare feet into the thick wool slippers his sister had made for him, the sister who still lived on—and clung desperately to—the family ranch. The sister, who still believed, even at forty-eight, her prince would someday come and help her on the ranch, herding the cows and sheep so she could milk the goats.

Felix's toes curled and dug at the home-sheared, washed and carded wool. He humored himself to think his toes could feel the difference in the yarns where her thumbs worked the spin instead of the looser, small fingers in a trailing feed of the large wheel spinning wheel. The small upright would have given her more consistent yarn, but she insisted on using the spinning wheel, which was taller than she stood—because it was the one their grandfather had made for their grandmother when she had to leave hers behind in Boston.

The sweet smell of rosin in the soldering flux curled up from the last soldered connection. Unplugging the small iron, Felix placed the iron in the holder and gently placed the remaining wad of soldering wire in the cubby next to the iron's cubby.

The last of the forty pieced-together wires were complete. In less than a week, they would just be small pieces of copper once again. Bits and pieces easily lost amongst the debris after an explosion in a store. He pushed them into a long cubby set into the porch's exterior wall.

Felix pulled a square box from its cubby. The box contained tiny vials made of thin glass, the size of a large vitamin pill. He withdrew the first vial and wiggled the small pea-sized drop of mercury inside. He smiled at the memory of coming up with this way to make a progressive explosion without long wires or fuses. The mine he and his father had been sealing up was over a mile long. They had wanted not just to seal the entrance but to collapse the entire tunnel.

The problem was they did not have enough wire to make the multiple runs of wire back to progressive loads of explosives. Felix figured out the small capsule of mercury inside a little plastic pouch to be nailed or stapled to the timbers. Stuck in the bottom of the pouch were two wires hooked to a battery. When the concussion wave from the first explosion hit the tiny pouch, it shattered the glass capsule, and the mercury closed the connection between the wires.

This set off the next explosion, which set off the next—until the entire mine tunnel had been destroyed with less than one hundred feet of wire and a few small batteries.

Felix had soldered the short wires to a small stack of watch batteries. These would be connected to the blasting caps during the setup. There was just enough energy to set off the tiny blasting cap igniting the larger package of explo-sives. Felix smiled as he slipped each glass vial into the plastic pouch, sealing it all with a touch of clear fingernail polish, completing the small pressure switches.

This next job would only require sixty of the small compression switches and a few of the larger explosive triggers. The bottles of propane and white gas in the sporting goods store would do the rest of the job for him. The idea was to create many small indistinct explosions, which would become untraceable, instead of one or two large explosions that would leave a traceable starting point at the center of a blast ring. Felix's success came from his explosions going unexplained—unlike arson that would reek of accelerant and have definite start points.

Felix looked at the clock, stood up, and pulled on a brown uniform shirt over his white sleeveless undershirt. He checked the polish on his boots and picked up his keys. Putting the last items in their proper cubbies, he placed the sections of boards back on the wall. He felt as much as heard the click of the small, rare earth magnets drawing the boards into place. The wall looked as it had for the last sixty or eighty years... once painted but now left to chip and weather. He peeked in his now empty coffee mug. He had hoped for one last swallow. He would pick up a couple of donuts and more coffee on his way to work.

Walking in front of the old dining table pushed to the wall and used as his workbench, he pulled the strings on the two old gooseneck desk lamps. Reaching the door, he turned back for one last check. Everything looked the same. It was a musty, almost bare, seldom-used screened porch just like dozens of other porches rimming the bay.

He turned off the overhead light and gently closed the door. The key clicked in the lock, and then the house joined the early morning silence, muffling the retreat of the crepe-soled boots down the hall toward the front door.

The stork standing on the end of the grass fluffed its feathers about its head and resumed sleeping. Dawn was still hours away. The foghorn on the Golden Gate Bridge started its early morning ritual. The long lonely sound echoed down the bay and blended with the engine of the old panel truck starting and finally crunching its way down the gravel driveway.

2

DRUNKS AND ICE CREAM

The cross wrench spun in Hooker's left hand then stopped. He moved it to the next lug nut and spun it with his right hand again. This was quiet work Hooker did without looking. Spin one, skip one, spin one, skip one, and one around the wheel. He looked up at the man weaving drunkenly. Even at quarter past four, the man was well past the limit of anything close to preserving composure. Hooker figured the man had hit close to toxic levels at two o'clock when some bar threw him out. With luck, he would get back behind the wheel and simply pass out before he could start the car.

Hooker let down the jack and restored it to the back of his truck. The giant vehicle was three times longer than the man's Chevelle and weighed six times more. To someone who didn't understand Hooker, they would have thought the truck, nicknamed Mae West, was overkill for a flat tire, but for an auto club driver, these 'T-1' calls were the 'T-wonderful' butter and jam lining the bread of Hooker's living. Hooker only got $3.12 for the tire change while Mae burned through almost a gallon—or sixty cents of fuel—but it all added up at the end of the night. The dead batteries, flat tires, and 'locked my keys in the car' were the auto club calls keeping Hooker busy during the night when he didn't have a wreck or commercial, and therefore, more profitable tow.

Lately, his nights had been nothing but the sparse butter and not much bread. The dead business wasn't what was eating at him—it was the quiet.

Hooker dropped the trunk on the Chevelle and turned toward the drunk. "Okay, sir. You're all set except twenty-six bucks."

The man fished some wadded bills from his pocket, leaning back against the car. He fingered through the money. Finally, looking up, he held out two twenties. His speech was massively slurred.

"Does this cover it?"

Hooker realized the man could not even tell what the bills were. He sighed. The man was beyond redemption. Still, Hooker could hear Candy's voice comforting these same kinds of people where she worked at the all-night diner. It was one of the main reasons Hooker had been drawn to her.

He leaned into the fog of alcohol from the man's lungs. "Let's see what you have here," Hooker said, not unkindly, as he fished through the man's bills and found the five and one to go with one of the twenties. Gently taking the rest, he pushed the bills down into the man's pants pocket so they did not end on the ground.

"Here, let's get you into the backseat for a nice nap, shall we?" He started to guide the man into the back of the two-door. It would make it harder for the guy to get back into the driver's seat.

"I have to be at work at eight o'clock," the man slurred.

"I think this is going to be a sick day for you today." Hooker watched as the man took the direction and stretched out on the small bench seat in the back. The first snore was wafting its way out the door as Hooker quietly eased it shut after sticking the keys on top of the visor.

Hooker grabbed the microphone from behind his head as he drew his left leg up into the cab of the truck.

"1-4-1."

"1-4-1?"

"Show me 10-97 on this red Chevelle, and you might advise PD, I put the guy in the backseat to sleep it off. Hopefully, he'll stay there until the afternoon brings him a huge headache. If an officer checks on him, warn them not to be smoking within twenty feet of the guy's breath."

The young dispatcher giggled. "10-4, Hooker... drunk at Pearl and Blossom Hill. Will advise PD and at least, have them watch so the car doesn't wander off. We aren't holding anything for you at this time. Dolly says Stella and Manny are playing gin right now, so you have a choice of breakfast with them or leftover beef stew here."

Hooker dropped his right hand and found the single ear of his partner. The twenty-plus pounds of orange tabby started to purr. Hooker looked toward the eastern hills. He knew there would be nothing left for the night unless someone decided to park creatively on the freeway.

He keyed the mic. "10-4, Dina. Tell Dolly thanks for the offer, but I think Box and I will mosey on down to the hacienda and see what creative thoughts Stella has in mind with last night's leftover barbecued pork."

Dolly's voice came back over the speaker. "If you're thinking of stopping by Thrifty's for any French vanilla ice cream—don't call back. I don't want Dina to go mush-brained on me her first week back."

Hooker snorted. The ice cream gave Hooker what Dolly called 'bedroom voice' and made the dispatch girls squirm in their seats. Dina had been out for a few months while she had her baby. Hooker was surprised to hear her voice back so soon, but he guessed the rumor might be true about IBM going through another round of layoffs.

"10-4, Mama. I wasn't thinking about ruining my break-fast with the folks."

Hooker hung the mic back behind his head and squeezed his left foot down on the clutch as he set the truck in sixth gear. Looking down at his partner, he smiled evilly. "How about it, Box? Should we go get some ice cream and then call Dina from the payphone?"

Box was always ready for his dab of ice cream in his small red bowl while Hooker usually got a triple scoop in a sugar cone. There were a few things Box always seemed ready for in life. Ice cream was right up there with beating the snot out of a dog or two and lying draped across the expanse of Dolly's chest. At nearly a quarter-ton, Dolly's exposed chest above her perpetual Muumuu was a perfect fit for a large cat and produced a lot of heat. Dolly was one of the few who could touch the cat—much less pick him up. Box was his own man and had very established preferences.

Hooker nosed the eleven tons of Mae West out onto the street and headed for Monterey Highway and their twenty-four-hour ice cream pit stop. The cops all joked (especially when the weather was bitter cold), about it being perfect weather for Hooker to show up at an accident with a triple scoop of French vanilla ice cream in a sugar cone with the window rolled down in the truck. Winter was when Hooker was at his most memorable.

Tonight, the window was down, and Hooker reached toward the small rack of eight-track tapes. His fingers hovered over Tex Ritter and then moved to the Riders. His forefinger and thumb even embraced the cassette, but then he leaned back in the seat, opting for the quiet of Mae West's 1,600 horsepower and the matching purr from below and beside his seat. He knew Box had his only eye closed and was leaning into the blast of heated air.

Hooker felt out of sorts.

A short but eventful year had started with him jamming his fork into a street punk's hand, which was stealing tips from Hooker's girlfriend. The punk turned out to be her younger brother, and Hooker ended up having to pack the kid around while his hand healed. Those fourteen days had been cut short when the kid saved Hooker's life. The indentured help eventually became the second set of intelligent hands and was now sleeping in a bed ten feet from one of Hooker's beds. Now the Squirt was attending the police academy, compliments of the San Jose Police, the Santa Clara sheriff, and the California Highway Patrol. All had lost officers to the serial killer the Squirt ended up killing.

Hooker was happy for the kid, and he would make a great cop... but now Hooker missed the warm body in the other seat.

As Hooker pulled up in front of the Thrifty Drugstore,

he could see the only two people standing at one of the check stands, talking. Hooker was sure the topic of conversation was either how the 49ers had been robbed or how the Oakland Raiders had become nothing more than thugs on the field. The manager was the 49ers fan, and the night cashier's uncle had once played a short career with the Raiders. For Hooker, it was the green light to break the health code law and let Box come in with him.

The manager, Randy, had heard stories about Box eating ice cream but had never met him. Holly had seen Box and always loved watching him delicately slurping his share.

Hooker grabbed the little red dish and swung open the door. "Come on, buddy. Show time."

The large cat slid between Hooker's legs and seat, beating him to the door. Holly was standing at the open glass door as Box strolled up.

"Well, hello, Box... Your place awaits." Looking up, the tall, athletic young woman smiled at Hooker. "We were just talking about beat-up street tuffs."

Hooker snorted. "Raiders tonight, eh? You know you'll catch your death of cold standing out here in the freezing weather."

Holly snorted a muffled laugh. "I love winter. I don't celebrate it with French vanilla ice cream and drive around with my window down, but it's my favorite time of the year." Hooker stopped and frowned. He could tell she was serious.

Still sober, she summed up her childhood. "When everything is cold or frozen, there are no rows to hoe, no smell of steer-blood or shit on the fields, and my hands are clean—or at least not stained black from gathering those stinking black walnuts." She followed Hooker into the store. "Nope, winter is my time to relax and enjoy—cold, rain, snow and all."

Randy chuckled as Hooker walked in with Box. "Actually, it's not the Raiders at all, this time. The ruling came out tonight and should be in the mercury this morning. They're going ahead and fining the Steelers and Green Bay for some of the underhanded stuff they pulled this year." He eyed the large orange body of fur and scars. "So this is Box?"

Hooker offered the man the small red bowl. "And this is the famous dish."

"Of course..."

Holly took the dish and headed for the ice cream counter. Hooker watched the way she moved. At almost six foot, she flowed with the fluid nature of a surfer who logged thousands of hours of water time off Capitola Point, except her hair was dark instead of blonde. Hooker knew her seemingly constant tan came more from working on the family truck farm in Gilroy since she was a tiny child, instead of any time floating around on a surfboard in the sun.

Hooker nudged Randy softly with his elbow. "How's the anatomy class coming, Holly?"

She looked up and smirked as she rolled her eyes. "Candy told you about...?" Looking down at the ice cream, she shook her head. "Yeah, of course, she would."

She set the dish down for Box and handed the cone to Hooker. "It was horrible *and* embarrassing. I don't skip lunch anymore. I'm sure they're already making up a nickname like Faint Girl, or something equally mean."

He gave her the famous Hooker one-sided smile. "Nah, I think you're good there. Nurses aren't mean by nature. After all, you didn't faint on the Squirt or anything like that." He watched as the deep red flushed up from under her shirt.

"What did John say?"

"Nothing. However, the day *he* was your massage body —he was very quiet for the rest of the day... So what did happen?"

Holly glanced at Randy, who held up his hands and rolled his eyes. "We're all adults here, Holly, and you know you don't have to share anything you don't want to. After all, I'm happily married, and it probably isn't anything I haven't experienced before."

Hooker could see her stiffen. "It wasn't anything sexu— well, you know. It was his scars." She blushed again. "I've never seen so many and so fresh... I-I urped."

Hooker stopped mid-lick. "You threw up? Where...?"

Holly was now in full flush. "In his pants." She realized how it sounded and rushed to explain. "They were on the floor."

Hooker pictured the scene and drew the final conclusion. "Which means he shucked them down around his boots..."

Holly buried her face in her hands and nodded, her voice muffled as she finished.

"I filled his boots as well."

3

BREAKFAST AT THE HACIENDA

Hooker parked the large truck on the thick driveway pad specifically built for her 22,000 pounds. As he grabbed his paperwork, he could feel Box's tail rubbing under the back of his knees as he absently opened the door. Set into the concrete pad the size of a gas station was a small patch of lawn. There was only one reason this existed. Box, hopping down, made it clear it was his turf.

Two doors down, the man who lived there had a young dog, barely more than a pup. For whatever reason, the dog's name was Mike. The owner had already suffered through Box coming down and beating the snot out of his previous older Doberman. Mike was a beautiful yellow Lab, and the man did not want cat scratches all over the young dog's mug. So the agreement was he would mow and edge the patch, and Hooker would keep Box at bay until Mike turned at least two.

Hooker hesitated to tell the man about Mike coming down, and Box taking a liking to the pup. Hooker had caught them more than once, wrestling quietly on the grass, which upfront to perfection. To keep up appearances, Hooker still called out loudly for Box to leave Mike alone until he was at least old enough to know fear.

Box threatened, Mike shied, Hooker bellowed, and the lawn stayed mowed and trimmed to excellence. Life was good in the neighborhood, except for the familiar '63 Dodge Dart convertible parked up close to the wall on the driveway instead of down in the garage where it belonged. At five in the morning, there had to be an explanation. Hooker looked at the heavy morning dew collected on the cold car.

As he walked through the front plaza with the fountain, Hooker could see it had been another one of those nights. Eight years since a bullet shattered its way through his spine, putting him in a wheelchair, and ending his career as a police detective, Manny was still dogged by nightmares.

As he reached the door, the angle was just right. Stella could see him from the kitchen counter, and she reached for his mug. Hooker knew she had heard the heavily baffled exhaust of Mae West and was prepared.

When Hooker remembered, he switched the exhaust to the 'silencer' as they climbed the hill filled with expensive homes. But as he settled her in on the parking pad, he ran her in standard exhaust for a minute to clear her pipes and make it easier to start.

Hooker opened the heavy front door, and the orange streak beat his foot to the interior of the slate floor.

"Lucy...you have some 'splainin' to do..." His Cuban accent was terrible, but his imitation of Ricky Ricardo never missed securing at least one smile from the family.

As he closed the door to the silence of being ignored, a slender hand grabbed his left butt cheek.

The immediate laughing of the three others helped to mask his high-pitched squeal of fear. Spinning, he found Candy still in pink pajamas with little red hearts. He settled down and grabbed her laughing neck in the crotch of his elbow and drew her in as she tried to wiggle out of his grasp. The giggling got worse as his right boot tried to swing up in a good-natured backhand slap. They danced in the entry much to the amusement of Manny and Stella. It was good to see the two having some pure laughter. Hooker knew, all too often, it was just the opposite.

"What are you doing up this early, you little scamp?"

Stella put his mug of coffee down on the table next to Candy's. "She was in your room..."

Hooker looked up and over at Manny. The man was nodding and no longer smiling. It was his 'I'm not going to talk about this' face. Hooker eased the arm grip on the now messed up head of hair. He leaned over and kissed the top.

Quietly, he muttered only for Candy, "It's something we all have to get used to around here."

Candy looked Hooker in the eyes and nodded slightly as he let her go.

Hooker frowned as he looked back down toward the hall leading to his bedroom suite as well as the Squirt's room at the end.

Candy snorted. "Are you kidding? The Squirt wake up from just a tiny little scream? Hah! Try a bomb, maybe."

The sound of the muffled zombie came through the door as it opened. "I heard that, sis, and for your information, I was already up and studying."

Hooker spun around and laughed. The Squirt had not come from his bedroom but had been in Manny's office. "Good morning, sweet cheeks. Holly says hi."

The kid blushed but smirked as he carried a large coffee mug toward the dining and kitchen area. "She owes me a massage... and dinner." He shuffled over to side-hug Stella and got a kiss on the top of his head as he poured more coffee. Turning, he looked at Manny as Hooker and Candy —still playing mild grab-ass—took the morning side of the table. "If I place the evidence bag on my desk and go to the bathroom for a couple of minutes, the chain of evidence is broken... but if I throw it in the bottom drawer, and leave on vacation for two weeks, it's not."

"Implied reasonable circumstances of security."

"But if I didn't lock the desk, where is the security?"

"I said, *implied*. I did not say it *was* secure."

"...and so it's defendable in court?"

Manny leaned back in his chair. Hooker knew the Squirt being at the academy invigorated the old detective as nothing else could. The man's eyes were electric with possibilities and training.

"I can think of a couple of great lawyers in the counties who I wouldn't try to run this past, but for most of the bucket-scum oozing through the courts today... sure, I'd run it."

Candy looked at Hooker. Hooker shrugged and wobbled his open spread hand. The meaning was maybe he understood and maybe not. There were a lot of cop protocols Hooker had picked up over the years. Some of those were the fine details of being a cop that did not matter to Hooker's job, but he still picked up from being around Manny, as well as other cops, for so many years.

"It's like if I tow a car and leave it on the street outside a shop's fence, then someone breaks in and steals the radio or something, it's on my insurance. But if I park it in their parking lot, the implied is, I left it in their care—even though I didn't stick it in their locked yard."

The Squirt snorted a laugh. "What about stashing trailers and cars in Safeway's parking lot?"

Hooker shot him an evil smile. "As long as I don't leave a trailer full of color TVs in the median dirt area in the middle of the 101. But then it goes on the trucking company's insurance. Their assurance was for the driver not to break down and to safely deliver the TVs to the stores—which he didn't."

Manny laughed as he remembered the incident. "Wasn't it Ace who left it there after the Chips had cleared it?"

Hooker laughed then saw Candy was lost. "Ace got a tow. The Chip hauled the driver away because he found a second time-log in the cab—that he searched after the guy failed to walk the white line. Drunk or too many hours on the road still makes you a ticking time bomb.

"Anyway, the Chip had pulled the guy over because he was high-balling in the fast lane on the 101 in the section where they have to stay in the two slow lanes. So the guy pulls off into the middle play area. The truck Ace is driving is only a deuce and a half—a two-and-a-half ton truck, and can only take the tractor and trailer one at a time. He uncouples the rig and hauls off with the tractor to go stash it somewhere close. He gets back, and the back doors are swung open... and a whole lot of tire tracks everywhere. He was gone, maybe twenty minutes..."

Manny snorted. "Which was about ten more than was needed."

Hooker tried to calm down and finish, but he was laughing too hard.

Stella just wagged her head. "There were just nine TVs left in the whole trailer." She held up her hands about a loaf of bread apart. "You know those little black and white TVs you get for a kid's room or something?"

The Squirt finished the punch line. "Only then was when Ace looked at the side of the forty-foot trailer. The whole thing was one big billboard. It said 'Another Load of Fine Zenith Color Televisions.'"

It was not clear if everyone was laughing at Candy's horror-struck face or the story, but Stella could not get up to start breakfast for at least five minutes.

As she stepped to the sink and from the corner of her eye, she saw a person just leaving from the front door across from the entrance plaza. She stepped over to the next window to see them walking out through the front gates, which pierced the fourteen-foot tall wall enclosing the plaza.

"Hooker, the Sunday Missile just got hand-delivered to the front door. Would you be a dear and find out why?"

The Sunday Missile was the only newspaper they got all week. Mostly, it was because Stella did not want Manny to cruise all the crime news. He was seven years retired with full disability, and still, the urge to figure out crimes was only held below the surface by his thinning skin. It was bad enough Hooker occasionally dragged home cases the police had no competence or interest in solving.

Stella saw Hooker glance at the newspaper and then run

toward the street. A few minutes later, he returned, picked up the paper, and came back in.

Stella's question was written on her face as she stood with her hands splayed on the large stone island's top. Hooker deadpanned and quietly offered out the large roll of newspaper in the plastic condom. They stood staring—both holding deadpan faces—the battle was on.

Finally, Stella realized she would have to heighten the conflict. "Did you want breakfast with your girlfriend?"

"Remember Lloyd Summers?"

She nodded. "Retired about two years ago... What about him?"

"He's your new missile boy. He got bored with fishing every day... and wanted something exciting to do. Out of respect, your missile will be placed, not thrown, at your doorstep every Sunday. I'm sure if you want, he'd even bring it in and place it in your hands. But then, you might have to give him coffee, and the others would get their paper late." Hooker smiled his quirky grin. He knew he had won the battle, and he loved stroking Stella's heart at the same time.

"I'll call his wife later. If the door's open, he's always welcome to coffee. He and his wife have done their share of canning in our backyard."

Hooker's face collapsed. "He got the job because... she passed away a few months ago. He sold the boat and moved back up from Monterey. Evidently, he fished because she loved to fish."

Stella looked at Hooker as she thought. "The door will always be unlocked on Sunday mornings." She looked over at Manny, who just nodded with his eyelids. Cops were always family. It was the reason Stella started what had become a huge canning project involving hundreds of volunteers. Every year, they helped can many tons of food, which was then stashed in large storage larders about the city—for those in need. What had started for comrade cops in need had grown larger through firefighters, city workers, county workers, and other civil servants. As Stella always told people, those in need are the only family ties needed.

With breakfast finished and cleared, the household settled down into a quiet routine. The Squirt was sequestered back in the office. The large, professional reel-to-reel tape recorder oozed out classical music into the equally professional-grade headphones. Pages of textbooks were turned and memorized. There were four large stacks of books. As the Squirt memorized a book, it went into the correct box to be returned. The boxes were labeled: County Library, Paul—the County Commissioner over all police matters, Chet—a California Highway Patrol captain, or he simply stood and returned the book to the proper space on the office's bookshelf.

With his photographic memory, he had no reason to mark them up or keep them or bother with reading them in any certain order. Every book was read, memorized, and ready for almost instant recall. What the Squirt would like to happen was to forget most of his growing up with his sister as much-abused foster children.

What the two had stumbled into was Hooker—and his family. Hooker and his sister had also grown up in the worst the foster care system had to offer. Like the Squirt and Candy, Hooker and his sister had ended their torture in foster care at the ripe age of fourteen and sixteen respectably. John was uncertain, but he had a feeling it was the commonality which first drew Hooker toward Candy at the all-night diner she was working at then.

On the other side of the wall, Hooker slept the sleep of the dead, with a soft slender arm thrown over his side. Candy had her nose buried in the back of his neck and hair and behind her knees, curled into a large orange furry package, lay Box. Even as a small kitten—which had not lasted long—he had a way of taking over the bed, and Hooker had taken to closing the door so he could have the bed to himself.

The large sunroom was off the dining area. Manny and Stella had designed it for afternoon lazy lounging days. The custom-made couch was a large "L" shape running for fourteen feet along the solid wall and then hooked left, running another twelve feet under the south wall of windows. The floor-to-ceiling wall of glass looked east across the Almaden Valley, and the south looked down the valley. The two had bought the large property back when the road was nothing but a dirt track. They would bounce their way up to their knoll just to picnic and gaze upon the unmolested valley. Later, they built their dream home, as did so many others. Eventually, the developers came and overbuilt the beautiful valley into just another tract of ticky-tacky boxes. However, the Romeros had their slice of heaven and were not interested in leaving. Therefore, they had designed the hacienda with its two-foot thick adobe walls and windows open to the expansive view and morning sun. The large expanse of lounging area, enough for the whole family, was a bonus.

"Huh." Manny almost sat up. The effort was too much, and he resumed his relaxed state. He waited.

The large grandfather clock in the dining and entryway great room ticked with its dull metered pace. Manny pinched his thumb on the line of news and continued to read. A few minutes later, he heard the other section of the newspaper slowly fold down at one corner.

He never had to look to know his wife's eye was studying him through the space where the corner of newsprint had been a moment before. She waited.

"It says here the old sporting goods store out on the Guadalupe had a gas explosion last night. Evidently, one of the propane canisters was defective and blew up. It must've set off a chain of other stuff because it's a total loss."

The newsprint in Stella's hand curled the rest of the way down into her lap as she reached out to the coffee table for more of what she called *her thinking liquid*. She sipped slowly as Manny waited.

The two had married just at the beginning of the Korean War. They were married on the dock by an Army Padre right before Manny boarded the troopship. On his return, they had slowly gotten used to the mechanics of how they collectively thought about things. As Manny's old partner used to tease, Manny got more productive deducing accomplished on a Sunday afternoon at home with Stella—than he did with the whole squad all week.

Manny never told Paul just how close to the truth he was.

"About two months ago..." Her hand and mug hovered in the air.

"...upper Stevens Creek Boulevard area..."

"... a machine shop or something?" Stella took another sip.

"Some kind of manufacturing..."

"...but it was natural gas or something..." She put her mug on the table and then leaned back into the couch.

The clock ticked. The minds both ground along.

"But it never caught fire... just exploded."

There were a couple of minutes of silence, and then the newspapers returned to their positions.

Across the valley, a bald eagle searched one of the last fields, hovering and watching for the tiny spot of red that meant movement. The predator was patient as he waited for the mouse or mole to move again. The wan winter sun did not heat the ground anymore, so the bird would only need the last twitch or step to zero in its targeting. The rodent was caught—they just didn't know it yet.

4

ANOTHER BOMB

Felix slid the key into the door. Through the tiny window, he could see there was another fat envelope. Two in one month—someone was in a hurry. He didn't mind the extra money, but there was always the risk someone would put explosions together and see patterns.

He opened the mailbox door and withdrew the envelope. This was the only reason he had this mailbox account—fat envelopes with instructions and money—lots of money.

Felix closed the little door and turned the key. Slipping the large envelope under his shirt and down the back of his pants, he fluffed the tail of his work shirt and walked out of the store. He wouldn't look at the envelope again until he was on his screened porch and safe from prying eyes.

The afternoon hadn't improved the light drizzle. Felix guessed there must be a large storm coming out of Alaska, pushing the cold down into the Bay Area. The weather in February usually could get nicely calm and allow the sun to bring the temperatures up into the balmy fifties. Felix thought of it as T-shirt weather.

The 1949 Ford panel truck squealed and creaked as the man nosed it off the street and up the gravel driveway. The salt air didn't help any of the offenses visited on the old truck, but they did no worse than the once or twice a year hosing down Felix squandered on what had once been his work truck. The house paint slapped on the side panels barely hid the old signage of *Rocky Mountain Mine Services*. Even the lead paint was taking a beating from the Back Bay's brackish salt air. The truck's once glossy finish had taken on a matching appearance to the house.

Felix turned the key to the left, and the old engine chugged and rattled its way to silence. The man's hands hung in his lap. His shoulders curled from a long-endured weight. He was home, and there was no joy in it. He looked over at the equally battered Volkswagen. He ran his fingers through his already graying hair. At forty-seven, Felix felt he and the two vehicles had seen better days. His left hand pulled the door handle up as his right hand grabbed his lunch pail, just another battered reminder from a better time.

As Felix walked the short walk to the entrance, the door opened. The scrawny woman in the threadbare coat with hair to match jerked her way out as she pulled the door closed behind her.

"I got her fed and bathed today. She be 'n fresh diapers now and was already sucking at her blanket when I left her. Sorry I can't stay longer, but I'z gots ta get home to my babies."

Not once did the woman look up. Her sunken features

were as threadbare as her clothes. Felix called over his shoulder. "Thanks, Edwina. See you tomorrow."

The rusted German relic rattled to life with a few pops, and the transmission whined as she backed out of the driveway onto the road. She ground the gears like every day and then drove off down the road just as fast as she had backed out of the driveway.

Felix closed the door. Not much ever changed.

He looked into the small room. He would turn off the tiny nightlight later. He stood listening to what was left of his wife of twenty-nine years as she suckled on the corner of one of the blankets. In an hour or two, she would be mercifully asleep. He drew the door mostly closed so the light from the other room would not intrude.

Almost to himself, he whispered to his love, "Sleep well, Thelma."

Felix stepped out onto the screened sleeping porch. He pulled the strings on the two gooseneck lamps. Drawing the envelope out from his back, he settled heavily onto his chair. He looked at the return address. The man or the address had moved from Fremont to San Leandro. Felix guessed neither was true. The pinched handwriting was the same as when it made out paychecks to the miners in Colorado.

Felix absentmindedly reached under the table. His fingers curled around to the backside of the table's apron and found the knife held there by two magnets. He slit the top of the large envelope and carefully poured out the contents. He fished about the pile with the knife. There was nothing there that could hurt him—just all of it. He placed the knife back on the magnets and began to read.

An hour later, he folded up the letter and maps and

placed them in the envelope. He removed the boards from the wall and stuck the folded envelope into an empty cubby. Fanning through the three bundles of bills, he then stuck the $30,000 into another cubby and sealed up the wall.

Turning off the two lights, he rose and walked to the end of the porch. The iron bed squeaked as he sat to take off his boots. As he stretched out, pulling the two blankets over himself, he listened to the night noises of the bay. There would be a lot of work to do in the next week.

5

BLOOD ALLEY

Bill Talbert walked through the large entryway of the main offices. He waved at the guard who was always there. They changed, but on Sundays, they seemed always to be the same—the stupid one, the old one, the zit-faced one, or they simply drew the short straw. It had to be a mind-numbing boring job... the job a person would have to be severely desperate to take.

Bill turned right down the second hall. He chuckled sadly about the guards. Since graduating from MIT, he never had to take a job he did not want. The recruiter came to him from Advanced Systems when he was a senior. When Connie was pregnant with their first child, she did not want to deal with the snows in Boston anymore. They had taken a vacation once to San Francisco, and she had fallen in love with the Bay Area. Bill picked up the phone, and two weeks later, IBM was moving their new engineer across the continent.

At the end of the long hall, he fumbled with his key to the Ram Core Design wing. Entering the large open area used for brainstorming, he walked along the southern row of small offices. Sundays were his time to get some serious work done in the silence. He reached his office and opened the door.

Putting his briefcase and coat on the couch, he turned to his desk. There was an envelope in the middle of the desk. Typed in the middle was his name. He opened the envelope and withdrew the letter and check. He glanced at the letter and then sat down heavily in the chair and reread. He looked up at the large clock in the main room, positive the long blur was both hands pointing in the two o'clock position.

Three o'clock was early for the phone to ring at the Romero hacienda. Manny mumbled into the wireless extension in the sunroom. He listened as he saw the door to his office open. He nodded his head toward the hall at the Squirt. "Yeah, Karen. The Squirt is getting him now. How bad...?"

He reached over. Pulling and dragging, he sat up with his legs hanging over the couch edge. Stella had one eye half-open—watching him. She never trusted phone calls at the wrong hours.

Hooker walked into the office with only his jeans on. His voice joined the conversation. "Hooker."

"Hooker, Karen. CHP rolled up three minutes ago. A single car heading south—crossed the line into a set of doubles. First response says at least a dozen vehicles and three are rigs."

"Blood Alley again... "

"10-4, Hooker, just south of IBM. I'll call Jose for you—the car punched a cab-over, and witnesses estimate he was going well over eighty. The cab-over sounds like toast, but there are also the other two rigs—"

Hooker didn't even listen to the last part. He hung up on her and moved to his bedroom. As he turned into the room, the end of the hall caught his eye. The Squirt was already dressed and pulling on his boots... not the police academy boots, but his real work boots.

Candy lay curled in the blankets, but both eyes were open.

"Large pile-up out by IBM..."

"Blood Alley..." Nobody lived in the South Bay for longer than a month before they knew and understood the name applied to the worst eight miles of highway—two lanes of highway separated by a set of double six-inch yellow lines. The new 55mph speed limit did nothing to slow down the drunks, sleepers, or suicides who had no respect for the people on the other side of the lines. When a car crosses the line traveling at 60mph and slams into another going in the opposite direction at 60mph, the combined kinetic energy is five tons of steel moving at 120mph comes to an instant rest at zero. The energy has to go somewhere. Hooker knew from street education the smaller energy would now be buried and flattened into the tractor of the truck and trailers. The engine of the truck would be pushed up into the cab or possibly out the back of the cab if it were one of the thin cabs called stand-ups.

Hooker dropped a fast kiss as he slid his feet into the boots with the tops of the socks turned over the rims of the top. He didn't even check to see if his T-shirt was fresh—it wasn't. It was the same one he had worn all day and night from the previous day.

Turning, he strode through the door as his left hand grabbed the leather jacket off of the hook. The Squirt strode by in identical uniform—black leather jacket over a starched white T-shirt, tucked into jeans over eleven-inch-tall engineer boots.

The Squirt made the corner and grabbed the doorknob. "Box. Go time." He looked back with a self-satisfied smile at Hooker with his lips poised to say the same thing.

The large orange streak was out the door before either of them.

Hooker smiled back at Candy as she stood hanging in the corner at the end of the hallway. She blew him a kiss with her hand. Hooker watched the Squirt grab the hammer and start pounding a fast route on the tires, checking for flats or wrong inflation. Even in a hurry, it is an important job taking less than a few seconds. Hooker shook his head and smiled. *I missed this kid.*

Candy watched from the long floor-to-ceiling windows making up the south wall of the hallway and the north wall of the plaza. Stella watched from the small observation window set in the wall of the kitchen. Together, they were thinking the same, simple caution—*be safe.*

The whine of the turbo had only run up about halfway when Hooker pushed the small silver button—lighting the controlled explosions in the engine. Mae West's 1,600 horses roared to life. Hooker blipped the throttle a couple of times as he passed the gears into sixth. He thought about the late afternoon and Sunday. The traffic would be heavy on Blossom Hill Road, but it would be several extra miles to go down and around through Uvas Road. The choice of route determined which way he dropped off the hill and into the Almaden Valley.

Hooker pulled the mic from behind his head. "1-4-1," he called the night dispatch as he glanced at his watch. He knew, at this hour, it could go either way. Karen was managing the day shift, but Dolly may be an hour or so early taking over command of the city.

"Go ahead, Hooker." Dolly was in. It told him the wreck was bigger than they do not just seal the entrance thought. Dolly's house was only a mile from the office, but she lived in the gray pumice brick building with the thick armor-plated steel door.

"Better from the Hill or Uvas?"

"The entire southbound is backed up past the 280, but they have it blocked, so the lanes are open to the south. I'd run Uvas and just open her up. Jose and Manual are on their way, and they're bringing both lowboys just in case."

Mae had already started rolling south down the street, dumping them out a short distance from the Uvas turnoff. Hooker shot the Squirt a glance. The young man had a look on his face, which could have been Box at go time.

"10-4, Mama. Let's have a great Sunday."

"Let's keep it safe, Hooker. Keep your powder dry."

Hooker hung the mic behind his head and jumped two more gears. He loafed the truck down the back road filling up with new homes. Every one of them larger than the next, and none of them looked like they belonged.

Glancing at the kid, he smiled. "How's school?"

"Finals for this section are next week. I'll be glad when they're over." The Squirt turned his head to the open window. The day had warmed up to a pleasant forty degrees. In the Squirt's world, as well as Hooker's, this meant it was just about right for leather over T-shirts with the heater running full bore. The winter wind through the open window felt good. He had missed his time in the truck.

"Tough classes?"

The Squirt snorted and looked over at Hooker with a sneer. "More like boring. I could have taken these tests two weeks ago. I'm just ready to move on to some of the more practical classes, like the shooting range and physical training." He smiled down where Box was leaning into the blast of the heater. "Heck, I think Box could take these courses and pass."

Hooker glanced over as he rolled to the stop sign. "Not everyone can read a book only once and have it memorized for life." Hooker set the gears into fifth and turned right, falling in behind a Camaro.

The Squirt watched how close Hooker rolled out behind the muscle car. The Camaro was smaller than the working bed on Mae West and barely stood taller than her wheel wells. He started to chuckle. He knew Hooker could not resist showing a Ford or Chevy what the real muscle on the road looked like.

The guy in the Camaro thought he was safe when he took a power turn onto Uvas Road. Eleven tons of yellow and blue rear end drifted in the corner. The back eight drivers howled.

As Mae straightened, the full force of the enormous engine churned the rubber—now gripping the asphalt—the front end rose.

Hooker hit the switch to move the exhaust dumps. Underneath the cab, the cylinders rotated, and the exhaust took the nine-inch shortcut—pounding the asphalt directly below. Mae responded to the lack of backpressure, and the tachometer jumped 380 RPMs. Hooker shifted to keep up with the new power range and eased into the oncoming lane. The Camaro aired out his exhaust the best he could, but the giant lady danced past him like it was a wallflower at the barn dance. Long before the back hook cleared the front nose of the Chevy, Mae was dancing a high-step. Hooker shifted twice more as Mae left the 120mph mark in the dirt with the Camaro.

The Squirt giggled harder as he cinched his belt tighter and considered reaching behind the seat and pulling the shoulder straps out for the four-point harness. Hooker grinned. *The kid had missed this girl, too.*

Hooker reached over his head and hit a large red button on the new header console. "1-4-1."

"Go, son." The Squirt marveled at the new hands-free radio mic.

"We're on Uvas—ETA is sixteen—any updates?"

"Hooker, you are breaking up, nine-by-nine. I hate the new mic Willie installed—but I can only guess as to why you are using it. The total looks like twenty-six shorts, four talls, and seven blackouts."

Hooker's throat filled. Dolly had just given him their shorthand for the number of small vehicles, rigs, and deaths. He knew the statistic with a wreck this big. The number of people who didn't get to emergency care in time would drive the last number up by at least another fifty percent.

"10-4, Mama." He hit the red button again.

The silence in the truck was a blessing.

The dangerous curves were coming, and Hooker did not

have time to drop down to the recommended forty-five. He drifted down to seventy and held it at the top of the power band. Cycling the exhaust dump gave him back the Jake-brake that fed air into the engine and let the backpressure slow down the truck the same as a regular gas car does. The curves were not banked right and could take a person unfamiliar with them through the curve and continue across the field in one curve or up a sand hill with another. Hooker became familiar with them by towing drunken locals off the hill and out of the field when it became an overflow for the creek running through it.

As Hooker wrestled with the snaking flat track, he remained calm. "So, after finals, are they giving you wannabe cops a break?"

The Squirt looked back into the cab. He wasn't sure Hooker was seriously asking about school when he was hauling eleven tons through some nasty road. Then he looked down at Box. The cat hadn't changed. His single eye was closed as he leaned into the hot air. As the truck shifted, he just leaned into the turn. Nothing seemed to faze the cat. Rolling his eyes behind his closed lids, the Squirt took his cue from the expert and flowed with the go.

"We have two weeks off. You need some help?"

Coming out of the curves, they raced around the top end of the small lake. At the near midpoint, Hooker stomped on the brake and clutch. Dropping the transmission five gears, he mentally lined up on the next turn—a sharp left onto the road leading them out to the bottom end of Blood Alley.

Hooker reached to the top of the large steering wheel boosted by two instead of only one power steering boosting pumps. This gave him the steering of a sports car at a tenth of the weight and a dozen times smaller than Mae. He flinched the wheel to the right, and then pulled down hard and around left. He mashed harder on the brake for a brief second, which broke the rear end loose. The view in the cab became a carnival ride as the back of the truck slewed around on the sand and gravel covered the intersection.

"Nah, it's as dead as a door knocker in a mausoleum." He dumped the clutch and tromped on the throttle as the truck lined up on the new road. Mae responded, and the tires bit into the asphalt, and the sliding truck became the usual yellow and blue missile. Hooker glanced over at the kid.

"I'm so bored that I was thinking the three of us could go and invade the Apple Farm and see Sissy."

The Squirt pursed his lips into a prune to keep from screaming. As he watched the posts on the barbed wire fence turn into a blur, he knew they were traveling at speeds most police cars could never obtain.

"Sure," he squeaked. "Sounds good."

Hooker took his last chuckle. In a few minutes, he knew they would be awash in a sea of sorrow. He wouldn't know any of the brain donors, but it was the sadness of how something could have been fixed with a simple fence of concrete down the middle. Something the state of California said it was too broke to do even if it meant saving lives.

As they rolled up to and into the carnage, Hooker and John were both evaluating the wrecks. In Hooker's mind, John had long ago stopped being the Squirt or a know-nothing new guy when it came to working an accident. In fact, the kid's first accident had been about half this size only a couple of miles north.

The kid pointed to a farm road breaking through the fence line and over the railroad tracks. About a hundred yards in, there was a large flat area where the farmer would park his trucks and tractors. Hooker nodded. They would stash tows there and come get them later when the mess was cleared.

Hooker snatched the mic from behind his head. "1-4-1."

"Hooker..."

"Who are the little trucks coming to the party?"

"Ace is returning from Gilroy and is behind the brothers. Mike and one of their new guys are coming in from uptown. Stan just picked up the Chevy and will be out in about ten. Don is on his way in to get their two-ton, and Karen says there are a few more, but they're coming from Clara."

"Hit Ace and Mike on their sidebands, and tell them there's a large stash lot just at the bottom end and to the west of the mess. Warn them it's over the tracks so they don't try it with any dollies. With luck, we'll have this all cleaned up for the Monday morning slugfest."

"10-4. West of the south end of the mess."

"Thanks, Mama."

He hung the mic and looked along the road littered with twisted metal. The stench of spilled gasoline and oil hung heavy in the air.

"Where do you want to start?"

The Squirt pointed at the steel pipe truck trying to mount a Monte Carlo. "Let's back the truck off... the drivers still look good, and we can recharge the air hoses for the brakes if we have to. We can stash the prom queen before the others even know we're here. If we have time, we can bone the Monte Carlo in the field and throw it to someone for a favor, but let's clean our way into the shit storm so we have some breathing room. We already know the crap upfront is two pieces of toast. We may or may not get a payday out of the trailer."

Hooker wound Mae around in a left arch and began to back her into the nightmare. The Squirt jumped out to guide him. As the afternoon dark became cold night black, the sky began to weep. Hooker did not have to explain how to do something, or what was next—even once. While Hooker shuttled twisted steel and rubber into the distant field, the Squirt worked the broom, shovel, and pail. Every small tow truck pulling out with a car also had a full debris pail. As the wrecks disappeared, so did the debris of shattered glass and peeled bits and pieces of what was left of the cars.

As they were down to a few last problematic hulks, the CHP captain showed up. Hooker was raising the busted end of a trailer as the captain walked up and quietly looked back down where the wreck had been.

Hooker looked at the man and then down the highway. He knew what the man was thinking, so he just shook his head. "It wasn't me, Chet. I've been jerking steel all afternoon." He nodded his head at the dark figure on the side of the highway, sweeping.

Chet snorted. "Is that the Squirt? Why isn't he studying?"

Hooker gave him a stupid face and hound-dogged his eyes. "He's bored. He reads the books and reembers them word for word. Dinner at Monterey Steak House says he aces every single test."

The captain just laughed. "No way am I taking a rigged bet. I've seen how his mind and memory work." He watched the kid as he swept and then dumped the pail in someone else's debris bucket. "Bored, huh? I guess maybe it's time to find some more classes he can challenge."

"Good to see you, Chet, but I need to jerk this Prom Queen and stash her. I think I saw Taylor over near the fire truck."

"Thanks, Hooker. I guess I'll be seeing you Wednesday night for dinner at Dolly's?"

"10-4. Dolly mentioned getting some salad fixings for you." The two laughed about the three pounds he had gained while he was off active duty.

Hooker looked at his watch several hours later. "Holy beans in sauce, Squirt. Do you have any idea what time it is?"

The kid rolled his eyes into his head, "Time for a nap?"

Hooker thought about the appeal of a nap. In another hour, the sun would be coming up. "Well, maybe... but first, it's time for ice cream."

6

BREAKFAST AT SWEETS

The drizzle had dithered about all week. It was as if the clouds were thinking about raining, but maybe not.

This afternoon it decided a little ray of sunshine on the South Bay would lull the inhabitants into a sense of safety so the streets could become snot rinks in the evening. Hooker had one of those feelings about plenty of work during the Friday night date time.

Even if it were dead batteries, it would still put fuel in the tanks.

Mae pulled up along the curb. The excellently tended front yard and the house stood out as the step above the neighborhood. It had nothing to do with a black family living in a mostly white neighborhood. This was the work of the oldest son, Danny. Everything about and around him was as well cared for or detailed as the 1968 Lincoln Town Car in the driveway. Hooker knew without looking there was not even a fingerprint on any of the chrome—even the door handles were clean and polished. Hooker believed it was the only reason Danny carried a handkerchief in his left back pocket. He had seen the giant of a man pull it out and make a final wipe every time he used the doors.

Mae's large engine, as quiet as it was when running, though, the dampening exhaust was noisy in the quiet neighborhood, so Hooker shut her down. The last vibrations echoed through the empty working-class neighborhood in the dying light of the winter day. Breakfast at the Sweets' was the same time as Hooker's beginning of the day—mid to late afternoon.

Sweets was the youngest son's name as well as the family name. In a high school accident during metal shop, Sweets traded eyesight for a unique set of other skills. He had always loved music, but in his blindness, he could remember all the liner notes and all the statistics of all the artists he had ever heard or even heard of. His skillset for talk and knowledge of music lead him to a career as a disc jockey for a local radio station. His shift started at midnight. Danny was his driver, caretaker, bodyguard, and minder. He was also Sweets' personal attendant when it came to clothes. Even though Danny's uniform of the day varied little beyond the black dress pants and shoes below the heavily starched white French-cuffed dress shirt and brown leather sports coat, Sweets dressed like a fine dandy. Danny's eye of décor prevailed everywhere within his reach, except for their much-loved mother.

The door swung open as Hooker reached for the doorbell. "Tilly, my dear."

"Hooker? Oh, my stars and garters—I almost didn't recognize you. You are simply wasting away from lack of food. Get in here. This is an emergency intervention."

Hooker laughed at the family joke for all of them and stepped into the same padding Stella provided with hugs. Tilly wasn't quite the level for him to snuggle into a fat neck, but he knew she giggled anyway.

"Stop that, Hooker. It just isn't decent. I'm an old woman." Hooker started to withdraw, and she grabbed the back of his head and pulled him back in. "I didn't say for you to stop now... just sometime in the far future." She giggled and squirmed some more.

A deep rumble like a mountain moving echoed with the giggles. "Are you molesting my mother?"

Hooker didn't stop. He turned himself and the focus of his attack to the left so he could stick his right hand and arm out.

Danny took the smaller hand and shook it. "You two hurry up with this foolishness. The neighbors are going to talk, and this hand is nothing but bones."

A voice of pure warm molasses came from the dining room. "I hope we're having more than bones for breakfast. I could swear I heard a sound like Hooker at the door—but it sounded weak and distant."

The teasing never stopped through the entire meal. It was always like this when the four got together. Hooker had been adopted into the family long before he was eighteen and legal to drive a commercial tow truck. He first met the two Sweets men one night outside the radio station when he was fifteen and driving with a bogus license.

Sweets had introduced Hooker to his other questionable gift from the injury—or skill set, depending on your perspective. Sweets could not see Hooker visually, but he could see Hooker was much younger than he was projecting. Sweets had a sixth sense or saw visions. He didn't know how to interpret them, but he knew who they were for. Hooker didn't always like what he heard, but he did pay close attention.

"How has the business been, Hooker?" Sweets touched lightly with his two smaller fingers for the edge of the plate as he put the knife down. Tilly's biscuits were legendary.

Hooker mumbled around the last bite. "Goomf." He swallowed with a sip of coffee. "

"Good, Sweets."

Danny snorted.

Sweets nodded toward his brother and smiled. "Even Danny doesn't need my sight to see there was a stumble of the truth."

Hooker blushed. "Okay, slow."

Danny was the moneyman. He told Hooker the first night when he handed him his card, 'If you get in trouble, you call Dolly. If you need money, you call me.' The man now stared at Hooker. "Do you need anything?" The unspoken yet understood word was *money*.

Hooker thought about his large family. Above all else, they were always looking out for everyone else. Family—by blood or bond. Hooker laid his napkin on the table. "Nah, I kissed Uncle Willie on the ear last Monday and hugged and nuzzled Stella this morning, so all the rents are up-to-date. I need fuel, but I've got some credit left with the Fly."

Danny smiled. He knew about the credit and why. "How are her daughter and Dog getting along?"

"I'd give them until this spring or maybe summer before they find a place together."

"Good to see both of them finally find the right person."

Hooker started to ask how Danny knew the man who worked sorting the vehicle cadavers for the Fly, much less the Fly's daughter, and then he remembered Danny was the same as Hooker—he knew everyone worth knowing, whether it be in high places, in the gutter, and everywhere between. Hooker just nodded, agreeing.

Sweets laced his fingers together in a tent over his empty plate as Danny silently cleared the table. "How much do you know about explosives?"

Hooker thought about where the question may have come from. "The dime killer used napalm the one time—"

"That would be more about flames."

"Well," Hooker continued delicately, "there were a lot of explosions out at the base when I killed my sister..."

"Close, but still not large enough."

"Then I would have to go with the answer of nothing." He frowned at the line of questioning. "Survey said?"

Sweets sat still. His face was passively quiet. "I'm not sure, but there wasn't fire... just one drawn out explosion or explosions."

"Did you see anything else?"

"Trees, but they didn't make much sense. They were too close together."

"How close?"

"Like they were touching... Like a fence made out of trees, but I could see the explosions like there were windows through the fence. It was like a large building, and I was looking in all the windows, but the explosion went from right to left instead of all at once."

Hooker looked at Danny, who just shrugged. Hooker looked back toward Sweets. "Usually, when they blow up a building, there are some smaller explosions all over inside, so the walls collapse down into the building area and don't blow out into the neighborhood."

Tilly laughed. "Kind of like you boys growing up. The explosions were all in the house."

Sweets snorted with an evil smile. "Except when Danny ate too many beans—"

"You want me to rearrange the furniture on you?" The bigger brother growled, but all four could tell it was hiding a laugh.

Tilly slapped his arm but still shook with a silent giggle.

Sweets looked in her direction. "You do know I can hear the wet slap of your teats when you giggle, don't you?"

The four burst into laughter.

It was breakfast at the Sweets' house, after all.

7

FRONTIER VILLAGE

"Squirt, Box—Go time." Hooker hung up the phone at the Whole Donut. Turning, he found himself in a hug with Mai Lynn, the owner. Her head barely reached his chest, but her hugs were always as welcome as any other hug he received in the Bay Area.

"Cherie, I gotta go to work. Besides, your husband might catch us." He looked up and reached out to shake Ralph's hand. The man smiled at his wife.

"She knows we never know when you'll leave and return or if we have to go up to the hospital to see you again." Hooker shrugged at the truth of the statement. Everyone joked about Hooker's third home being the Valley Medical Center and its emergency room.

Mai Lynn pushed back and shook her finger in his face. "You go to hospital. Very expensive for Ralph and Mai Lynn to come see you—we have to bring many dozen donuts to bribe our way in."

Hooker laughed at the tiny woman who had stolen

Ralph's heart in Vietnam. He had convinced his superiors he had knocked her up and, subsequently, was married by the village priest. The State Department let her come to America, but they couldn't marry for three years—until she was eighteen. Manny had signed on as her godfather and guardian and then gotten them jobs up the peninsula working in a bakery.

To raise money, Manny and Stella had spoken to every cop, firefighter, nurse, and doctor. The donations had come in pocket-change and small bills. Eventually, they raised enough to buy the land and build with a parking lot big enough to hold many cop cars and fire trucks, as well as entire county work crews. Everyone had bought in to sponsor a donut shop for the madly in love couple. The donut shop was not about the couple or a few interested friends. It was about the whole situation and what they represented. The walls were plastered with nothing but photos of all the city, county, and state workers who frequented the shop.

The only thing on the one wall—other than photos—was a large saying in a simple frame:

No matter where your travels wend,
And take you in your life, my friend.
No matter where be your travel,
No matter what be your toll,
Keep your eye upon the donut,
And not upon the hole.

Ralph's long recovery had never reached completion. He still moved with hitches and stutters in his muscles and bones—but he had never lost his focus on the whole donut or on his wife.

As Hooker and Squirt moved past her, she popped a round donut hole in each of their mouths. Ralph and Mai Lynn followed the two men out the back door and stood by the screen door, waving as the large yellow truck drove away. The painting of Mae West as a pin-up on the driver's side waved back.

"What do we have?"

Hooker pulled on the steering wheel as the truck followed the cloverleaf up and onto the 101.

"A bobtail delivery truck broke down this afternoon in the back parking lot of Frontier Village. The driver caught a ride, but they want the truck hauled up to Ivankavitch's so he can work on it first thing in the morning."

"I thought the Frontier Village was dead and gone..."

Hooker snorted dryly as he cleared his side mirror and rolled onto the freeway. "Probably should have been years ago, but there are people who went there as kids and who now take their kids there."

"But isn't it closed in the winter?"

"Maybe the guy was just driving by, and this is where he broke down."

"Or this is where he left it to go *meat* someone... and where it was when he got caught." The Squirt held his two fists next to his waist and pumped them back and forth.

Hooker laughed at the Squirts double-entendre. "How did you spell the word meet?"

"Just the way he was using it..." The kid laughed and played his hand in the wind out of the window. Distractedly he asked, "Have you always had your window down?"

Hooker had never thought about it. "When I started driving, they gave me the junkiest truck. They figured I'd wreck it anyway. I didn't know if there was a window in the door or not, but it never rolled up. By the end of the year, I got into the six-year-old Ford. I never even tried to see if it had a window. The little trucks never get a break. Your whole shift demands your butt in the seat, so you never have a reason to roll up the window and lock the rig."

The delivery truck was full of auto parts. Hooker looked over at the Squirt and smiled. "Looks like you nailed the Lothario to the bed."

"Why wouldn't they just come down and drive it back themselves?"

They slid out of the cab and headed toward the back end of the two trucks. "Maybe it did break down, and there's some face-saving going on. Either way, we get paid a commercial job out of it."

The kid slung the J-hook and chain under the back end of the bobtail and followed it in. Hooker threw his hook and chain so the kid could hook it all up while he was underneath and turned toward the utility door covering the controls for the working bed and boom.

The echo gave the Squirt the sound of almost being the size of Danny. "Were you serious about going up to see your sister this week?" He slithered out from under the truck and nodded. The chains were all hooked and secure.

Hooker pulled on the twin levers and started the cables lifting the back end of the truck. With trucks, it was always slow work in the raising. As the truck changes attitude, the driver has to listen carefully for any creaks or snaps that could be a problem. Hooker quietly told the kid to go check the steering to see if they would need to tie it off. The weight on the rear tires of the truck reached zero. Hooker could see the tire move sideways a half-inch as the truck settled into the towing sling.

Waiting for the kid, he looked along the extended building, which stretched for a city block. During the summer, the many large doors would be open to allow people to drift in and out as they moved from one carnival-like game to the next. The large windows dotting the length of the building were set into the fake log cabin walls. These narrow logs were vertical, like the fort walls instead of horizontal like a real log cabin.

Hooker was wondering what was taking the kid so long, but also half of his brain was filled with red lights flashing and the dull sound of klaxon alarms going off. Something was there just outside of his grasp...

The kid was sitting in the small truck. The steering was locked and, therefore, good to tow. As he started to slide back out of the cab, his height advantage allowed him to look over a low fence. An old white panel truck was parked on the end of the building—like it was hiding.

In the last window, there was a flash. The yellow flash turned into a white-hot flash growing into the next window. Then another flash joined the first flash and grew into the next few windows. A new flash continued within a split second joining it.

Out of the corner of his eye, the Squirt saw the panel truck pull out. It hesitated when it came into full view and then turned and drove away. By then, the noise of the explosions had become deafening and had his complete attention. The white panel truck was just a memory—a momentary distraction gone as quickly as it was seen.

Hooker watched what Sweets was seeing. Right to left,

the whole series of explosions had not taken more than a couple of seconds or even one very long second. The speed of sound deafened him, and he dove for safety as the windows of the building all reached out in shards of glass searching for something to burrow into.

Hooker's face pushed against the damp asphalt. Something was wrong. An explosion rips through a building hundreds of yards long should have deafened the bum on upper Ninth Street twelve miles away. It should have rocked Mae West from the concussion. And yet, she stood solid and unmoving.

"Squirt?" Hooker called out. His hearing was ringing, but he could hear.

"Yeah..." The kid tumbled out of the passenger side door of the smaller truck. "I'm good. I ducked, but the other window wasn't so lucky." He stood up, dusting off the crystals of tempered glass. He looked back into the cab. "Holy fireworks, what happened?"

Hooker stood. Shards of glass had knifed their way over and under Mae. Hooker looked back at the building seventy feet away. The distance of the thrown glass was also wrong for an explosion. The shards should have been thrown at least a hundred yards or more. And then there was the building. It stood there silent, still structurally sound in appearance, and not burning.

Hooker walked around the front of Mae. The 1950s heavy metal skin had turned most of the assault away from everything else behind her. A couple of the larger shards had the energy to puncture the working deck box doors. Hooker and Uncle Willie had folded the custom doors out of only twenty-two-gauge sheet steel, similar to the skin on the bobtail truck's cab. The large cargo box on the other truck was covered with thin twenty-eight-gauge sheet metal and now looked like the nose of a dog who kissed a porcupine. There was a shard for every six square inches. Even small, thumb-sized shards had planted themselves in the skin.

Hooker let out a low whistle. "Man, the Fly is going to love this." He turned to look for the Squirt.

The kid had taken a glance at the prickly scene and had then gone into cop mode. He was already walking the scene. Hooker watched the measured steps. He knew they were preliminary to the kid figuring out the energy spent throwing the shards and to still have the energy to plant them into the truck's steel skin.

Hooker leaned against the back corner of Mae to watch him work. In six short weeks, the kid had grown way beyond any other rookie in the academy. This was the result of spending so much time with Manny and Paul, as well as his other friend and CHP officer, Micha. Hooker knew he was done for the night. The trucks were part of a crime scene or, at least, a scene of an explosion. There would be no hurry to do anything but wait.

He watched as Officer Squirt walked to the end of the building and peeked into each window—or the hole where a window had been only a few minutes before. Hooker knew what was next. He turned and walked to the passenger side of Mae's cab. Tucked behind each entry door was a small hatch. He opened the door and reached in, grabbing the familiar long tube containing six D-cell batteries. Glancing at the orange blob of fur leaning into the hot air, he turned and handed the flashlight to the Squirt before the kid could ask. Both smiled at the silent teamwork.

As Officer Squirt walked back to the building to restart his exam, Hooker walked around the nose of Mae. He patted her on the heavy bar rails of her four hundred-pound front bumper. "Sorry, girl. We'll make this right."

Climbing into the cab, he grabbed the mic from behind his seat. "1-4-1."

Dina's voice giggled out of the speaker. "Why, Hooker, I'm shocked. It's after the witching hour, and you're calling me without your French vanilla ice cream voice."

"Give us a few hours. We'll be here for a while. Could you please call PD, and I think they may have to send the bomb investigation team as well. The bomb went off, so they won't need Max."

Dolly's voice took over. "Hooker?"

"We're fine, Mama. The explosion was in the long building at Frontier Village. It went the entire length. I've never even heard of anything like it, but the PD will have to cordon off the area, and the bomb guys will need to do their thing. I'm going to need some downtime, though. Mae got hit and needs some bodywork done. Maybe it's time to get some touch-up paint done, too. I didn't get to it last year."

"Hooker... Are you sure you're okay? You're running off at the mouth."

"I'm fine, Dolly. We're just a little shaken up."

"We...? Where's the Squirt?" By her voice, Hooker could see her head down on her arm and desk. The knock of the lollypop microphone tapping the top of the desk confirmed it.

"Oh, crap, Mama... you should see him. He picked himself up, dusted off, and went right into investigation cop mode. If Manny were dead, you would think it was reincarnation."

"Don't let him screw up the scene..."

"He knows what he's doing. Just get the PD out here. Tell them if they take too long, the Squirt will have it all figured out, and he'll take the information to the sheriff himself."

"10-4." The radio shorthand still couldn't mask the sound of Dolly laughing at the idea of the Squirt figuring it all out in a few minutes. But then again, he was very instrumental in breaking the last three cases Hooker had worked on—even though the first case almost killed both men.

Hooker hung the mic and went back out to watch the Squirt work. The Squirt was standing back up near the start with both hands holding the large flashlight across his thighs. He was looking at Hooker.

Hooker smirked and rolled his eyes. Walking over, he noticed the interesting pattern of the glass. He stopped.

"It's okay. You're still in the path I took to get over here, and you don't scuff your feet. The patterns are consistent all the way down. It's thirty-seven or thirty-eight small bombs. They went off in sequence, so I'm sure we'll find the wires once they start digging through the debris. You're okay on the porch here. The first throw pattern starts out there about twenty-nine feet."

"Not twenty-eight? Not thirty? How can you be so exact?" Hooker smiled at the younger man.

"Laugh it up, chuckles. The deck here is sixteen feet.

The overhang is an extra four for shade. The first small shards are out another twelve feet."

"Which makes a combined thirty-two feet, not your twenty-nine?"

"But where they're lying is not where they first hit. The scatter pattern of the close pieces did not have the high-energy to throw them far, but glass always hits and then skips. In the professional investigation community, we have a specific term for the shattered-glass phenomenon called 'hit and skip.' It even has changing parameters like hitting concrete, dirt, asphalt, or your fault." The kid stood with a solid deadpan face.

Hooker held his face as a mirror for only about three seconds. Laughing, he turned and looked down the long porch. "Get your best jokes in now, because PD will be here shortly, and you'll have to have this all figured out by then. Why? Because you know they won't let you near it again." He looked back at the Squirt—sober and serious. They both knew how true it was. Three times, they had broken the case ahead of the PD, which did not sit well with the current officers. Their attitudes would now be even more hostile, with the Squirt being an academy snot.

John waved his head back toward the end. As they got to the last window, he shined the powerful flashlight at the wall. "See where it looks like a phone once was?" Hooker nodded. The Squirt moved the bright center of the light about eight feet over to a warped metal sign. "The metal sign is where it started. My guess is there was a small timer attached to the face of the charge. The metal plate directed the blast. The timer vaporized in the first five feet."

He walked down about sixteen feet and pointed the light

at a support column. "The next charge was attached to the face of this post facing down the building. If the first charge had been bigger, the crack in the post would be on the other side. But the next explosive was on the downside and cracked the post this way."

He pointed the focused beam of the flashlight down to each of the upright support posts. "The same is true for all the rest down the line. Every single post is cracked—with the crack on this side and the blast facing the other way. This is the good news. As each blast went off, the blast radius behind was preserved. If the guy had put even a smaller charge on this side of the posts, it would have messed up and confused all the evidence."

He turned to face Hooker. "This building is toast. Those supports can never be safely replaced. I'm not even sure if this building will remain standing through the week. We get little earthquakes through here every day. All it would take would be one aligned north and south and be enough for us to feel."

"So it was intentionally set."

The Squirt nodded.

"Motive?"

"You said it yourself... the place should have gone belly-up a long time ago."

"But kids love this place."

"Sentiment goes only so far. This is business." He stepped over to the wall and knelt down. "Let me see your knife."

"I don't carry one."

"Sure you do. Manny gave it to you years ago for Christmas. And if you don't trust me, take the money out."

Hooker smiled and fished the money clip out of his pocket. He left the money in as he handed it to the kid.

The Squirt pulled the tiny knife blade out of the clip. He tested the edge on his thumbnail. It was sharp but not as sharp as he had seen it. He took the tip and pushed it against the faux log. A solid board would have stopped it after an eighth of an inch—but the blade sunk in almost the entire two inches. He pulled it out and continued to sink it into the boards until he met resistance, about four feet up.

"A good piece of lumber comes from the heart of a tree where there's some hardness. The entire outside of the tree is new wood and very soft—which makes it useless for lumber—but explains why these fake logs are made from the trash part of the log. The soft outside is susceptible to bugs and rot." He folded the blade back into the clip and handed it to Hooker as the first police car drove up and right into the glass scatter pattern.

The Squirt leaned close and muttered. "We won't tell them about the dry rot."

The two men stood there like a matched pair of mannequins—engineer boots, jeans, starched T-shirts, and leather jackets. Only Hooker's beard was the general difference. The spotlight seared the night as the officer focused on the two men, then stepped out onto the slippery glass shards. He immediately slipped and fell on his butt.

Hooker leaned close to the Squirt and muttered, "We do get to talk about this, don't we?"

The Squirt didn't show any sign of moving or talking. "Oh, hell yes. Chet and Micha will love this. Maybe Dolly will invite this crime scene spoiling rookie for dinner one night—for a nice roasting." They both knew almost all of the

Wednesday night dinners were spaghetti with Dolly's secret marinara sauce with Sicilian sausage from Chiaramontes.

Hooker could not resist. "I hope he didn't hurt himself. We already know he's going to be a pain in the ass."

The Squirt shook silently.

"How did you spell it... p-a-i-n or p-a-n-e?"

8

MILPITAS REGRETS

Felix sat in the panel truck cursing. His hands gripped the steering wheel. His fingers and knuckles were the same aged-white of the Bakelite.

"Damn it to hell." His mind replayed looking over the fence into the face of the man sitting in the broken-down truck. The truck he had left there to draw any attention while he worked. Rigging the succession of explosions took him over an hour. Even though it was a simple rig, the sheer quantity had taken time.

The small trigger went on the side receiving the blast from the previous charge. The new charge was on the side facing the building toward the end. A small piece of tape for the trigger, and a thumbtack or more tape for the small charge, and a tiny battery—all would be destroyed by the blast.

The battery was bonded inside the plastic explosive, which was in the small baggie. The baggie was just a convenient way to carry the pre-made bomb. The short, constructed wire was wound up and stuck in the baggie. As long as the glass vial didn't break, the rig was safe. On-site, he would pull out the wire and trigger, then nail, tack, or tape the baggie to the post or wall. He would then run the short wires and pressure switch to the other side of the post and tape or pin the small plastic bag.

Felix had carried the entire thirty-seven charges in the cotton duct grip bag. The Gladstone bag had been his father's tool bag in the mines. In the old days, his father would carry the dynamite or TNT in the Gladstone and stick six or eight blasting caps between his lips and teeth like a carpenter does with nails. Sometimes, ignition fuses would be hanging from the caps in small coils. On large jobs such as this, the mass of caps and white fuses made the man with prematurely white hair look like a malevolent Santa Claus.

Thinking of his father did nothing to ease Felix's mood. He knew the driver in the truck had seen the distinctive panel truck. Felix waited for the first explosion, hoping the attention would be on the bright light, not on his license plate. But he also knew he would now have to get rid of the last vestige of his father and better times in Colorado's high country.

He sat in the truck as if an extra few minutes would be enough to soak up the essence of the memories embedded in the walls, seats, and floorboards of the truck. His father had been using a stripped out old Chevy sedan from the 1930s. Mining was never a game of much money, other than with some of the big corporations or a lucky wildcat miner who had hit a valuable vein, or series of veins, in one of the metals having paid a decent day. Even gold wasn't much of a payday unless the ore was rich or a visible vein could be worked to produce heavyweight, instead of just dust or tiny nuggets in a cold-cream jar.

Most of the hard-rock mining was coal and salt on very large scales. Whole mountain tops were removed in some states, but in Colorado, the veins had to be chased inside the mountains. Felix knew from personal experience there were many seemingly large mountains, which were nothing but a large pile of Swiss cheese. He and his father had collapsed tunnels only to find they had done nothing but open an even larger cavern. A web of tunnels, drifts, and shafts fed these caverns running not only below the tunnel they'd tried to collapse but also above.

One series of tunnels they had blown up in the mid-sixties became a cavern over a half-mile in height with a floor covering twenty acres. The mining company sold it to a storage company and then contracted to clear the debris. The last Felix heard before moving to California was the mining company was still cleaning the chamber and processing the silver, gold, and mercury along with other trace minerals. He and his father worked for three long, backbreaking weeks. They were paid less than what the company was taking in each day from the residual work.

Felix wasn't mad about the inequity of the income, but he did miss his father. Being a powder monkey and setting charges paid more than most other jobs in the industry, but it hadn't protected him from the black lung, which took so many miners. In the end, his father would review the plans with Felix—between the coughing and hacking that would turn the man's face purple with strain. But, in the end, it was Felix alone who carried the bags into the mine and set the charges. Luckily, he never had to use a hammer and star drill chisel to bore holes into the rock faces like his father. The fine dust blowback went straight to the lungs and stayed there.

Felix was tired, and he would have to be up early in the morning for his shift. He pulled on the door handle, and the door of the Ford truck creaked open. His body felt the same as he crossed the front yard in the dark.

He checked on his wife. She was hours past sucking on the corner of the blanket, and he could hear her little squeak as she breathed in her sleep. If not for the memories of their life together, it could have been him checking on a small child. He turned off the nightlight, knowing she wouldn't wake up again until morning when it was time to change her diaper and feed her. Tomorrow would also be bath day. She fussed about the water.

He retreated from the room and drew the door almost closed.

He unlocked the back porch door and stepped out into the screened area that defined his life. He sat heavy on the chair and slowly removed his boots. Moving them near the bed, he then pulled the board from the wall. He counted out six of the hundred dollar bills and put the rest back in the cubbyhole.

Replacing the board, he looked at the bills. They were used, but still too close to new. He began to wad and rub them on the underside of the table where there was a thin layer of axle grease and caliche clay with a touch of lamp-black soot. The mix transferred to the bills and then got rubbed in. He picked at a corner on some of the greasy bills with his fingernail and made a crease more prominent in others. In a few minutes, the bills looked well abused, probably more than any respectable bank would ever let back into circulation, but for the street, they were perfect.

He placed the bills in a used envelope and set it aside for tomorrow to pay for his wife's care. The sum was three times the monthly rent on his house, but Felix knew it was the woman's only income.

He slid into bed and pulled the blankets over his body. He looked at the alarm clock. Five hours of sleep. He pulled the button up. He reached over and pulled the string on the lamp. The dark settled in. Out across the bay was a glow as light as the predawn before sunrise. The light caused gray shadows on the lighter gray wall.

Felix was used to the gray. His life was gray. His eyes drifted closed. The gray heron at the end of the lawn shook its feathers to fluff.

9

GOING NORTH

The Speedwagon was the vehicle of choice for the three. The backseat provided the Squirt room to read the new stack of books his cheer-squad had provided him.

What had started with the librarian Maddie, the Police Commissioner Paul, and the California Highway Patrol Captain Chet had now grown by a sergeant in the Sheriff's department and three of the professors at the police academy, one of which was the director.

If the Squirt was successful in challenging the next round of courses, the thought was he could possibly graduate with the class ahead of his normal cycle. As if he was not unique enough, he would be the first to have ever succeeded in jumping their graduation class cycle.

Hooker glanced back at the kid, hunched against the side. His book was face down on his lap. His eyes were closed, but his face was working through gyrations of thought.

"How are you doing back there?"

There was silence.

Candy turned and looked behind her. "John?"

His eyes fluttered open, and he turned and sat up. "I'm fine. I was just thinking about the other night."

"The explosion...?"

"Nah... the truck."

Hooker glanced back. "What truck?"

"There was a whitish panel truck parked behind the short fence at the end of the building. As the explosion started—it left." The Squirt looked up at the rearview mirror. "I've been trying to see the license plate, but it's all wrong."

"Wrong how?"

Candy's head moved back and forth through the volley of the conversation. She had never seen how the two worked almost like a single brain.

"The color...it should be yellow letters on black. But I keep seeing white letters, same as the truck."

"Can you see any numbers or letters?"

The kid shook his head. "Nah, it was too dark. It's why I'm not completely sure about the plate. Color washes out in the dark."

He pulled his legs and feet up and leaned his back against the other side. Picking up his book, he went back to reading.

That night, the four sat around the small table in the heated porch. The cheery fire dancing lazily in the wood stove was more than enough heat for the large porch. The storm windows had been hung over the panels of screened mesh months before.

Sissy suggested playing cards. Hooker and Candy had said nothing but looked at each other. The silent communication wasn't complete, but it was getting there. Hooker had no personal experience with the Squirt and cards, but he could imagine. Candy's glance all but confirmed it.

The hand was halfway played when the Squirt spoke up. Sissy had just led with the king of spades. The Squirt laid his cards face down on the table.

"You have five of the lesser hearts, and you're fishing for the Queen." The Squirt pointed at Hooker, and then Candy. "They each have a heart. Hooker picked up the king when Candy ran out of diamonds. Candy got her nine of hearts when I ran out of diamonds. You may think you're strong enough in diamonds, but no matter what you played—even if you had the two hearts they have—Hooker is still holding the Ace of hearts I passed to him."

Sissy slowly put her cards down as she examined the kid's face. She turned deadpan toward her brother. "Let's take him to Reno."

Hooker shook his head.

Sissy frowned. "Why not?"

Candy started laughing. "The table limits are too low."

As the laughter settled down, Sissy slurped the last of her cocoa. "So what games can we play where Mister Superbrain doesn't have an advantage?"

The Squirt smiled but with a slight blush. "Anything with dice."

"Why dice?"

"Because every roll is random—there is nothing there for me to memorize."

"So the cards you memorize?"

"If I've seen it, I've memorized it."

"Seriously?" She looked at Hooker and Candy, who were both nodding.

"So if I wrote down a string of numbers twenty-six numbers long..." The kid nodded.

Hooker thought a moment. "What was the book Maddie gave you last fall? The poetry book..."

The kid rolled his eyes toward the ceiling for a moment. "The Collected Poems of Robert Service, published by Dodd, Mead, & Company in New York."

Candy turned over her hand and counted the cards. "Page thirty-three."

John's eyes rolled up, and he lost any life in his face for a moment. Hooker and Candy were used to this face of his recalling. His voice had a faraway quality about it as he began to read the page, burned forever, in his mind. 'The Cremation of Sam McGee.' His head rotated forward as he recited:

> There are strange things
>> done in the midnight sun
>> By the men who moil for gold;
>> The Arctic trails have their secret tales
>> That would make your blood run cold;
>> The Northern Lights have seen queer sights,
>> But the queerest they ever did see
>> Was that night on the marge of Lake Lebarge
>> I cremated Sam McGee.

The kid opened his eyes and smiled softly at Sissy. She sat quiet—digesting. It had been many years since she had heard any poetry. This was not dainty woman poetry; this was the kind men forged from a hard life spent on the razor's edge—something she could relate to.

Candy and Hooker watched her.

Finally, her voice was more of an echo of a lover's sigh, something more a part of the night air than a voice. "Was there more?"

Claire and Harold listened from the other room as the young man recited of the Yukon and men struggling and dying in the snow or on battlefields. Claire had looked toward the wisdom of the former psychiatrist in her husband. He had covered her hand with his and nodded with his eyes. The shared time with her brother and growing family would heal old wounds more than any number of hours talking with Harold in sessions.

Therefore, they leaned back and listened.

10

QUIET ON THE HOME FRONT

Manny put his pencil down. He had been trying to write down some notes on something, but the lack of noise distracted him.

He looked up. Stella shook the Sunday newspaper in the sunroom. Everything was as it should be. Peace, quiet, good coffee, and the newspaper after a late Sunday breakfast.

Manny looked about the room. The dishes were rinsed and in the dishwasher. His mug was still half-full of coffee. The grandfather clock was ticking, and he had drawn the weights up yesterday, which meant it was wound for the next eight days. Stella had her coffee and newspaper. Even a slim patch of blue sky was helping with some sun in the large sunroom. He looked toward his office... the door stood open to the darkened room.

Manny picked up his pencil to write. Staring at the paper, he realized he had forgotten what he was going to write. He gently placed the pencil down and pushed the pad away from his eating area. He pushed back from the table.

Turning his chair, he moved to the archway defining the boundary between the dining area and the sunroom.

He sat staring at the two hands and the newspaper they were holding.

The clock ticked.

Slowly, the one corner of the paper curled down. Stella's right eye became visible.

"I don't like it," Manny grumped as he pushed down on the arms of the wheelchair. The weight of his butt lifted from the seat. It wasn't about comfort because he couldn't feel his rear end—it was about adjusting his mental state.

The paper curled down a tiny bit more.

"Do you want me to bring the Caddie up, and we'll go for a drive?"

"No..." His voice trailed off before it turned into a whine. He turned and gave a halfhearted push on the wheels. "I just don't like it."

Stella laid the paper in her lap and watched her retreating husband, best friend, and love. She closed her eyes in commiseration. "The kids will be home tonight."

"I just don't like it when they're gone." He disappeared into his sanctuary and office.

Stella stretched her legs out on the couch. She knew he would swap out the large sixteen-inch reel on the professional tape recorder for something more violent like Vivaldi or Frank. He had been listening to Brahms the night before. On a day like this, it would not suit his mood. She thought about the music. "Put on the Vivaldi and leave the speakers on. I want at least an eight on the volume, Mr. Romero."

She was rewarded with a soft chuckle. She knew he would turn the volume up closer to halfway and come back out to lie in the sun and maybe nap. It wasn't the sound of the kids, but it helped. She didn't like the silence either. It was the wrong kind of silence.

The shadows in the sunroom had long changed sides of the room and disappeared with the early sunset. The sound of two soft snores vibrated through the room. The Vivaldi tape had only lasted for three hours and twenty-nine minutes. As designed, the phone rang in the office first. The distance softened the awakening tone ringing next in the sunroom.

Stella's hand reached behind her head at the buzzing wireless handset phone. As she pulled it back to her head, the thumb finding the button with the green phone icon. "This better be good," she growled.

Her matched voice growled right back. "Oh, shut up. I'm in early. Where's Hooker?"

Stella relaxed, but her entire body went on high alert. Her sister didn't start work on a Sunday until what most people would consider a late dinner. "What time is it?"

"Almost four."

Stella swung her legs over the edge of the couch and sat up in the gloom. She looked over at the other stretch of couch. She could see movement. "My guess is somewhere around the city, maybe even up or down."

"He's not answering the radio." Dolly was irritated, and Stella could hear her fussing with papers on her desk. A few years separated the two, but for the way they read each other's voices, they may as well have been twins.

"They took Willie's truck. Mae was getting a facelift this week." By the little sounds in the room, Stella didn't have to look up to know Manny was making ready to transfer into his chair.

"They should have been down by now. We woke them at four this morning."

Stella stopped herself. She almost asked why but stopped because she didn't want to know. She leaned forward and put her face in her left hand—thinking. "Did you call Willie?"

There was silence. Either she had just tripped up her sister, or she had asked a stupid question.

"Gotta go." The metallic click vibrated around the room. Stella smiled. It was a great day when she could trip up the great Dolly at her own game of communication.

"What do you think she—"

"Manny Romero, you know I don't want to know. It's Sunday, and I was having a great dream where I was shopping for a wedding dress with my daughter."

Manny smiled. It was less than a year, and mama bear was already protective of her new cubs. He remembered when Hooker first landed in their guest bedroom. There ensued a certain love and hate relationship in the house for all of them.

Stella loved her quiet house, but Hooker's schedule of towing at night, coupled with Manny's detective shift during the day, filled the hacienda with another breathing soul in residence at all hours. It never had time to irritate her, though; she had quickly taken to mothering Hooker as much as she did Manny.

Hooker, on the other side of the coin, was a distant, reserved entity, who was uncomfortable with close contact. He had become accustomed to Willie, but when the household went to war, it was hit the streets and find shelter. Dolly vehemently told him he had no choice—if he didn't bunk at Hacienda Romero, he could go find some other state to live in—because the Bay Area just wouldn't be big enough for her and him. Luckily, he chose to become family.

But the new children had turned on a new side of Stella that Manny liked seeing. The Squirt was actually young enough (and innocent enough) to be mothered. His sister had done a great job with what she had, but it was more of a child raising another child.

However, it was Candy who opened Stella's heart to full motherhood. She finally had a daughter that she could be a mother and a friend. Manny quietly hummed to himself, for he was also content at the blend the large household had become. He just wasn't sure whether they were part of Stella's and his family or if they were all part of Hooker's family. Either way, it all worked for him. He pushed his way to the office.

ACROSS THE VALLEY, Hooker nosed the Speedwagon onto the approach apron large enough for most small airplanes. The gigantic door was built for small lookout dirigibles. The oversized motor quietly rolled the monolith of corrugated steel back from the closed position.

Uncle Willie walked out as the door rolled back. His dress of the day was florid pink and lavender paisley floral pattern. The burn marks and small holes bore testimony that it had also been a welding day. The holes were consistent with not only a torch but also either the heliarc or the standard stick arc welder—Hooker didn't want to look close enough to find out which. Willie smiled as he grabbed the long dress and pulled it out as he took a curtsy.

Candy stepped out of the passenger side. "Oh, now Willie, those are definitely your colors. The lavender really sets off your highlights, and the pink just adds a certain *devil be damned* flair."

Hooker reached out and grabbed the last of the Squirts leather jacket and pulled him back into the Speedwagon. The Squirt turned around with an evil, mischievous smile on his face.

Hooker looked at him and growled. "If you encourage him, I swear...I'll stick a fork in you. *Again*."

The Squirt snorted. "Oh, look at it. You know you didn't have to tell me. Good gosh, it's paisley, for God's sake." He continued to climb out of the backseat of the Speedwagon.

Willie smiled as he hugged Candy. Willie was always happy to see the young man. His right hand stuck out, but his left arm didn't let go of the Squirt's sister. "It is always a pleasure to see you, Jonathan."

He took the man's hand and winced as the man squeezed. His smile turned to a quiet chuckle echoing his sister. Willie pulled the young man in closer and whispered, "Hooker hates the dress, doesn't he?"

Candy shook even harder and pressed her face into both the dress and Willie's chest.

The Squirt nodded slightly and chortled. "Willie, it's hideous. Good job."

The older man smiled broadly. "I searched through the entire bag of dresses from Goodwill this morning. Many of 'em had potential, but I just knew this was the winner."

The three watched as Hooker slowly pulled the Speedwagon into the giant air hangar-turned-into-an-acre of garage. Willie called out, barely in control of his voice. "Go ahead and take it all the way back to the grease rack, Hooker." He knew they needed the extra minute to get the laughs out of him and the other two. As they stood laughing, the large DeSoto convertible pulled up.

Willie's boyfriend, Hank, sat staring at the dress. Slowly, he rolled the window down. "William, I'll be forced to take your Goodwill privileges away from you if you insist on wearing only the ugliest of the dresses. Now please, go put on a nice rose color or at least a blue. I bought wine, and we have company."

Candy put her finger to her lips. "Hanky, shh. Hooker is parking the Speedwagon."

The man rolled his eyes and pulled the DeSoto through the door. "I have wine...children"

Willie called after the car, "I have shine..."

The glasses were mixed. Hank and Willie shared the vino while Candy sipped on the moonshine Willie had mentioned. His childhood friend and fellow car fanatic came from a family of moonshiners, but recently, her brother had been branching out from the standard mash and had been mixing in some of the local fruits. This one happened to have a distinct peach flavor with an apricot aftertaste.

Hooker was on the phone with Dolly. He and the Squirt were holding off on any drinking until it was determined if the early morning wake up had been resolved. The conversation was going a lot longer than Hooker's usual talks with Dolly.

To not feel useless, the Squirt sat doodling what he had been thinking about. What he saw in his mind was the cartoon face of a Chinese dragon. The truck had been in the dark, and when the front came out from behind the fence, he only had a split second of a look. He was looking at the round eyes, but they were wrong—they were below the nostrils. Then, too, the teeth were wrong...

Willie leaned over and looked over his shoulder. "It's a fucking Ford. Don't buy it."

Hank's hand reached out and slapped the other man's arm. "William!" Willie looked at him from the bottom of his second water glass of wine.

"You owe Hooker's swear jar a quarter for the word, and a quarter because you said it in front of the children." Hank's pencil line of a white mustache twitched. He was also drunk. "I don't care how you feel about the cars from Dearborn, we have rules, and you are not above them."

Willie smirked and growled at the slightly younger man. "You know I can still take you."

Hank drew himself up straight. "We will not be discussing our bedroom activities in front of the children either."

Candy giggled, and the Squirt blushed. Willie glared at Hank and then returned his attention to the drawing as he laid his head on the Squirt's shoulder.

"At least someone still loves me." He pointed at the semi-teardrop nostrils. "Those are the vents they put on some of the late 1940s Ford trucks. If the grill ran horizontal, as you are intimating here, then it's 1949. It actually wasn't a bad truck."

The Squirt snorted. "It just wasn't a MOPAR."

Willie rested his hand on the Squirt's arm and pouted at Hank. "See...at least *he* gets it."

Hooker hung up the phone and looked at the table arrangement. Hank, Candy, and Willie draped all over the Squirt's arm. "What's going on?"

They all stiffened into a guilty silence. The Squirt broke the stall. "What about the wreck."

Distracted, Hooker sat. "They got it handled. A car cut off a small bobtail truck in the early morning. The truck flipped and scattered the box all over the 680. They found some bodies, but there was evidence there were several other people in the back of the truck."

Candy frowned. "The truck was hauling bodies?"

"No... people." Hooker sagged at the implication of what he had just spoken.

Willie whispered, "Who?"

Hooker was slow to look up. "Asian. Probably Vietnamese..."

Hooker and Willie had spoken about slavery in the Asian cultures before. Chinese and Japanese workers brought over as little more than indentured workers built California in the early years of the gold rush. What followed were the women in the form of sex slaves along with the opium. San Francisco's Chinatown was built on the needs of the Chinese workers, and eventually, the needs of the white residents of the city. Asia provided the cooks, maids, laundry workers, seamstresses, and sex workers, along with the means to forget your cares in the opium dens.

The Squirt leaned forward. "Where on the 680?"

Hooker looked at the Squirt. He could tell it was the future cop asking.

"Near King and Story." It was the new center for the Vietnamese gangs or the Mafia.

The Squirt thought for a moment. He picked up the mason jar of clear liquid and held it up toward Hooker. Hooker almost laughed at the look on the kid's face. It was almost more eager than asking. Hooker nodded, and the top was off with a single twist.

Hooker stood and stepped to the phone. He knew Stella and Manny would want to know their plans.

As the phone rang, Hooker looked back at Willie. "When do you think I can have Mae back?"

The man closed his eyes to clear his thinking. Hank's hand had slid up inside his shorts. The evening of entertaining was rapidly ending for the two older gentlemen.

"Um, I believe she called...yes, the Fly called, and said they couldn't match the pearl flake in the clear coat until at least next week. However, if you need her now, the color is all shot and pinstriped. I think this would also be a good time for Candy to add the two dimes on the tote board. And if she's up to it, not that I'm an expert on womanly anatomy, I've always felt Mae looks slightly under-endowed."

Hooker nodded and turned toward the wall to hide his laughter at seeing Hank invading Willie's privates. He had to give it to his uncle... he hadn't broken under fire. He could hear the two chairs slide back as the phone picked up on the other end.

"Romero's... Okay, Hooker... What's so funny?"

Hooker giggled harder.

"Willie and Hank are plowed and just beat a fast retreat. Listen, Manny, we're staying here tonight so I can pick up Mae in the morning." He turned back toward the Squirt as he spoke. "Could you put in a call to Paul and have people start looking for a—"

The Squirt chimed in, "A 1949 Ford F-1 panel truck with a funky white paint job. License plate is not California. It's white letters on a black back."

The former detective, on the other end, mumbled while he wrote.

"Got it. Anything else?"

"Just a squeeze for Stella."

"Got it. A major suck up for not calling earlier."

"Thanks, Manny. You're a champ." Hooker hung up.

11

ANOTHER ENVELOPE

The new envelope was fatter than any Felix had received as a down payment. This one had almost not fit in the large mailbox. Any larger, and he would have drawn attention to himself by having to ask for the package. He didn't like the size. He could feel there were five bundles of money instead of the usual three. The sheaf of information was also much thicker than usual.

He sat on the screened porch without any lights. Only the dim light from across the bay illuminated the envelope dully. Felix did not like this one bit.

He thought back to what the woman said when she'd left. *That man from the county was here again today. He's not just going to disappear. They are going to take her.*

He moved from Colorado because they had tried to take his Thelma away from him. In his soul, he knew the woman he fell in love with and married so many years before was no longer in the shell lying on the bed, ten feet away. The body suckling on the corner of a blanket until she drifted off to sleep only looked similar. He had resolved himself to this fact many years before. The accident took all of her away from him. She was never coming back. However, it did not mean some soulless state facility could warehouse what was left until it expired from lack of food and attention. Felix would rather die than let such a thing happen.

Reaching out, he pulled the strings on both of the lamps. The envelope looked even larger in the bright light. The yellow-cream was wrinkled where the center bulged. The large stone in Felix's stomach sunk lower and rattled somewhere near the pit. Whatever his old boss had contracted for him to blow up was large or important. The usual half down payment, as well as the twenty-five percent for expenses, was normally twenty plus ten thousand—three stacks. These lumps were thicker, and he was looking at five distinct lumps. His right hand moved under the table to the commando knife. One smooth pass and his hand returned the blade back to the magnets behind the table's skirting.

His hands rested on the table, bracketing the envelope. He closed his eyes and drew in an even slow breath. Pinching the two back corners, he lifted as his eyes opened. A sheaf of papers slid out with the ten packs of hundred dollar bills. One hundred thousand dollars—the job wasn't small or huge but rather, it was complicated—so it was also important.

Twenty minutes later, Felix started rereading the instructions. He had done something like this only once before in Colorado. Actually, the job had been in Amarillo, Texas, just across the border. The job then was a car dealership. Felix didn't understand why they wanted him to blow it up. The people who usually hired Felix were the sort of people who had been cooking the books on a business in trouble, or they were skimming so hard it was about to be in trouble. The idea was a large insurance payday to make it all go away or to cover everything needed to restart the clock ticking on the scammed business.

Felix did his research on the car dealership. The dealer was anything but in trouble. In fact, he was making money at such a rate he was paying out bonuses to even the receptionists. The dealer supported three little league teams, had just installed lights at the local high school so they could play night football and had a new hospital wing named after him and his wife. He wasn't hurting, but someone wanted to hurt him.

Felix leaned back as he thought about the long-ago night. It was more than just to hurt the guy's business—it had been much more.

It was Christmas Eve. Felix thought it was from the owner because they provided keys and security alarm codes. The lot was loaded with cars, and he had set lines of detonation cord wound into a rope of five lines. In confined spaces or wrapped around something, each of the cords burning at the speed of sound provided an explosion. Then multiple cords were wound into a rope around a thin line of Felix's homemade plastic explosive, and the cars over the rope lifted forty feet in the air before crashing to the ground. To hide the evidence, Felix had hosed out thin pools of diesel fuel. The fuel burns slower than gasoline, so it was a confusing curative instead of an added explosion. The fires also guaranteed the cars and trucks were a total loss instead of repairable.

Felix didn't like the idea of explosions in the open air. However, with all of it contained within the area of the car lot, he figured it would be okay. Only he was set up by someone who had shown up shortly before he had. Many of the cars had been bathed down with gasoline in the engine compartments, or fuel lines were shaved where they would be slow leaks under the outer perimeter cars.

The building had a whole different gemstone of things wrong. Felix was to set up the showroom and the cars there. Usually, he would use low-grade explosives, which would cause massive damage but would be contained within the building. If a window blew out, it would be from the rapid expansion of the explosion, not by the explosion itself. This time, it was different.

The payloads were almost three times the size he felt would have done the job—but the instructions had been explicit. Where the explosives were to be placed, the size, the blast spread, and even what chemistry to use. Felix had the feeling whoever had ordered the job was also an explosives expert. Felix had been so right.

At exactly 3:41 in the morning on Christmas day, the local radio station played Elvis's *Heartbreak Hotel*. The start of the song was obvious, but the disk jockey even announced it. The song was Felix's signal to explode the dealership. The total time for all the explosions to go off was forty-three seconds.

While Elvis sang, nineteen telephone switching stations tasked with routing telephone, radio transmissions, alarms for security systems, and a myriad of other transmissions vaporized. The plastic explosives planted in those switching boxes the previous day left nothing but bits of twisted copper, steel, and aluminum. Fifty-nine windows, a motorcycle illegally chained to one box, and a row of prized Texas yellow roses had also ceased to exist.

What nobody knew until two days later was sometime during the explosion, which lit up the sky and captured everyone's attention, the floors in the vaults of seven local banks also turned to rubble from below. By Boxing Day, or as the locals would call it, the day after Christmas, the local banks were drained of over eleven million dollars and heaping mounds of personal possessions once filling the hundreds of violated safe-deposit boxes.

The local media had tried to keep some lid on the banks being breached, but eventually, the word spilled out. Keeping quiet about a bank staying closed longer than three days is next to impossible, especially when businesses need to deposit their holiday receipts. The firestorm that followed never even got close to looking at the car dealer with anything other than an after-mention. The focus was all on the banks. The funds Felix was paid provided what he needed to find and purchase the house on the bay using a fake identity.

Moving his wife had been more problematic than the complicated explosion. Wiping out a car dealer with over two hundred cars and trucks was child's play in comparison. By the time Felix was ready to move her, Thelma had the mental acuity of a one-year-old. Still, Felix and Thelma had disappeared only one step ahead of the law. Colorado felt Thelma's care was not up to the standards of a state institution, which would be covered by Medicare.

Felix put the paper down on the desk and looked out into the gloom sprinkled by the distant twinkling lights from across the bay. His hand went to the scar on his forehead, which continued into his thick head of dark hair. His left ring finger found the furrow and rubbed it as he thought. The wording was similar—too similar. He had trouble remembering names, but patterns he recognized—the patterns of speech, the details of the explosives, how much and where were the same. Even down to a specific record, playing at a fixed time on a named radio station in the middle of the night was the same, or it was close enough.

It had been five years since the job in Texas. Felix now wondered where he would have to run to next. He knew he couldn't do this job and not to be swept up in the resulting investigation. You don't get lucky the second time, and whoever these guys were—he had a feeling he was going to be the patsy this time.

12

BITS AND PIECES ON THE MUDFLATS

"Hooker." The small Asian woman yelled across the muddy parking lot. She wasn't getting any closer to the mud than the doorway, porch, and two steps. The deep overhang of the roof over the porch was designed for sunshade during the long hot summers. The Fly knew, in the bottom of her heart and soul, it was to protect her from the nuisance of the South Bay Area rain, which begets mud.

She turned in the doorway and spied one of the new workers. The man was already dressed in his rain gear and mud boots.

"Hey, slug."

The man looked up. She called all the new guys slug or slug-bait until they proved themselves—in her eyes and on the balance sheet.

"Go tell Hooker that Dolly try to get him on radio for twenty minutes. CHP and Sheriff have panties in twist... they screaming for him."

The man lumbered out the door and across the nasty

mud lot and rain. He never looked to pick a dryer path. He just went straight to work. His only nod to the rain was wearing a stupid Dodger's hat. Everyone knew she was a Giant's fan, but she liked how he was about his job... straightforward and to the point.

One of the office assistants walked by and glanced out. "Looking ugly today, Fly—don't go out there."

The Fly turned slowly with her smartass scowl prepped. The young woman was chuckling and had beaten her to the scowl. Everyone knew the Fly hated this time of year. "Okay, smartass—who is slug I just sent out there?"

The young woman peeked to confirm her suspicion. "Bradley. You hired him last fall when Spider took to the wind. I think he is one of Dog's nephews or cousins or something. He's a nice kid. Smart too." The woman took one more peek as she set the Fly up for the punch. She looked over her shoulder as she walked away. "You should fire him... so he can go find a better job."

The Fly muttered as she looked out at the young kid walking back into the yard. Hooker was climbing into his cab and then waved. Her job was done. She shivered and closed the door.

Hooker grabbed the mic from behind the seat. "Go, Dolly."

"Head for the flats at the south end of Moffett field, I think they meant where you killed your sister last year. When you get close, find Chet on tack five. Your number will be Tango-Tango 4-1. He's in the command car, so he's Charlie Alpha One."

Hooker put the mic up to his mouth, but before he could key—she walked on him. "Just so you know, this call is now twenty-eight minutes old. Your perfect record this week is shot to slime and guts on toast."

Hooker chuckled. "10-4." He had taken three calls so far this week since picking Mae up. All three had problems in the front end, which started them already running late. He was also still waiting for at least one commercial tow—something to start putting a down payment on the new paint job. The insurance would only cover so much. The fancy layers of clear coat with mother-of-pearl floating in it—giving Mae her iridescent look—were never covered on a commercial truck and were expensive as hell.

The afternoon traffic had started. Monterey Highway was still the fastest way up through San Jose to grab the Guadalupe Parkway and out to the 101 North. Hooker was starting to understand all the work Willie and his lifelong friend Maddie had done when they revived Mae the last time. The 1,600 horsepower engine with the top end of over a hundred and sixty was a gas for sure, but the special rig Maddie cooked up took the cake every time Hooker got stuck in traffic.

Maddie was a slight built librarian by day, but it was the other side where she shined. She was born into a family who knew three things—driving moonshine, driving fast, and building the right car for the job. When she left Salinas for a more respectable life, she had never stopped loving the last two. Being a librarian meant nothing more than ready access to more knowledge of how to go faster and better.

Hooker had seen Maddie covered in more grease than he'd seen on Willie, and when it came to the quarter-mile speed, they were equaled no matter what the bracket. However, for overall crazy top-end speed—Maddie won hands down. For eight years out of eleven, she held the title of the fastest land speed record holder in her brackets on two or four wheels. The only endeavor better than Maddie's racing as the years started to take their toll was her family's other product—moonshine.

Hooker rolled to a stop at the light. Flicking the small lever down, he shifted the large shifter from the twelfth gear to the sixth. Maddie's research had removed the transfer case with an extra gearshift and dropped the gears from twenty-four to sixteen. The important differences were how the gears were laid out, and the new engine with an increase of four hundred horsepower. A large conventional Peterbilt with high-weight load dual rear end now towed like a light-weight Cadillac.

The light changed, and Hooker rolled forward behind the stock-blue Nova. He knew the young kid driving the Chevy was staring at the four hundred pounds of chrome ramming bumper in his rearview mirror.

"Hook?"

Hooker smiled. Danny was the one person who did not see a reason to waste energy on words, even to the extent of shortening his name. The former most promising lineman for USC had been scouted by the NFL when he was still playing for the blue and white of Branham High Bruins. He was now his brother's bodyguard, driver, and caretaker of anything other than the music his brother lived and breathed.

His little brother, Sweets, had been hit in the head during an accident in high school. Danny walked away from a full scholarship and a promising career. He stepped on the train, and seven hours later, he was walking the head nurse of the ICU backward because they had entered his brother's name wrong. He never stopped being the man he had chosen to be.

Hooker grabbed the mic and shifted again. "Go, Danny."

"Mama says, breakfast tomorrow. Bring Candy, and I have your grand."

Hooker frowned. "Grand?"

"Sweets says you need a grand for the new paint."

"10-4, Danny. See you three at three, and thanks."

Three clicks rattled over the speaker. Danny had reached the end of his word limit.

Hooker shook his head as the Nova turned and left the road onto the parkway clear. Hooker up-shifted as his face pulled into his trademark quirky smile.

He knew nobody had told Sweets about the damage to the truck or about Mae getting a new paint job out of the deal. Sweets *knowing* was just part of the package deal known as Sweets.

When the welding gas cylinder hit Sweets in the head, it took his sight. What replaced it was a second kind of sight as well as a memory for everything music. Sweets knew who made what, who really wrote the song, or who had done the lyrics, and who had done the music. He knew every word printed on all the liner notes of all the records. He was a walking encyclopedia when it came to music. Billboard writers regularly called him for interviews or background information. The checks were an endless stream of cash flowing to the young black disc jockey. Sweets the man went to work at midnight and played old country and western music on a rock and roll station... and got paid top dollar for breaking the rules.

Twenty minutes later, Hooker took the off-ramp leading to what used to be the southern part of the Moffitt Field Air Base. The old part had originally been part of the large push for dirigibles. The largest two were the Akron and the Macon. The original thought was for the Macon and a newer ship to be stationed here at Moffitt. The first hangar was built and still stood. It was named creatively, Hangar One. The Macon did come and did not fit. Today, the building housed a large office building and the entire squadron of P-3 Orion Subchasers. Each of the airplanes was the same size as PSA's commercial jets flying up and down the coast.

Hooker turned right at the cross street, away from the southern entry gate. A mile south, he rolled out onto a three-mile-long runway he had blasted down the previous summer. His speed, while over the state limit, was much more docile this trip. From his vantage point high in the large cab, he could look across most of the open area and spotted the red domestic fire engines as well as the lime green or fluorescent orange base emergency response team trucks. Mingling in the static scene were smaller cars of the familiar black and white variety.

Hooker nosed the large truck left and across the last of the large balloon tie-down stations. Parking at the edge of the large gathering, Hooker checked in with Dolly and then slid out into the light mist.

"What's the matter, Hooker? Couldn't you find any ice cream on the way over?"

Hooker veered toward the familiar voice. What Chet missed was it being before eight at night. Hooker rarely stopped for a triple scoop of French vanilla in a sugar cone before eight at night. Usually, it was after midnight, but always when the temperature had dropped down to a low enough temperature to guarantee cops would be stomping the feeling back in their feet as they cringed at the sight of Hooker enjoying his large slurp of pleasure.

"I picked up some street mackerel on the way. Probably wasn't killed more than a week ago, still a little squishy on the inside, but the outside has the tasty asphalt tough crust you like so much." He offered the CHP captain and friend a piece of the strange-looking homemade salmon jerky one of Dolly's friends had given her.

The man didn't even look. His hand was already out. If Hooker was eating it, it was good enough to eat. He had seen it in Dolly's refrigerator but wasn't going to be the first to try it. He chewed as they both looked across a field dotted with dozens of little yellow plastic tents. He was hyper-aware of the rookie PD standing on the other side. He thought he had heard a muffled 'urp' as Hooker was describing the food. He thought it was his duty to urge things along.

Chet leaned to Hooker, and in a loud grumble, commented, "I saw this on the way over. I thought it could use a few more days to rot before I'd pick some up. I see I was right. You did leave the rest to age up, didn't you?"

Hooker glanced leisurely behind Chet as he watched the young cop run for the distance. The kid made it almost twenty yards before all parts of the last three meals reminded him he was just a rookie.

Hooker smiled and bit off another piece. "Well played."

"Oh, I wasn't just going to leave it lying on the table. I heard him flinch as you were walking up. I think he is of the mind..." Chet waved his hand at the field, "...out there, in all this mess, is a possible body."

Hooker looked at the field of short winter-burned grass and bits and pieces of twisted steel. "What am I doing here, Chet? This is something for a skip loader and a dump truck."

The man started walking. "Let's go take a look."

As they walked, Chet thought out loud, "Where do you think the Squirt is about now?"

Hooker looked at his watch. "The Hacienda... having dinner. Why?"

"Let's take a look and see if we need him or not."

The debris field and little yellow plastic crime scene numbered tents covered the better part of a pair of football fields. Everywhere Hooker looked were small pieces of twisted sheet steel and some recognizable auto parts. The two started by walking around the perimeter, but Hooker still scanned outside the specified area just to make sure nothing had been missed.

Hooker stopped and knelt down to examine a piece of twisted steel the size of his hand. Chet handed him a pair of latex gloves. Hooker looked around as he pulled the tight gloves on before picking up the piece of sheet steel. One side was a thin, smooth coat of white paint, the other a thick white paint with brush stroke marks.

"I believe you are looking at the Squirt's funky white color paint."

Hooker frowned as he looked closer. "It looks like—"

"House paint. There's some writing underneath, but it's anybody's guess if we can put Humpty Dumpty together again. The explosion did a real number on the body."

Hooker slowly flipped the piece over as he examined the

ripped steel edges. "It looks like the explosion came from inside this. But this piece wasn't blown in the center of the piece, just the edges."

"The bomb squad from up at Moffitt—who worked on the thing with your sister last summer—they said it looked like cordite or detonation cord. It burns at the speed of sound and is sometimes used to cut metal. But they all agreed this would have taken a hell of a lot of det cord."

"Sure cut the truck up into tiny pieces." Hooker carefully put the piece back next to the little tent with the number 217 on it. He let out a winded whistle as he stood up.

Chet snorted. "Not all the pieces were so little." He pointed then walked downfield, carefully picking his way through the little markers.

In the distance, Hooker could see two guys working with a camera and a large clipboard. "Who're the two file clerks?"

Chet looked over and smirked. "You know when you really screw up? I mean screw up so bad Dolly won't talk to you for a year or even a lifetime?" Hooker started chuckling quietly. "Well, this is the job you end up with. They're charting every single piece and where it fits on the grid, which is about a hundred and fifty yards each way. Those guys are the newbies of the bomb squad and have either unsteady hands or just sweat too much."

Hooker thought about what some of the graphing and mapping Chips had done at wrecks when someone dies. "Tedious work."

Chet raised an eyebrow. "Don't ever screw up this bad." He pointed to the hunk of metal they had been walking toward.

Hooker frowned, and then slowly realized what he was looking at. "How in the pickled peach soup can you cut an engine block like...?" The chunk of metal was the front four cylinders and the top half of a straight-six engine. The rest of the engine had been cut away explosively. Hooker could see the fracture marks from the instantaneous beheading of the engine.

"The guy looped a couple of wraps of det cord over the engine and hoped it would destroy the top part. They almost succeeded."

Hooker and Chet turned toward the voice and watched the man in khaki slacks and a leather flight jacket approach. The sewn-on nameplate read Cpt. J. Thack. Hooker smiled. "Hello, John. Good to see you again."

"Better to see you survived the last time you came out here, Hooker." They shook hands.

"Chet, this is Captain John Thack. His people were the ones who blew me up the last time I was out here."

"Glad to meet you, John. I'm glad your crew was a bunch of screw-ups, and Hooker is still dodging bullets and bombs."

John laughed. "Yeah, I hear the only thing he can't dodge is a dime or three."

Chet's eyes lowered as Hooker laughed. "Yeah, well, Chet has the same affliction."

John turned with the light going on in his eye. "So you're the matching two-bit—"

Chet cut him off. "Nope, I'm just a one-bit. The Squirt, who is also a John, is the other bookend to Hooker. He was also the one who ended the rampage."

The naval officer turned on Hooker. "I'm not so sure if it's safe to be friends with you."

Chet leaned over the engine part. "Oh, I can guarantee it isn't safe...but it is interesting." He leaned close. "Hooker...?"

Hooker stepped over and looked at the area where Chet was pointing. The raised area was dirty and flash-smeared from the heat of the explosion. Hooker squinted—all the serial numbers were there.

Hooker turned his head to smile at Chet. "Unlike Giovanni and his Chevy, this guy screwed the pooch."

They stood as Chet shook his head. "I'm telling you, some criminals just want to get caught."

The Navy captain smiled. "It gets better. Take a look at this over here." He led them over to where four men in dark blue jackets were working among the pieces. John passed his outstretched hand around an area. "These guys are the Navy's answer to the ultimate jigsaw puzzle—putting crashed airplanes back together to find out what went wrong. The first thing Poncho and the guys saw was a field of glass scatter. This large field is where the front windshield went. About thirty yards is a fine spread of the left window and about forty yards over there where the yellow pole is—is the other side window. So working within those boundaries, they could start narrowing down to find this." He knelt and picked up a small twist of sheet steel and handed it to the gloved hand of Hooker.

Hooker laughed. He was looking at the stamped piece of tin every car after 1954 contained. Henry Ford had started the original number system for his Model A. When he started churning out cars from different assembly lines—and different plants—he wanted a way to trace where a specific car was made, on which day, which line, and presumably, by whom. Soon, the other automakers in Detroit saw the advantage and adopted their own. In 1954, the federal government saw an advantage to the system and standardized it to seventeen numbers.

The vehicle identification number—more generally known as the VIN—became universal. The tin was intact in the oval opening stamped into the dashboard. Hooker knew this would tell them who was supposed to own the car. He handed the metal shard over to Chet.

13

SLOP IN THE STREETS

When the jet stream pushes down at steep angles, the storms come straight out of the Gulf of Alaska. When there's a large tropical depression off Hawaii, the rotation drags moisture up out of Mexico and creates fire-hose-like rain. Mix the two together, and you have a Monday like no other.

This Monday morning had been nonstop for three days, except for the occasional short nap in the sleeper. Hooker pushed the broom along the highway. With each reach of the arms, it opened his leather jacket just enough to take in air. When he brought them back, the expelled air could just about knock over a horse with the stench.

Hooker was starting to have fantasies about getting a break long enough to go grab a shower and fresh clothes. He knew if he were at Willie's, the clothes he was wearing would be washed with a cutting torch. Realistically, he didn't care. He had just gotten another whiff.

Hooker laughed at the thought of Willie. The man had spent so much time in the jungles of Korea and Vietnam and, as a POW, had gone weeks without any kind of reference to hygiene. And yet, as frugal as he was, if an article of clothing were passed a certain point, he or his boyfriend Hank would rather burn it than allow it to enter his clean washing machine.

As he once told Hooker, his machine was for *soiled* clothing, not dirty street grim. Hooker knew if he made it past soiled point, it was far wiser and frugal to take it to a laundry or have Stella do it. Even Maddie had been known to carry a pair of jeans out into the garage area at the end of a stick. Once there, she would take vicious pleasure at striking a three-foot flame on the cutting torch, her flame of choice.

The trick would be how to sneak into the house, get fresh, and escape with the dirty clothes without being caught by Willie or Hank. The latter had been spending more time at the house lately while he changed the whitewashed walls to a new paint palate he called Tuscan Morning. Hooker thought the new color looked like it was a little smudged with dirt but still basically white.

The whistle bridged the time gap between the flare of lightning and the crash of the resulting thunder. Hooker pushed one last sweep at the pile and turned. The CHP officer in the yellow slicker wound his finger in the air—he was releasing the traffic. Hooker waved and grabbed the dustpan out of his back pocket. He carried the small pile scooped up back to the working deck of Mae. As he passed the crushed Gremlin, he reconsidered, and his hand flashed. The dustpan was empty, and there was a little more weight when the AMC car went on its journey to the crusher. Dog wouldn't even bother taking the seats out. Only the rubber tires would be removed. Nobody wanted the clown-car rims.

As Hooker closed the door, he glanced at his watch. It was half-past three. Sticking the truck into gear, he looked across the freeway. He evaluated the off-ramp on the other side—leading straight up to Willie's place.

Hooker looked in the mirrors for the CHP officer. He was looking north at the oncoming traffic. Hooker and what he was doing was the least of his concern. Hooker smiled and reached to the large new overhead command board Maddie had built and installed for him. He would be safe, as long as he stayed away from triggering the siren.

Facing the two lanes of oncoming traffic from the south —the front of Mae West lit up in red and blue rotating lights. Hooker had chosen a break in the traffic, which had a little stopping room. The mass reared in panic at the monster truck and stopped. Hooker spun the wheel and stomped on the go-pedal. As he invaded the space of the two lanes, he reversed the switches, so when the officer looked around, it just looked like a bunch of kind drivers had been nice and gave Hooker the right-of-way.

Hooker bounced over the low break curbing separating the freeway from the off-ramp and turned the nose up the hill. The traffic resumed, and two minutes later, Hooker pulled up in front of Willie's giant garage.

Even with the cold of the storm, the door was half-open for ventilation. The heat in the acre of garage was provided through the thick concrete floor courtesy of the hot water artesian well in the side of the mountain.

Hooker hurried quietly along the one wall as he kept his eye on the hunkered form bent over the blue-white glow of a welding arc. It was too big for Maddie, and he knew Hank would never get close to something so potentially dirty.

Hooker figured it was his uncle, and he just might not lose a set of clothes today.

As much as Hooker wanted to curl up on the floor of the shower and let the water beat him into sleep, he knew he had a car to drop before his compulsory appearance at the Wednesday night dinner at Dolly's. Turning off the water and grabbing the plush white bath sheet, he dried his hair and started down. As his eyes cleared the towel, he noticed the empty floor. His wallet, money clip, change, and keys were on the counter. He closed his eyes and kept drying off.

Dressed, with hair brushed and a semi-decent shave, he walked out into the general living quarters. Hank sat at the large dining table, sipping his tea and reading the racing forum. He never bet, but he loved handicapping the ponies. On occasion, Hooker had placed a two-dollar bet at Hank's suggestion and came away a winner almost every time. If Hank ever caught wind of Hooker betting any real money, he would never speak of the ponies again. However, the occasional nice dinner paid with a two-dollar bet was okay in his book. With his knowledge, it wasn't like it was gambling or anything.

"William is washing your rags out on the concrete." Hank didn't even look up.

Hooker remained silent and headed for the garage. He knew Hank would not take his pleasure and smile until after Hooker had cleared the door to the large garage.

As Hooker stepped out into the garage, two things were askew. Willie was standing over a smoldering heap of rags while wearing a short square dance dress. Hooker assumed the burn pile had been his clothes, but the hulking form in the welding booth was still welding.

Hooker shielded his eyes and saddled over to Willie. "Who's burning the arc?"

"The Squirt."

Hooker frowned and started to look.

"Don't look. It makes him nervous."

The static snarling stopped. Hooker could hear the strikes of the welding hammer breaking off the slag. The pounding went on for a couple of minutes. It was a very long weld.

"You want to check this, Willie?"

Willie smiled at Hooker and swooped his turn with an arm up like a dancer. "Coming, dear..."

The two men walked over to where the Squirt was standing next to two long pieces of railroad rails—now attached. Hooker didn't ask—he knew the railroads never sold their rail. They smelted them back down and made more. Therefore, it was illicit to be in possession of any rail... but the steel made a nice anvil. Hooker recognized the two-foot-long double-width form.

"Planning on doing some bodywork, Squirt?"

The Squirt smiled. "Nah, I just wanted to learn the welding. But I think Chet and Willie are planning on some bodywork."

Willie bent over to examine the weld. "We found the frame for a 1929 AC Runabout."

Whatever he was saying after that was lost in Willie's mind. Hooker knew he was already folding and pounding into shape sheets of steel. The short dress and petticoats exposing most of the man's legs—was not lost on Hooker. Long past any stage of being repulsed by the sight, he was also long past any compunction at using it to get his uncle's attention back.

Hooker grabbed the large industrial drill with no bit in it. After checking to make sure it was plugged in, he started to place the drill between the man's legs. The hand on his arm stopped him. Hooker jumped and looked into Hank's face. The man had pure devil in his eyes. Hooker handed the drill to his uncle's boyfriend.

The one-second goose of the electric drill produced a reaction none expected.

The man didn't jump. He didn't scream. He just started to straighten and then spoke in a slightly higher octave, "It must be Hank. Because that Jacobs Chuck is way too large to be Hooker."

The four were laughing twenty minutes later as Hooker and the Squirt were leaving for Dolly's and the Wednesday night dinner.

As the two young men stood poised at the large garage door, the two older men stood with their one arms around each other's shoulder or waist. Willie snapped his finger and looked at Hank. "The phone call."

Hank raised both eyebrows, which lifted his forehead. "Oh, yes, Hooker. A very nice Lieutenant named Miller called today from up at Moffitt Field." Hooker stepped back into the garage, and the Squirt followed. "He said the explosive cord the person had used was a unique kind... it was only used in hard mining or something."

The Squirt stepped forward and stood next to Hooker. "Did he say hard-rock mining?"

Hank snapped his fingers and pointed at the Squirt.

"Exactly the term he used. Very good, Jonathan. I'm proud of you."

Hooker muttered with a teasing bored smile, "Get over it. He read it somewhere once."

Willie growled.

The Squirt ignored them both. "It means the mining is done in a confined space, and the explosion needs to be constrained or restrained. Making a large explosion is not the objective, but instead, is made to be used for precision."

Hank rolled his shoulder. "Well, I don't know about that. It sounded like a big bang was the idea. They estimated he used about one hundred pounds of the rope. This Miller fella seemed to think he glued up a cord every six-inch square. It sounds to me like he wanted more than just a quiet whoop-de-do."

Hooker gave a low whistle. "Wow. What kind of person is this?"

Willie had a serious look on his face, and his arm around Hank's waist applied a little bit more squeeze. "This is a very dangerous person, Hooker. You be very careful... which goes double for you, Squirt."

The two young men saluted the former Navy Seal and recipient of the Congressional Medal of Honor hanging ten feet away. Hooker placed it there to remind everyone Willie had earned his right to be the man he wanted to be—the hard way. If any person had the right to speak of danger, Willie held the honor—in spades.

Turning, the matched set of black leather jackets, starched white T-shirts, jeans, and boots sauntered out into the midwinter drizzle. Hooker grabbed the large hammer and bounced it down on every one of the ten tires. Dropping it into the bucket, he climbed up into the cab of his first love —the giant truck known as Mae West. As he closed the door, Willie smiled at the new rendition of the early screen star waving from the side of the truck.

Hank purred his approval. "Oh, those new extra-large bumpers are just perfect."

Willie leaned into his boyfriend. "So she doesn't look like some anemic adolescent tenth-grader anymore?"

Hank slapped him on the chest. "Just stop. I never said such a thing. She just didn't look so...well, Mae West."

The two men waved as the truck rolled, and leather-covered arms waved from both windows.

They turned, and Willie hit the switch. The pig-sized electric motor across the large doorway started to close the forty-foot tall and wide corrugated tin door. He knew the boys wouldn't be back until after the storm was gone, he just hoped Hooker would get some rest.

Willie caught Hank staring at him. "What?"

"Nothing... other than the kid looked like hell warmed over."

Willie's lips rolled into barrels. "It's the job. You make hay while the sun don't shine."

14

DOLLY'S TABLE AND A COLORADO PLATE

The seating arrangement at Dolly's table on any Wednesday night was up to Dolly. One phrase a guest would never hear Dolly say is, "Oh, just take a seat anywhere!" It just would not happen. Everyone knew the seating was part and parcel of Dolly's selection of who was invited for a certain night.

Until the previous year, no woman had ever sat at the table—not even Dolly. Those few women who had broken the tradition were powerfully connected women in their own right.

Tonight's agenda was even obvious to the Squirt, who sat at the foot of the table. Hooker, quietly amused, sat at the head. There were five seats down each side. Sitting in the middle seat on Hooker's right was the Highway Patrol Captain, Chet. Hooker was silently enjoying watching the man squirm. Dolly had let Hooker know the local CHP office had six new openings for patrol officers. Hooker was aware the official title was Patrolman, but if Dolly had her way, it would become patrol officer or just officer.

Seated down Hooker's left side were two field officers from the sheriff's office, two patrol officers from the San Jose police department, and a Deputy Fire Chief from Moffitt Field Air Base. The five women smiled prettily at the Squirt, Hooker, and especially Captain Chet Davis.

Flanking Chet was the county commissioner Paul, who kept watching his plate for fear he would start laughing at the uncomfortable spot Chet was now in. Nothing official would happen tonight, but Paul and Chet knew the pressure from Dolly's table could be worse than an investigation from Internal Affairs. Both of their careers had experienced and enjoyed the power of the table.

Sitting between Paul and the Squirt was the large mass of the happy Filipino, Officer James Aligo. His right hand slid a small snapshot of his new partner, a black German Shepard, over to the Squirt. The man was positively radiant... like a proud new father.

The deputy on the end leaned forward as she recognized the type of photo. "New K-9?"

Aligo beamed. "Zaafir. She's just a year old. I start training next week. Her name means—"

"Victorious." The black eyes flared.

Aligo smiled.

The female deputy continued. "My mother is from Lebanon. They met when my father went to Israel on a sabbatical to study in the original scriptures. She was on holiday. It was love at first sight. Her parents said it would never work because of the differences."

"Because he was Jewish...?"

The deputy laughed. "Oh, no. Jewish would have been

fine. My mother was Jewish. No, it was because he was an American."

The Filipino frowned, as did the others who were now listening. "Your mother was Jewish, but from Lebanon?"

"Certainly. Why not? There were large Jewish ghettos in both Beirut and Tripoli. Most of the major cities of the Muslim world had large Jewish populations and ghettos. Usually, they were the commanding population in the medina or old central district of a city." She passed the dog photo down the table on the female side.

Chet was happy the object of discussion and focus was off him. "So the only problem was your father was from America?"

She chuckled, "No, because he was married."

The table was silent. She continued to explain. "Nobody thought to ask about the ring on his finger. Even my mother wanted to ignore the ring. In those days, jewelry was something most people in the region couldn't afford. So for the man to have a wedding ring... it spoke volumes about the importance of the marriage."

The lieutenant in the Navy whites leaned forward on his elbows and rested his turned head on two fists. "So, obviously somehow, they resolved the issue of this marriage which was in the way of their own, otherwise... he wouldn't be your father."

She blushed. "Well, if he had been married, he would still be my father. The truth came out after my mother had discovered she was pregnant with me. The wedding ring was just a ring. When my father was only nineteen, his parents had died in a train derailment. They were in New York on the elevated train over Jamaica Bay. The train plunged into the deepest part of the bay. After the bodies had been recovered, my father was given their jewelry. It was their simple thin rings and her gold earrings. He had them melted down and made into a ring for him to wear and remember them by. He just never thought about it being on his wedding finger—honoring their marriage."

The Navy captain in khakis mused, "It's amazing sometimes how wrong, or misplaced beliefs can be... when understanding can sometimes be as close as a simple question."

Chet shifted in his seat and cleared his throat. Then he looked up to see Dolly with two hot plates in her hand. "Incoming. Nobody move."

Dolly nodded a thank you and started placing plates of her spaghetti with dispatch-cooked marinara sauce and a Sicilian sausage from Chiaramontes in the north end of the city in front of each of them. The banter changed, as Chet relaxed and did what was expected of him. He asked the female officers about their experiences with being a female in the field.

The conversation led to the many factions of the law enforcement culture, and how it was changing. The consensus was slowly and not often for the better. Chet and Paul both got the full blast of the female viewpoint. All five of the officers had been coached on the nature of the table. Nothing in conversation went beyond the door, and even then, it always answered to Dolly. Hooker was enjoying his dinner. He was certain a few—if not all—of the officers would be seen at the table in the future. He gave Dolly a knowing smile. They both liked the idea of change.

Dina called from the other room, "Aligo, your watch

commander wants to know if you will be swinging by the precinct. I believe he has someone for you to meet."

"Ladies, it has been a pleasure to meet you this evening. We hope to get to know all of you better. Hooker and Squirt, I have a commercial in San Francisco going to Auburn. Pack an extra T-shirt."

Hooker stood first, with Aligo a fast second. "James, as always, it's been grand. Good luck with your new girlfriend. She looks a little young for you, but I'm sure it will all work out. Please keep her safe out there in the Knife & Gun Club of King and Story."

Turning to the left side of the table, Hooker smiled winningly. "Ladies, the protocol is you do not touch your plate." The deputy quietly placed her plate back on the table. "Thank you. You place your napkin on the table, push your chair in, and thank Dolly for dinner. Hugs are optional and your choice. However, I recommend considering them. We'll clear the security cameras and meet you at the door. Gentlemen, please be seated once the ladies are gone. I'll be right back."

Hooker cleared the monitors and gave Dolly the nod. Dolly opened the door and received five hugs. She enforced the exchange by telling each she would be in touch. The last was one of the deputies, and she held her hand to keep her a moment. Quietly, she leaned in. "I know you're getting the promotion you put in for and heading for Sacramento."

"The selection hasn't been released from—" She frowned at Dolly. "Not even my supervisor knows I put in for the position." Her voice trailed off as she remembered where she just had dinner.

Dolly had waited to see the light of understanding cross

those deep, black eyes. She smiled as she recognized she had just secured the friendship she was looking for.

"I wanted you to know your new job doesn't let you off the hook with my table. Whenever your new schedule involves the South Bay, you make sure it also involves dinner on a Wednesday night—just let me know you're coming. I also don't want you to think this is about you being special. Besides, I need a set of eyes and ears in Sacramento attached to a sharp working mind."

The woman hugged her again. "Thank you again. The dinner was fantastic..." She stopped and struggled with what she needed to say next. "All my life, I have lived and eaten halal. Halal means I don't eat pork... But after tonight..."

Dolly smiled as she put a finger to the young woman's lips. "This is our secret. The dinner tonight was kosher. I knew about you. I made... um... accommodations. Nobody comes to my table without me knowing how they eat and a lot more about them."

The woman slumped. "Of course, you would. It was silly of me—"

Dolly cut her off again. "Never think less of your beliefs or who you are, and so you know where you stand in my eyes, say hello to Lynnette when you get home tonight. Give her a large hug for me. If I thought I could do her any good, I would bring her to the table also. I understand your relationship will be a strained long-distance one with her. But I've also heard there may be a need for a good nurse at Central Valley."

The two smiled as the understanding sunk in. Sarah leaned in for a last hug. "Of course, you would know about us. Thank you for being a friend. When the announcement comes out next week, I'll remember to act very surprised."

Dolly squeezed a little tighter. "You have my numbers."

Dolly watched as the woman crossed the parking lot and safely drove off. As she closed the door, she kissed her two fingers, and then pressed them to the badge welded to the thick steel plate door just above the doorknob. She could hear the men going over the strange new case taking up Hooker's attention. She knew they would need more coffee.

Captain Thack leaned forward and looked down the table at the Squirt. They were chuckling at Chet, who had asked, "How many feet of det cord was used, John?" The two Johns had started to answer at the same time.

The Squirt settled it. "Let's just stick with Squirt and captain. That way there's no confusion."

Paul snorted and muttered. "At least, for now, there's just one captain."

Chet cleared his throat, and they all laughed.

Hooker leaned back as he realized his mug was empty. "Okay, Squirt, as you seem to have the answers... how many feet of cord?"

The kid walked them all through the problem, and it became obvious he had not previously worked out the answer. The two naval officers had never watched the Squirt's mind work like the other three had. Even Dolly had not seen him crunch information and stood amazed as she leaned against the counter with the coffee carafe floating ineffectively in midair.

"Assuming the box of the interior was roughly twelve feet long and five feet wide... the walls in a standard panel truck are almost five and a half feet tall. The end-for-end runs would be twenty-nine feet. Accounting for the way he cut up the dashboard and firewall, let's use an integer of thirty because he used more under the dash, but he didn't need any for the glass. There would be eleven of those runs if we assume one running at the edge of the walls.

"The inner circumference of the cylinder would be twenty-one with a basic sum of fourteen runs. All of this gives us eight hundred and eighty-five feet... but that is the bare minimum. As we didn't find much in the way of seats and other interior parts, I would assume the bomber used at least an extra hundred and forty feet, wrapping extra loops under the dashboard, around the seats, and the steering column. The drive train didn't receive as much attention. From what I could see from the photographs, it would appear he made several loops over the rear end and suspension, as well as down the driveshaft. I would estimate he used only an extra couple of hundred feet there. The transmissions condition, or the mess of the gearbox, would suggest he made several loops about six feet each and draped them over the transmission. My guess is there were two sets of loops—one in front of the shifter and one behind. All total, about an added hundred feet." He paused a moment to take a sip of his coffee. In the room, a pin could have dropped and startled the listeners.

"The blast deformation changes with the engine compartment, the front end, and the fenders. The blast shifts from inside to dual blast and or shell compression." He looked at the two naval officers. The man in white smiled and nodded.

"He wanted the front end of the truck to be obscured. He knew it was a unique shape and design, so he used most of his remaining charge line to destroy the shape. I'm going to go with about two hundred feet of cord, which... out of a pair of one-thousand-foot rolls of mining detonation cord, he only had a few long hanks left to try to blow the engine. My guess is we are dealing with someone who knows their way around a mine and explosives but is not automotive inclined."

Paul leaned back with the thumbnail of his left hand pushed into his lips. Where Dolly's mind was stunned into a stall, his was whirling with information. "So two-thousand feet...?"

The Squirt looked at Dolly and held out his coffee mug. Dolly jerked back to the world she knew and started pouring. The Squirt looked at Paul. "Two-thousand would be my guess. I did a little digging around, and a regular person can buy small rolls of two-hundred and fifty feet or even five-hundred feet if they have a blasting license like a farmer would have for clearing trees and such. However, someone who knows explosives, especially if it is their profession, would be buying the more economical roll of a thousand feet. So, two rolls."

He looked back at the lieutenant. "But there was something I was curious about. The pieces of the hood and inner panels of the engine compartment seem inconsistent with the shearing of the body. There wouldn't be a change of the metal's thickness. So, did your squad have any conjectures about what would account for the change in the deformation?"

"We thought maybe your figure of two thousand might have been close, but not close enough. We think in the front he used a smaller roll of the more common form of cord—

which would be standard use with the farmers you mentioned. The cord would be tighter and less contained in its explosive nature. It wouldn't be used in a mine but would be the right thing for use on a stump or large boulder." He leaned back as Dolly filled his cup. "We think he ran out of the cord he normally used and had to supplement it with a two-fifty roll. We're hoping the police can find a roll bought locally in the last few weeks."

Hooker smelled his fresh coffee and took a sip. Setting the mug down, he weighed in. "So how did we do with the numbers, Chet?"

"A strange mixed bag there also. The truck was last bought by one Helmut Lysander. However, it seems Helmut died in 1968 in a mining accident, but he continues to drive and register his truck each year in Colorado. I've reached out to the sheriff in a place called Fairplay—he hasn't gotten back to me yet."

The Squirt pinched the bridge of his nose. The information was not making sense, or whatever he was processing, and it seemed to hurt. Speaking into his hand, he continued to pinch his nose.

"In 1963, a woman in Tulsa, Oklahoma, was found guilty of fraud. Her husband had died the year after returning from the war in the Pacific where he had been injured. She buried him in the backyard and continued to receive his disabled veteran benefits checks. When the VA required a check-up, she convinced her brother to stand in. Nobody at the VA hospital noticed the blood type had changed. It was only when someone took an x-ray of his gut they saw the lower half of the left lung as well as the kidney had grown back. The woman had maintained the ruse by continuing to pay the registration fees on his truck, which sat disused in the barn. She also paid his Masonic Lodge dues as well as his Shriner dues. The Master of the Masonic Lodge was reported as saying they regretted hearing of the brother's passing as he had been a regular attendant of the lodge, and he would be missed." The Squirt released his nose and looked up.

Hooker looked at him with a deadpan face. "Did they charge the Master with collusion?"

All five of the men laughed. Hooker, Dolly, and Paul knew the Squirt had just read something he had seen at some time. The Squirt shrugged. "It didn't say."

The other five stopped laughing. Captain Thack opened his mouth, thought, and then shut it. "That was real?"

The Squirt nodded. "The point being—we're looking for a relative."

15

HELMUT'S SON

Helmut Lysander's son sat on the screened porch and looked across the bay. The panel truck was history, but he had a bad feeling about it. The two large rolls of det cord weren't beyond his budget, but they also were not cheap. His supplies came through strange roundabout routes to hide their final destination and took time. With this new job, time is what he did not have.

In addition, the new van was a connection he did not like. He had to buy it in his own name... a name where, for the last five years, had all but remained outside the system of records in California. Even his work shirt only had Jake stitched on the breast.

His right hand reached out and grabbed the soldering iron from its stand. The left fingered the wad of solder and fished out a longer end. The two met on the small asbestos mat. The flux seared, and the tendril of smoke enveloped Felix in memories.

Felix could still smell the wet, pungent odor of the rotting timbers mixed with the damp earth and leaking seams of sulfur in what was left of the coal. He held his father's left hand, and the man carried the large canvas bag in his right. It was Felix's seventh birthday, and he had wanted to see what his father did with all the stuff in the large locked shed behind the house. He had always known it was dangerous, or he and Tommy Campbell would have broken into the shed a long time before—as they did with Tommy's older brother's room. At the time, the two boys did not understand the pictures of the women who were not wearing clothes... but it was only a matter of time.

The old mine was large to the seven-year-old, but later, Felix knew it had been just a short walk into the mountain. It was only a test hole. The entire shaft did not run a thousand feet or more. His father had spent the week before pounding on a two-foot-long rod with a hardened end in the shape of a cross. The rod was called a star drill. One man can drill a hole in rock wall by hitting on the rod, and between hits, turn the rod an eighth of a turn. Then two hits and turn. Two hits and turn. The first hit would break the nodes from the previous beats, and the second would drive a new star into the bottom of the hole—which created four new nodes.

With each hit, a small puff of stone dust would eject from the hole. Not enough to notice, but just enough to be breathed in. Over the course of a decade or two, the tiny pieces of stone would make tiny cuts in the lungs where they came to rest. Those cuts would fester and heal, fester, and heal. With age, the scars lose elasticity, and the lungs cannot expand and contract like they needed.

With the lack of fresh air to the lungs, combined with a daily pack of unfiltered cigarettes, the damage becomes either black lung or cancer. Either one was a short death sentence to a miner. Many like Felix's father had first gone in a mine not much older than Felix was on his seventh birthday. Many of those miners, like his father, had retired because they could no longer breathe—and would never leave the hospital where they ended up.

By the time his father fell in the mine and rushed to the hospital, Felix was already in the family business with enough experience to be running most of the day-to-day work. He had watched his father fade away. When he was young, he was in little league. In the summer evenings, his father and he would throw the ball. Nobody ever said anything, but if you stood quiet-like, you could hear the echo of leather balls smacking into leather mitts.

Few fathers could afford or felt a need to buy a glove for themselves. Most were just grateful they could watch their boy play high school ball. Some didn't even last long enough. The mines gave up their riches grudgingly, and occasionally, extracted a high price. Later it would extract a high price from all the miners—it was just a matter of when.

Felix counted the four-foot lengths of pieced wire... one hundred and seven. He banded the hundred and placed the packet on the shelf. Turning back to the table desk, he started making the next hundred. He would need seven bundles for the next job and one more for any unforeseen problems that may arise. The wires were always the same and adaptable as to length due to their construction.

Felix looked out across the black expanse he knew was lawn—or what passed for the lawn. Even in the cold of winter, Felix could feel the fresh-cut grass between his toes. The summer he played left field in the city league, he could feel the strength leaving his father. The mitt didn't sting anymore. They threw the ball until his father's television shows were on instead of until it was too dark to see. It was also in his step. He had caught his father sitting on a rock or old timbers, catching his breath. He took two days to set up a job instead of the morning to set up and then would blow the job when the four o'clock whistle blew.

When Felix was twenty, the two of them would go over the plans, outlining the job. Felix would then set the charges, and his father would come to examine the first few hundred feet. His pat answer was spoken with a shortness of breath. He would wave his large hand in the air, saying, *Felix, you set it up just fine. I don't know why you insist on my checking your work.* Then he would shuffle back out of the mine. As the years and stone dust took their toll, his shuffling became slower and longer.

One day, the shuffling stopped. The man collapsed, and Felix almost left him in the mine. The man had no one, but his son left. The woman he loved and thought loved him had left him with a six-year-old boy to rear on his own. For a moment, as Felix knelt there in the dark of the mine, he could feel the new radio detonator in his jacket pocket. It would have been so easy to simply carry his father deeper into the mine where the charges were larger—sit with him and hold his hand while he pushed the little button.

Felix had only dated Thelma a few times by that day. He had no plans.

Felix stuck the iron in the holder and gently placed the small loop of solder on the table. He leaned back in the chair with his eyes closed. This is what his father must have felt. Life had started with such promise—and then a little stone dust here, a bump there, and things turn out not like you had thought, even if you had planned.

Felix pushed back the chair as he stood.

He turned off the last lights in the house. He wouldn't need any to see his way around a house he knew so well. For a man who had spent most of his life in dark mines, the house in the middle of the night was almost like daylight.

He checked at the bedroom door. The cover was askew, so he went in. He straightened the sheet and folded the top three inches down over the blanket. He knew she would find the satin binding in the night and stick the corner of the blanket back in her mouth like a baby. He pulled back the quilt square to her shoulder, leaving just the top inch out to the cool of the night.

He ran his hand down along the quilt—feeling the pattern. Thelma and her mother had pieced the top from four generations of their family's clothes. When Thelma and Felix were first married, she could point to a tiny piece of cloth and tell him who had worn it and what it had been. It was a graph of her history. She was the smart one. She had even studied at the junior college in Boulder. A misplaced charge and a two-inch stone to the front of her head had taken it all away from her— had taken her away from him.

Felix ran his hand down along her shoulder and arm. There was almost nothing left of the woman. She would hardly take any food or water. She was disappearing in front of him, but his guilt and grief couldn't let her go.

The Colorado hospital had sent a nurse out to check on her condition and the condition she was living in. Felix hadn't blamed them. Even in the best of times, mining towns were not sanitary or comforting places. People were busy trying to dig a living out of the side of a mountain—even though the living they were digging was at the bottom of the barrel.

With Felix's side money, they were building a nest egg they thought would one day set them free. They dreamed of a day when they could just live in a clean town somewhere—somewhere they could both work nice clean jobs. Things like a fine new home and cars were never part of the dream. Their dreams were simple and down to earth—same as they were.

Felix looked at the small line of a rise in the quilt. The moonlight through the window barely cast any shadows on the bed. Like their dreams—the day at the mine having ended in the hospital had wiped out their savings and left only a small lump casting almost no shadow on a bed.

Felix walked back out to the screened porch. Glancing at his watch, he started putting the equipment back in the wall. In six hours, he would have to become Jake Smalley again.

As he removed his boots, he thought about the fateful night in the bar in North Platte, Nebraska. He had finished a job earlier in the evening, further east in Chapman. The old wood grain silo had blown just the way the man had described an old silo would explode if the heat built up in the grain. Felix had laughed. The site was instantaneously ready for an oversized cement pond.

He had stopped in at the roadhouse because most bars had some generally decent food to go with their watered-down drinks and cheap beer. The food was better than expected, and the beer was damn good.

Felix had ordered and then gone into the men's room to freshen up. When he returned, the waitress looked surprised. She stepped back a few paces and grabbed a plate a man was starting to reach for. She told the man sorry and brought the sandwich back over to Felix. Then she kept looking at him and then the other guy. Finally, she asked if they were brothers or something.

The two men looked at each other. In a rough sort of way, they could have been twins. The joke about *who's your father* was as instantaneous as the *let me buy you a beer.* Felix had long known about the existence of an estranged sister... but had never heard about a brother. This wasn't, but their lives would become perversely intertwined moving forward.

Felix wasn't forthcoming about what he was doing in the left armpit of the country. Jake, on the other hand, by the third beer, had mapped out a life gone all shades of wrong. He had a decent job, but he was dating the boss's seventeen-year-old daughter. Next thing everyone noticed, she couldn't fit in her ass-tight flowered jeans anymore. Her daddy had a shotgun, and soon, Jake found himself on the road with his thumb out headed west from Fort Wayne, Indiana. A trucker here and a drunken territory salesman there had landed him in North Platte. He was hoping to land a job on a tramp freighter in Seattle. If not, he would continue up to Alaska and the pipeline.

Felix had given his doppelganger a thousand dollars the next morning as traveling money and then explained how to get fake identification in a large city like Seattle. The man would no longer need his real driver's license and had given it to Felix. In exchange of good faith, Felix had promised he would run the trail cold.

True to his word, Felix had washed the ID through the

Texas system, rinsed it in Utah, and dried it in Colorado. By the time anyone asked in California if he was Jake Smalley from Terra Haute, Indiana—he could honestly look the man in the eye and tell him he had never been in Indiana. It was a simple truth.

As Felix pulled the light cord and pulled the blankets over him, he was hoping Jake had found his freighter. He just hoped he wouldn't have to do the same.

16

CAN YOU TOW A TRAIN?

Hooker leaned over and felt in the rack. Along the right outer edge were bumps on a tape that Sweets had put there for Hooker. Each of the eight-track tapes had a unique set of bumps. Hooker just needed to learn the Braille. They were the same bumps Sweets had on all the eight-track tapes at the radio station. Being blind for Sweets was the same for Hooker when it would be dangerous to take his eyes off the road at sixty while running up a dark 101.

Dinner had been a few hours before in San Luis Obispo across from where he had dropped a Mack tractor with a cracked engine block. The hotdog stand was everything the man had told him. What the man hadn't mentioned was the woman who owned it also loved cats. Box had gotten a dish of fresh caught Rock Cod. He had also failed to mention she served soft frosty. It wasn't his usual French vanilla, but neither he nor Box had a problem with any of it.

The tow was a special deal with the Fly. She wanted it towed on Sunday so she could charge weekend rates, and to force Hooker to take it, she had handed him the key to the lock on the fuel depot. Her instructions were to give it back sometime next week. He would have made the tow for just the three hundred plus gallons of fuel, but she also was implying a refill when he got back, on top of the long green for the tow. She knew he was working to pay Danny back for the extra special pearl paint job—Mae West's signature look.

Tex Ritter's boy was just starting into the steel guitar solo Hooker liked so much. Hooker smiled. The song would take him all the way to the top of the grade, climbing out of the coastal plain. The rest of the album would see him past Atascadero, and by then, he could pick up Sweets at shortly after three-thirty.

Hooker rubbed his face with his right hand. It had been a long day, but worth it.

The red lights swung onto the highway just after Hooker passed the cutoff to Santa Margarita. The cruiser fishtailed and then became steady. Hooker expected the Chip to pass him, but the officer tucked in behind Mae. Hooker looked at his speedometer. He was only about twelve over the limit. Hooker could smell chicken manure growing all over this.

Mae nosed onto the shoulder, and Hooker set the brakes. He considered making the officer work for the ticket by having him climb up and down to get to Hooker's window but then thought about the fairness. He had been speeding—a little. Which was nothing compared to what he had been doing when he dragged the dead tractor down, or what he was going to open up and do after Atascadero...

Hooker pushed open his door and slid down the side of Mae. He met the officer at the end of the working bed. The man was all smiles. Hooker could feel the weight of a rural ticket.

"Are you Hooker?"

Hooker stopped. "Yes, sir..."

The man turned and headed back to his cruiser. "You'd better come on and set in the passenger seat. Y'all ain't gonna believe this."

Hooker slid down into the low-slung cruiser, which sat purring a little rough. Hooker frowned and looked over at the man. "Do you take this home at night?" Hooker nodded his head toward the car's front end—which was not running a stock engine.

The man chuckled. "Sure."

"440?"

The look on the man's face soured. "Panty-attack crap? No way. I ripped that out years ago, son. That there is the sweet sound of pure Mopar. My buddy races and we built out a 340 Hemi to a 390 and got a sinker manifold to mount the twin quad Hollys. If I could get away with it, I'd trick out a shaker hood with a stack of six-pack."

Hooker stared at the man as he thought about the engine the man had just described. It was a unique design meant for only two cars.

"Did you pull this engine out of a Belvedere that went sideways on the Visalia drags and ended rolling through the weeds?"

The man laughed. "Y'all know Ben Robinson?"

Hooker smirked. "Sure—but I know his sister better."

"It were Maddie's boyfriend done rolled the sum-bitch."

Hooker nodded. "My uncle."

The man laughed and stuck his hand out. "Wa'll hell,

son—that there makes you family. Chester. Chester Duggins. Ben's daddy and mine done run shine together. They runned north, and daddy runned south." The man leaned back and just slowly shook his head. "Shoot... small world."

"Sure is." Hooker gave him a moment and then started to open the door. It reminded the officer of the unfinished business.

"Let's get dispatch on the horn here." He took the mic off the holder on the dashboard. Reverently he called his dispatcher. Hooker was amazed they had one at this time of night.

"Alpha 2-4."

The female voice crackled: "Go ahead, Alpha 2-4."

He turned toward Hooker. "Oh, good. She's still awake. I was expecting you an hour ago. They said you had a mean mill in that there rig." He keyed his mic. "Sugar, I have that there tow guy they was looking for."

"10-4. Let me call them back, honey."

Hooker looked at the man. "Honey?"

The smile was pure pride. "As you can guess, there ain't much out here in the weeds at night, so we have the phones and radio switched over to my house. My wife is a light sleeper and a hair-trigger. It don't hurt none that the phone and radio is right thar by the bed." The man blushed. "Of course, it makes being out here even harder knowing that there radio is a direct connection to the prettiest pink baby doll."

"Honey, they want to know if you have a *hooker?*"

"It's the man's name, sweet pea—and yes, he's here."

"The lady said to use the top four gears and head for

Fremont... he has a train to tow. Something about trying a county that don't work or something. Honey, I was in the middle of a nice dream, and then you called... I don't understand any of this... Oh, wait. She wants more."

Chester just smiled as his yoke was showing. "She's not the brightest star in the night..."

Hooker smiled. "But she's your star."

"You got that right."

"Honey, I think I get it now. They want him in Fremont code-three. There was some big train wreck, and he's the closest crane."

"10-4, Sugar. I'll talk to you in the morning."

"Love ya, honey."

The man hung the mic and looked at Hooker. He frowned. "Code three?"

Hooker rolled his eyes. "Trust me. You don't want to know. What can I expect between here and San Jose?"

"Cop wise?" Hooker nodded.

"I'm it until you hit Gilroy. Battle, Henry Battle, will come on at King City about five, but I'd 'spect y'all will be long gone by then."

Hooker stuck out his hand and shook. "Long gone, Chester... long gone. Thanks for the pullover. Good to know the killer engine is being put to good use. Also, it's always good to know more of the family."

He backed out of the car and loped back to the cab of Mae.

Chester tried to keep up but finally fell off at Atascadero.

17

COG IN A LARGER CRIME

Felix sat in the bar. The place smelled worse than the most disgusting mine he had ever been inside of. One would expect the bathrooms to smell of old urine and maybe even shit... However, when sitting at the bar, or even shooting balls on what was passing for a pool table, a person would expect to smell only stale beer and possibly vomit. Even Felix's nose could smell all four mixed with what he knew to be the coppery smell of old blood mixed with semi-fresh blood.

Someone recently bled more than just a nosebleed or small cut. Felix guessed it had been in the last few hours.

Felix chose the bar a few times in the last five years simply because of all the filth and neglect. Anonymity also came with the territory. The skanky barmaid with the skewed false eyelashes and a bra she should have upgraded three sizes ago—would never remember him. He would try hard never to remember her or her bad dental habits that matched the men's room and the corner of the bar. Felix could feel the wobble in the fourth leg of the stool. It had probably been the strike-point too many times. The repairs were getting sloppier and sketchier with each bar fight.

Felix didn't care. He was watching the ten o'clock local news. The flashing lights of police and fire were everywhere the reporter and the cameraman panned the camera. Felix inwardly smiled. *It must be tough to report on such a train wreck. Just point the camera everywhere and keep saying things like horrible and disastrous.* He raised the long neck to his lips. The cheap beer was biting in his mouth. He kept watching the television hanging off the side of the wall in the corner.

The scene changed back to the station's newsroom. The guy with the bad wig was talking to the young woman who was struggling to not look at his hair. Felix would have thought it was a comedy skit from Saturday Night Live, but he knew it was local talent.

In the corner, a large building appeared. Felix recognized the building. The caption read there had been a catastrophic failure of the floor in the building's parking structure. The TV switched to the reporter on the scene. To Felix, the guy appeared to have been either pulled out of bed or told to get out of his janitor's uniform and put on the company's jacket. He was having several problems with his microphone. It all seemed to match the fact his fly was open, and the cameraman either hadn't caught it or didn't care.

Felix didn't care either. His focus was on what news crews called the "B" roll. It was the footage of the destruction, which they had been allowed to shoot sometime in the previous hour.

The walk-up showed a secured loading dock surrounded by a heavy steel-barred fence and electric gate. There was only room for one truck at the dock at a time. Looking through the bars of the fence, the camera looked down into the large hole which seemingly had swallowed an armored truck whole. The concrete dust was still hanging in the air. A light powdering was everywhere the camera looked.

What the camera did not see, but Felix knew, was the back door of the truck was also blown. He hadn't been there for the door part of the job, but he had supplied the special charges and left them in the sub-basement. It was a simple peel-and-stick charge. It was one of his specialty charges.

He had seen enough. He threw a five on the bar and left knowing he would never walk into this bar again.

The underground parking with the secure loading dock was the transfer station for the Bay Area's Federal Reserve. Every bit of new money and every bit of old, used, untraceable money processed through the dock. Felix had no idea how much or what was in the armored truck, but he guessed there were pallets of conveniently wrapped large bundles. The news over the next week would give at least some idea of what had really been in there. A tingling in the back of his neck told Felix—moving to another state would not solve his problem this time.

As he drove the van, he repeatedly stretched and clenched his hands. Making the C-4 the way he did required him to knead the dough by hand. Once the mixing began, it could not be stopped until it reached the right color and consistency, telling him it had stabilized.

His special recipe malleable plastic was easier to mold and shove into cracks than a child's plasticized clay—which plastic explosives were named after. Felix's father had worked out the recipe when he was in the paratroopers in the Pacific. There were many ways to make the explosives known as plastic. The material went back to the late 1870s, but the clay Felix and his father always used was known as C-4—short for Composition-4.

Felix raised his right hand to his upper lip and smelled. The corn oil he used instead of the motor oil the paratroopers had used gave it the extra smooth thinner consistency. Felix was sure it might take a few hundred miles per hour off the 26,000 feet a second the shock wave was supposed to travel at, but even at 25,000 feet a second, the destruction was enough.

Felix learned to be a minimalist. Where a one or two-pound block of C-4 would be more than satisfactory to take out an eight-inch thick steel I-beam, many explosive technicians would go for the overkill and belt the beam with an eight or ten-pound satchel to leave no doubt of getting the job done. Felix believed in knowing exactly what the job would take and only adding an extra ten percent.

Where others would lean a case of dynamite against a twelve-by-twelve Ponderosa pine timber having rotted in a mine for sixty years—Felix would jamb a pound of C-4 between the timber and the stone of the wall. When the dynamite would blow, most of the force would be wasted in the air where the box was facing. When Felix's charge would blow, the force blew into the stone, amplifying the push toward the timber. The early force would crack the timber, but the rebound force would push the broken timber into the middle of the mine.

The frugal nature of his father and Felix brought them much work. Not because they were a bit cheaper than others were, but because they showed up on time, did not wreck the rest of the mine, and were always sober on a job. Even in the bar, Felix had only taken a few sips of the one beer.

Felix knew there would be a package or large envelope at the mailbox store. It would be either new bills he would have to wash and age or old used bills. Either way, it would be his last job. He had a large nest egg now. It was just a matter of Thelma and how to transport her.

He turned the lights off as he nosed the van into the driveway. It wasn't because the lights might disturb Thelma —she was beyond that. It was just habit. He jingled the keys in his left hand as he walked toward the door—one of his other habits. Thelma used to know whether it was Felix or his father who was coming up the walk. If there were keys jingling, it was Felix. If it was silent, it was his father who lived with them after Felix's mother passed away.

Felix tucked the one leg back under the covers and straightened them. His hand rested on her shoulder as he lightly bent over and kissed her hair. He could tell that somewhere in there, she had heard his keys jingle and would now sleep peacefully through the remainder of the night.

18

PULLING RAILCARS

Hooker eased Mae down into the mess. One look and he started missing the Squirt.

Hooker was on the outer perimeter of the response to the carnage. A fast count of what he could actually see was seventeen freight cars. Some had held new cars, some had boxes, and three contained, so far, unlabeled canned goods. Hooker wondered if any of the cans would make their way back to Stella's wonder rooms of food. The four Hooker had a feeling about were the tank cars. From experience, Hooker knew a standard railcar weighed thirty tons empty. The same held true for a tank car, but then you start putting liquids in a tank, and the weight starts to approach the weight of the locomotive engine—at a hundred tons.

Mae could not lift the railcar, but she could lift or shift one end at a time. Set with holdouts stacked or chained off to something large, her twin pulling power was rated at over one-fifty. This meant Hooker could roll a tank car, or even move it around, which was something a Class-A crane could not do.

Hooker's only worry was his cables were at the end of their lifespan. He had meant to get new cable wound last year, but a little problem had come up just before the holidays, and everything slipped his mind.

The scene looked like chaos, but to the eye of someone who worked in the middle of disasters, there was a system to the madness. Hooker scanned the workers. He was looking for the one person who did not have dread in how they were moving. This would be the person who had seen so much that they were in charge—if not for the whole event, at least some of it.

The yellow hardhat had thrown Hooker off. Yellow was usually the color worn by workers, where supervisors wore the clean, seldom worn white plastic hard hat. The man stood looking at the large tow truck. His eyes traveled over the massive scale from the diamond-plate front fenders to the oversized working bed on the back. His eyes did not miss any detail of Mae West or the slogan painted on the boom.

"I don't need a quickie, but I understand you know how to roll a tank car and do it carefully."

Hooker's head ground around to look at the man. Hooker almost laughed. Not only did the man sound like Wally Cox, but he also was the same size and even built like him. The thought of this small man behind a standard desk brought up the idea of him sitting in Dolly's oversized chair. He figured both of them would be uncomfortable in those situations.

Hooker looked back in the cab. "Box, stay. I'll find you some dry grass later."

Only the single ear twitched to signal the cat had heard him. Box leaned forward a little harder, maybe to get closer to the heat coming out through the vent.

Hooker slid down the side of Mae. He stuck his hand out. "The name is Hooker. What are we looking at?"

"Victor Mayhew. What we have is a very delicate situation. Are you familiar with caustic soda?"

Hooker looked down the jumbled line of mayhem chopped up by more and more work lights being set up. He looked back at the man who looked like he should be sleeping after a long day as an accountant. The only piece missing was the bow tie.

"Other than... it can strip the meat off a bone in seconds rather than hours... no, not much."

"That's probably the most important thing to know. The other is about a hundred yards and some. Over there in the dark are the title flats. In about five hours, the bay water will be at its high point. If one of these tanks were to rupture, the resulting fish kill would stretch up past Alcatraz by early spring. By the end of summer, there wouldn't be anything alive in the bay."

"What about boom barriers?"

The man smiled. "So, you've done this before."

Hooker nodded. "A couple of times."

"Good. I like experience. The barrier trucks are coming down from Richmond. They should be here in the next half hour. Arco is sending down skid diapers as well. We have forty tank trucks coming from all over the Bay Area, plus a pumper. This means we can only clean one car at a time. While waiting for you, we went ahead and surveyed the conditions of the cars. There is one with an expanded weld near the neck. I want to roll it first, but it's number three in line."

"How soon can I get Mae in there?"

"Probably not for another hour or so... I'm sorry... I know you rushed up here from somewhere down south, but there's nothing to do right now but hang tough and wait."

"I was in San Luis Obispo this evening. If it's all the same to you, I'll just get some sleep, but I'm going to call in my assistant. He's the only person I'm going to trust on this."

"That's fine." The man looked around. "If you want, you can park over there near those warehouses. I'll come get you when we can get you in."

Hooker climbed back in the cab and called Dolly.

"Ask him to borrow the Granny car and get up here. Stella can take Candy to school in the morning."

"Got it. Now get some sleep, and we'll talk to you when you know more."

About an hour later, the Squirt crawled in on the passenger side. "Go back to sleep. They still haven't cleared the way through. I just wanted to let you know I was here, but I'm going to go scout along the site. I'll come get you when they're ready for us."

John listened for the mumble or acknowledgment, but only got a couple of low snores harmonizing with the slow lope of Mae's engine. Quietly, he slid out and closed the door. Putting his hood up on his poncho, he faded into the dark and light misting drizzle.

After talking to a couple of men in white hardhats, he finally found the yellow hat with the VM on the back. "Victor Mayhew?"

The man turned, "Yes?"

The Squirt stuck his hand out. "Squirt... I'm Hooker's, um... consultant."

The man looked at the youth in the poncho. "Son, I don't know who you think you are, but this is an extremely dangerous—"

The Squirt cut him off. "I understand you have three tank cars running fifteen to eighteen tons over the legal limit, which I understand is one-thirty on these rails. Once you go past marker 741, which this engineer was just twenty-two minutes away from doing, it drops to one-fifteen. We have a low-pressure cell settling in, and this nice tropical evening we are enjoying right now is about to get train-wreck ugly. Pardon the euphemism. At this moment, Northern Pacific is only facing a $75,000 fine for each of those rail tankers, and if one splits, the fine will run into the millions before the caustic soda hits the bay. If the CS spreads north into the bay—by four this afternoon, the die-off of the fisheries will extend up past Antioch as the tide comes in." He paused for a moment as Victor Mayhew could only stare at the young man.

The Squirt continued. "Now, you can stick your head up your ass about my age and waste precious time, or you can stop being an asshole and help me do my job. It's your choice.

"Personally, I don't give a shit. Until you opened your mouth, NP was on the hook at a thousand an hour. You just removed any goodwill you might have enjoyed, and we are now standing at two thousand an hour from when you put the call in for us to come save your ass. Now, are you going to help us help you, or did you want to explain to your review board how you hired and wasted the only team who could save the bay and your job... and still got charged five thousand an hour starting from the time your engineer ran this hunk of shit off the rails?"

The man stood with his mouth hanging.

The Squirt gave it the old Dolly five-count and then turned to walk off. "Fine, I'll go find someone who knows what the hell is going on..."

It took Victor almost five heartbeats and the young man covering almost twenty feet before he could find his voice. "Where's Hooker?"

The Squirt only half turned—still negotiating through body language. "I have him working on some other logistics. There is a hell of a lot more going on tonight than your party."

The man thought and looked up into the dark sky. True to the kid's word, the rain was beginning to feel a little heavier. "Fine, let's look at the tankers."

Forty minutes later, the Squirt was directing Hooker as he maneuvered Mae up into a pocket where there were three large concrete bunkers. Set on the top of each bunker was a two-inch-thick steel loop. Originally, the loop was used to crane the bunkers into place. They had been the foundation for one of the log loading cranes used until the late 1950s. It became cheaper to build a smaller mill and rough lumber near the source, and then rail from there. After the timber was no longer trucked and railed, the bunkers were the only parts left standing.

Once the Squirt had seen them, he knew the fourth lay buried in the hillside. The three visible six-foot-high bunkers were only the top third. The other two-thirds were twelve feet deep, and each weighed close to twenty tons. They were perfect for what they wanted.

The two men stood in the rain as Hooker listened to the Squirt. "The smaller car only has a skin about a half-inch thick. She is the one we need to handle gently. This one in front of us is the prom queen with the stretched weld. The flaking paint is about six inches, so the stretch is probably a foot long—eighteen-inch at the most. The good news is she's the prom queen. Her maker mark is Gunderson up in Portland. She's one of the new double walls, and the outside is just under three-quarters of an inch, so we can manhandle her, and she won't whine. The third one with the graffiti on the belly is the lightest of the four, and we can turn her after these two. I think the cables will still reach, but we'll be at the limit if we still want to belay off these bunkers." He jerked his thumb behind them.

Hooker half turned. "And you knew about these... um, things, how?"

"Paper for Maddie last November had some information about the rails and why they run up both sides of the bay. Stanford was running food and people up the peninsula, but he was grabbing logs here from Oregon and then trucking them out to Pleasanton and the old mill. These bunkers were just part of the research, and there were some old photos of the cranes. I think there's another set about a hundred yards down south of here, but it useless for the fourth car—that one, we will have to snatch straight off Mae. I'm sure Mae is fine with the hundred and forty tons to roll, but it's the cables I'm worried about. You didn't get it replaced last fall, and they're stretched and worn out. Therefore, I figured we would leave it for last. We can take it from close in and do a loop-tie. But it's still the biggest risk."

Hooker looked at him. He studied the kid who had become a man.

The Squirt fidgeted. "What?"

Hooker laughed. "You really told him two grand an hour?"

The face was deadpan. "From when you got the call or cleared San Luis Obispo."

"I wouldn't charge the travel time, and I damn sure don't charge a grand an hour—much less two."

The Squirt looked over the long jagged line of tossed about railcars. "You do today." He looked back at Hooker and winked. "Are we finished screwing around?"

Hooker thought a moment, then put two fingers to his forehead and saluted the kid. "Yes, boss. Let's earn some easy money."

The weather had other plans. There was nothing easy about any of it.

A soaked Hooker looked at the wheel assemblies called the 'trucks.' They had leveraged the first and lighter car back onto the rails, but this one wasn't even close. The lead truck was at least twelve feet away from the rails and cocked.

"Hey, Squirt?"

The kid came around the head of the car. He nodded his jaw up in the dark and then realizing Hooker couldn't see the nod, called out. "What?"

"When we pull this up, she's not going to be even close to the rails."

The Squirt kept coming. "It won't matter. Not only does it not matter about the rails, but also we aren't going to right her completely. The weld stretch is on the downside of the manhole on the top. All we have to do is get the load chemicals down below the stretched weld." He pointed at the valves and pipes running along the underside of the car. "Once we have it done, they have trucks that will hook up to those nipples and suckle the tits until they get almost everything out. When she's empty, the car will only weight thirty-tons with maybe a couple of tons of soda left. From there, they can crane her with ease."

Hooker smirked. "I suppose you have some blocking material coming?"

"Eight to ten trucks with self-loading arms are bringing rail sleepers. They should be here by now." He looked around at the perimeter of the mass of trucks and equipment. "They were coming down from Antioch."

Hooker pointed out through the rain at a tractor-trailer making its way down along the other side. "While you go talk to the driver, I'm going to go put on the spare jumpsuit. This one's soaked."

The kid nodded. "You might think about hitting up one of these rail guys near their trucks. They have the heavy-duty work rain slickers. They don't tear every time you fart in them. I'm sure they'd let us borrow a couple."

Five minutes later, Hooker came back with two insulated jumpsuits, mud boots, and two sets of slightly used rain gear. They took turns changing in the cab of Mae. The warm-up break combined with dry clothes helped. The other critical ration was the hot coffee and sandwiches Hooker was already scarfing down in the backseat of Chet's cruiser.

The Squirt slid in. "We have a savior from the south?"

"Dolly figured Hooker would at least need coffee, and the food is always good. How's it going with the cars?"

Hooker swallowed. "The easy one is done, but we're just starting on the scary one. If we're lucky, we should have it up enough by sunrise for them to start emptying it."

Chet frowned. "Dolly wasn't sure what was in them."

The Squirt swallowed his coffee. "Caustic Soda—highly corrosive and deadly—if we get a spill out here, the fumes alone will require everyone to suit up in re-breathers and protective suits." He took another bite of his sandwich as if he was talking about flipping a Volkswagen back over with a full tank of gas.

Chet looked at Hooker. Hooker duck-lipped his mouth and rolled his eyes up toward his one raised eyebrow. They were both noticing how much the kid had matured in less than a year. Maybe having twenty-eight dimes shoved into you with a shotgun will do that to you.

Chet stayed and kept his distance in his cruiser. He watched the painfully slow dance of rolling the tank car back upright or close to it. The sky eventually lightened. Although filtered through the clouds, which, thankfully, had stopped raining, it still helped everyone to see. The work up and down the wreck site seemed to pick up the pace.

Chet wiggled the last thermos. There was less than a swallow left. He started the cruiser and backed off the outcropping, which had given him the vantage point. Like most highway patrol officers, he knew where he could get more coffee and maybe even some donuts. The sugar would help with the waning energy. Hooker had to be on the back end of at least twenty-four hours—if not thirty-six.

19

COFFEE RUN

Chet placed the three thermoses on the counter. The man in the rumpled white shirt, pants, and apron didn't even blink. As Chet looked over the early morning offering of donuts, the man refilled the thermoses.

"Do you want me to leave room for cream in any of these?"

Chet looked up. "No, thanks... black all around."

The man placed the thermoses on the counter. He reached behind him to a large stack of already made-up boxes. His hand paused, "One dozen or two?"

Chet held up his index finger, and the man swung around with a box. "Are you out at the train or the bank?"

Chet looked up at the man with a frown. "Bank?"

The man rolled one eye at him. Chet realized the weepy eye was glass.

The man tossed his head toward the left. "The feds have been through here all morning. I thought cops ate a lot of donuts and coffee, but you guys can't hold a candle to the feds. They've been grabbing the two-packs and a large thermos load. They tend to go for the fluffy with high sugar while you guys down at the train have been sucking up all of my old-fashioned and cakes."

"What bank?" Chet pursued.

"Actually, it's the transfer station for the Federal Reserve. It's where they take all the money they have to destroy, but also where they deliver out to the banks in the East Bay and maybe down south."

Chet was getting a bit exasperated with the guy's lack of information. "So, what happened over there?"

"Oh, it's been all over the news... "

"I don't have a TV in my cruiser—but I do have handcuffs, a nightstick, and if I need it later, a shotgun, and shovel to bury you." He glowered at the man. "Now what the hell happened?"

The man blinked. "Someone robbed one of the armored trucks. Blew up the floor under it and then blew the back door of the truck. I overheard a couple of the Feds talking, and one guy said it was three pallets of new hundreds. Millions."

Chet wasn't a banker, but he knew the man could only guess at what Federal Reserve pallets looked like. Chet had firsthand knowledge—there was an extra zero stuck in there. He threw a ten on the counter and grabbed the coffee. "I'll be back for the donuts. You know what we're eating."

He strapped the thermoses into the passenger seat then turned the selector on his radio to one of the tactical bands.

"C-C-1-4."

"1-4?" The voice was the day shift. Chet swore silently.

"Karen, is Dolly still there?"

"No, hun... but there is a large blob doing a mountain of paperwork over there in the dark. What can we do for you?"

"This is going to sound strange, but... how many explosions have you guys heard about in the last couple of years?

"Explosions?" Dolly's voice sounded tired and harried.

"Morning, sunshine... yes, explosions. Ones like... what was it... um, Frontier Village. I'm talking about businesses that went out of business—because they had some mysterious freak explosion."

There was silence. Chet watched the traffic with the eye of a longtime officer. The deep cloud cover was slowly burning off or seemed to be. Maybe they would catch a break today at the wreck and not have to work with yuck in the air, just the mud the rain had left.

Chet felt as much as he heard the cruiser's back door open and close. The donut guy never said a word.

"Chet, we think it's maybe about six or seven made the paper. Why?"

"Someone blew the Federal Reserve transfer station up here. I don't think it was the only place blown up last night."

There was dead air for a minute. Chet could smell the donuts, but he started the car instead. Swinging out onto the road, he headed back toward the train wreck.

"Mike at Alonge's mentioned a couple of phone company crews out... In fact, Fremont Alarm has a couple of crews out checking why they had a whole bank go down this morning."

Chet grabbed his mic. "Can you ask Mike the locations and see if they overlay Fremont's dead zone?"

"We'll get back to you."

"I'll put the outside speaker on, but I think we may be

taking a break here in the big yellow schoolhouse. The Squirt is here..."

Dolly knew he was talking about tapping into the kid's freaky memory. Anything the kid had ever seen, heard, or read was his for total recall. He also had a strange way of seeing math or geometry. "A good mind is a thing to use."

Chet chuckled. "C-C-1-4, out."

The radio clicked twice as Dolly or Karen double keyed the mic.

Chet pulled up near the giant yellow and blue tow truck. He could see Hooker at the controls and knew the Squirt was around somewhere close. He opened the door and started to get out.

"Oh, my, I smell donuts."

Chet laughed. Turning, he faced the Squirt, deadpan. "Nope, only day-old coffee."

"Uh-huh, and Mae West is a Volkswagen." The kid rolled his head in a shortened zombie roll.

They laughed and pulled the breakfast out of the cruiser. Hooker walked over, and they climbed up into the heat of the cab, exchanging places with an orange streak. Mud or no, Box needed his morning run and dump. The Squirt kept his foot bracing the door open halfway until Box returned.

Hooker sunk his teeth into a donut as he poured dry cat food into the little red bowl. The water bottle was always strapped to the gear shifter and handy for Box to lick the nipple from his place in his own box next to the driver's seat.

With Box taken care of, Hooker sat up. The crack and crunch, along with the deep rumble of purring, were music to Hooker's ears. "Thanks for breakfast, Chet." The Squirt also raised his cup while he quietly chewed.

"Oh, I brought you more than just coffee and donuts..." The man smiled and raised his half-eaten donut.

"What?"

"Just relax. Enjoy the break. It'll all be coming soon."

The radio crackled. "1-4-1?" Chet pointed at the radio with his donut and then took a bite.

Hooker reached over and grabbed the microphone from where it hung behind his head when he was driving. "1-4-1, go." His eyes were fixed on his friend—who ignored him.

"The Fed, the phone work crews, and dark alarms are all in a one-square-mile area. You are a mile and a half away from the center of the dark target zone. The train had derailed twenty minutes before the power, and phone lines went out. Nobody is giving out any information from the Fed."

Hooker looked at Chet and mouthed *fed?*

"Uh, 10-4." Chet was nodding.

"Fed?"

Chet nodded and swallowed. He took a sip and swallowed again. Hooker could see his mind was doing the same thing he was used to seeing in the Squirt.

Chet cleared his throat as his eyes rolled up into his head —looking for the information. "Let me see if I have this all straight. The train derailed. Twenty minutes later—while the police and fire trucks are making a lot of noise and racing here—several phone lines and alarm lines go down at the same time. Meanwhile, someone blew their way into the Federal Reserve Bank and popped an armored truck for several million bucks."

The Squirt choked, "Too much of a coincidence. The odds of even two of them happening on the same day are close to eleven million to one. Not going to happen naturally." The Squirt sipped his coffee and then closed his eyes as he bit into a chocolate-covered old-fashioned.

Hooker watched the kid. Finally, the kid opened his eyes with a sly smile. "That was so much bullshit. You just made up those odds."

The three laughed. The kid raised his mug to his lips. "You don't like my odds... make up your own number."

Hooker thought a moment. "I think for all three to happen together would be in the billions. It all smells rotten." He reached and grabbed the mic.

"1-4-1."

Karen's voice was laughing, "Took you long enough. Dolly's on the phone to them now."

"Fremont PD?"

"Oh, no... she's done with those idiots. She called the governor's office. She decided to start working top-down. I have a call holding for the Assistant Field Director of the FBI for the west coast down in Los Angeles. His secretary was a little snippy, so we're letting him cool his heels before I swap him out for the bozo answering the phone at the governor's mansion this morning."

"How did she get the mansion's phone number—oh, never mind. I'm sure I don't even want to know this story. Tell her we're headed out and are going to go walk the rails. I'm in a betting mood, and I'm willing to lay down good money on us finding something long before those transportation fools catch wind of this."

Hooker hung up and looked at the kid. "Where are the locomotives?"

The kid pointed up the bay. Hooker looked and pointed down. "Let's take a stroll."

He grabbed the long black flashlight from its holder next to the sawed-off shotgun. The kid nodded and grabbed the matching one from the holder on the passenger seat.

Even though it was daylight, it was still overcast. As they piled out of the truck, Chet stepped over to his cruiser. "I'll get mine too."

Forty minutes later, they stood with three officers from the transportation board and four supervisors from Northern Pacific. All eyes were on a small mangling of the wooden railroad ties. All it had taken was probably thirty feet of small explosives to blow out the bedding under the ties, then some explosive charges placed first on the ties where the rails were tied, and then along the outside of the rail to push it in.

Once the width of the rails had been compromised, the locomotive's wheels had jumped the track. Where the heavy wheels dug through the rail, the next dozen had cut the rail in half and started to work on the unsupported ties. A nine-inch square piece of wood cannot support twenty tons of railcar. They were quickly cut and torn apart with each consecutive car derailing. Effectively, the cars derailing at thirty-miles-an-hour had all but destroyed the evidence.

The one man knelt to look closely at where the bright flashlights were shining. He removed his helmet and ran his fingers through his hair.

"I would have never seen that." He looked up at the Squirt as he fingered the helmet with the VM painted on the back. "I've been at this game longer than you've been alive..." He stood and put his hand out. "I owe you an apology, young man. I would say you have earned every bit of the four-thousand an hour you last quoted me. I'll make sure the check gets cut this afternoon when you know all of your hours."

Chet snorted. "And that's why he'll be graduating from the police academy in half the time of the other cadets. The bottom line is—we cannot wait for him to turn twenty-one or lollygag around in school. We need him out here on the street where he can do some good."

Victor chuckled. "You're not even twenty-one?"

"Twenty, sir... and the two is enough."

"Not today, son. Not today. You just took this crap dump out of my hands and gave it to them and the FBI. My wife would insist on the extra. My vacation starts on Friday, and I'm taking her to Paris for our twenty-fifth."

The spare looking man in the blue jacket with the letters NTSB looked hound dog at Victor. "Thanks a lot, Mayhew... you just reminded me... today is my wife's birthday."

"Well, cripes sake, Neal. Just get her something on your way home and tell her it was in the car for a week. I love my sister dearly, but she isn't sharp enough to figure out you forgot a national holiday like her birthday."

Hooker laughed. "So this is a family affair?"

They grimaced and nodded. Then together, they said, "I got him his job." Obviously, this was an old routine.

Victor laughed. "If there was an opening, and he didn't like the politics so damn much, I have a brother with the FBI back in DC."

The brother-in-law laughed. "He's a pansy. He doesn't

appreciate our beautiful weather we get to work in." They both nodded and then wagged their heads.

"He's right. Teddy would rather fly a desk for twenty straight hours than be out here in the elements for twenty minutes."

Hooker and the Squirt begged out of further discussion as they still had two railcars to roll. The sun was threatening to break through in the east, but the clouds over the coastal hills were looking darker. Hooker and the Squirt both were eyeing the leading edges of the cloudbank for telltale wisps indicative of the clouds moving their way.

"How did the cables feel on the roll?"

"They were both warm, but not hot. I think we can get this done and be fine, but the last one, we'll need to do a loop pull. But I'm telling you, it's time to get Mae re-wound."

"Yeah, yeah, I know. Things just got a little busy."

"Well, four-thousand an hour will pay for a lot of cable rewinding."

Hooker stopped stunned. His head ground around to look at the Squirt. "Thousand? You told him thousand?"

"He was being a jerk."

Hooker read the kid's face. He could imagine what kind of jerk the guy had been to a mere kid. "Even so, my billing is only eighty an hour on a complicated tow, and one-fifty flat if it goes back to the Fly."

"Well, you heard the man. You can drop it to hundreds, but it's still four hundred an hour. What time did you clear SLO town?"

"Nine-twenty, but I stopped for some pizza and got pulled over by a Chip in Atascadero. I don't charge for inbound."

"This was the only way these could get rolled last night. They needed you no matter where you were at the time. For all they know, you were headed down to Los Angeles to go see what the big deal was about the Sunset Strip. They called—you came. End of story—four hundred an hour. Now let's go earn some paint and fuel."

Seven hours later, Hooker handed Victor a bill under the watchful eye of the Squirt. The man read it through and looked up at the kid.

"You read this over?"

The Squirt nodded.

"You approved it?"

The kid jerked his thumb back over his shoulder at the truck. "It's his name on the truck."

Victor looked at Hooker and then at the truck. Smiling, he looked back at Hooker. "So your real name is Mae West?"

He bent over the checkbook and dashed out a number closer to the Squirt's original statement. He tore it out and tossed the book back in the car. Handing the check to the Squirt, he showed a deadpan face. "I stand by my statement. You both were worth every penny."

The Squirt didn't even look at the check. He folded it and stuck it in his back pocket. The arguing could come later... or not. He stuck his hand out and shook the man's hand.

"Have a great time in Paris. There's a restaurant named Tour d'Argent. It means the silver tower; it's the oldest restaurant in the world. It's probably expensive, but they are known for their duck and the view of Paris. It's probably the best place to take her for your anniversary."

"You've been there?"

"Read about it somewhere. It was Victor Hugo's favorite restaurant, as well as Charles the first."

"...and someday...?"

The kid nodded. "Someday... When I have someone worth taking."

20

THEY TOOK HER

Felix gave the woman the pink notice from his box. He tried to look as bored as she did. She shuffled over to a large set of shelves and found the box. It looked like it had been used a few times or had gone a few times around the planet. Felix knew inside the box was a brand new and much sturdier box. However, even the outside box was new—just made to look as worthless as the millions of other boxes in the postal system too worthless to insure. She started to lift it and quickly adjusted her grip. Felix knew it probably weighed at least twenty-five pounds.

She plopped it on the counter, ignoring the fragile stickers. "There you go. Tell your boy to have a happy birthday from me, too."

Felix picked it up, nodded, and walked out. It was not the first time the package came addressed to a made-up son from his made-up grandmother with birthday stickers attached. What adoring grandmother would send some kid twenty-five pounds of cookies?

He placed the box on the floor of the van, went around

to the driver's side, and got in. As he started the van, the news came on. The lead story was still the train wreck. Felix knew the next story would be the armored truck heist. The T-shirt at his neck seemed to get tighter.

As he nosed the van into the gravel driveway, he saw Edwina sitting on the front porch. Her face was down in her hands. Her duffle bag of a purse was next to her. There was also a large paper cup with a lid and straw next to her. Obviously, she had been out at some time during the day.

Felix slowly got out of the van. The woman, who normally wasted no time leaving, was now sitting. He could hear her soft sobbing from the driveway.

"Edwina, what's wrong? What happened?"

The sobbing turned to wailing, and Felix confirmed his long-held belief. There wasn't a tooth in the woman's head. Everything in her mouth was pink with dark splotches.

He sat down next to her and waited the hysterics out. It was his experience from mine accidents that, after a few minutes of wailing, a woman who had been crying for an extended time would settle down and would finally be able to talk.

Eventually, the lips began to suck in and out. The blubbering turned to hitched sucking of air and moaning.

"What happened?" He knew it had something to do with Thelma, but he could feel the cowardice in his guts— the last thing he wanted to do was go check a dead body.

"There... there was nothing. Nothing I could do."

"It's okay. I'm not blaming you for anything. I just need to know what happened."

"They came. I... I couldn't... I couldn't stop them." She

looked up at him. Her eyes were red like a forest fire sunset. She whispered, "Thems had papers this time."

She rolled up on her one butt cheek and slid the papers out from under the other. Felix was almost certain she couldn't read. These could have been work orders for furnace repair or even his daily delivery logs. She would never know.

He unfolded the four pages. It was a court order from Weld County, Colorado. There were conforming stamps from Contra Costa and Santa Clara counties. They had run him to ground and bracketed him. He read through. Thelma was to be transferred to a locked care facility to wait for medical clearance before transporting her back to Weld County.

He stood. "Edwina, stay right here. You understand? I'll be right back." She nodded, and he entered the house.

He had never thought about not leaving fingerprints, but for some reason, he now didn't touch a thing. The quilt lay puddled mostly on the floor. Only one corner had enough weight to still be on the bed. The blanket lay pushed up against the wall. It lay bunched like a boa constrictor. The tongue was a frayed corner of saliva stained satin. It was all Felix had left of his wife.

"Dan?" The voice was more of a moan than a wail. Felix realized he had been standing, looking at the empty bed and room for more than just a few minutes. It was almost dark.

"Sorry, Edwina. Give me a couple of minutes more. I'll be right there. Don't leave." He rushed to the back door. His hand fumbled in his pants pocket. He stood with his head against the door as he thumbed to the right key and felt the ridges to know which side was up.

The door swung open. Three steps and he stood at one of the older hiding panels. He stuck the key in the crack and used it like a pry. The board bent and then came loose. He reached forward to one of the many bundles stacked in the wall. He knew each bundle was twenty-thousand dollars in twenties and fifties. Each one was an old, untraceable bill. He stood and left the wall open. He knew he would be opening it later, anyway.

He walked out and sat down on the porch.

"Edwina, this is very important. Do you have anyone you can go live with for a while?"

"My husband's old girlfriend." Nervously, she sucked her lips back and forth over her gums.

Felix felt the ground beneath him sway. "Where is your husband?" She had never mentioned anyone before—other than her babies, which Felix knew were stray cats in the back alley or something similar.

"Dead," she blinked.

Felix frowned. "When did he die?"

"After I shooted him."

Felix's stomach took a flop and a roll. He wasn't sure he wanted to go down this road, but he had to know, and now he was glad he had never really interviewed her in the beginning.

"Um...how long ago?"

"Boat maybe ten years or so." Felix sighed.

"What did the police say?"

"Never knowed about it—I jus' buried him in the back-yard and moved."

"And where were you living then?"

"Black Water, Mississippi."

"Is that where his girlfriend lives now?"

She snorted and screwed her face up into an ugly rendition of a smile. "No... course not. After we had done buried him and his brother, we lit out of there. She were here for a while, but she don't like the fag and cold, so she live now down Las Vegas way."

"You mean she didn't like the fog."

The woman frowned ugly. Her whole face was loose skin and seemed to move about. "Nah, she like the fog good enough."

"But you said—"

"No, the fag—the queer. The man we live withs. He lacks kissing other mens and thems parts."

Felix felt like he was losing ground. "So if I put you on a bus to Las Vegas, do you think you can find her?"

"Sure. I have her number in my purse if you can dial it." She reached for her bag.

He put his hand on her bag to stop her from searching. "It's okay, Edwina. I just wanted to make sure." He paused and thought a moment. "Listen, your car... is it registered in your name?"

She waved her finger and hand. "The bug? Oh, hell no. I found it one night a few years ago. It had the key in it and so I drived it home. No bodies looked for it, or found it, so I keeps just drivin' it."

Felix got up and went to look at the license plate. Sure enough. The registration was six years out-of-date, and it was an Idaho plate. He had never noticed it with all the mud splattered on and about the body and plate.

Felix wondered if the mud splatter and placement were by happenstance or design. Either way, he didn't care. It was about to become abandoned again. He sat back down on the porch. Edwina had been silently staring with giant eyes at the bundle of money he had left on the concrete.

"Okay, Edwina. I need for you to think real hard. Is there anything at your house you feel you simply cannot leave behind?"

"My..." She started to wail.

"I know—the cats. I'll have them taken care of. Anything else? This is very important. I don't want you to go back to your house. I'm going to take you to the bus station and get you on the bus to Las Vegas and your girlfriend. But I need to know now if there is anything you might think later was important enough to go back for."

The woman sat and rocked. Felix wasn't sure if she was thinking or had gone into shock. Finally, she gently shook her head. "I don't really got much. Jus some clothes."

"Nothing else?"

Her shoulders slumped when she realized her sum total amassment of wealth was basically her purse. "No... Nothing."

Felix brought the four-inch-thick block of money around. "Okay, listen. This is twenty-thousand dollars. This is enough for you to start a new life. If I thought you could do it, I would tell you to go to Mexico, but maybe Las Vegas is good enough. I'm going to put you on the bus. You need to think of another name you want to be. Those men today probably know your real name by now."

She shook her head. "No... no, they don't. My real name is..." she leaned in as she looked out toward the street, "Vesta Conworthy." She sat back and smiled. She just shared the biggest secret she had ever held with this man.

Felix felt the ground under him become a little more solid. He smiled back at her. This might just work. "Great, but you can't be Edwina anymore. They might look for you by that name."

"I had an aunt once I liked. Her name was Bina. I kinda liked that name."

"Okay... Bina, it is. So here's the money. I'll take you to the bus and see you off. Then you never come back here again. Okay?"

"Okay." Her hands started to shake as she touched the money. However, a second later, it disappeared into the bag.

"I need the keys to the car."

"I always just leaved it in the little hole so I knowed which way it go."

The system made sense to Felix. He had watched many miners use similar systems to order their lives.

Felix stood and locked the front door. "I need to move my van. I'll be right back, and we will take your car."

"Okay."

21

———

REVENGE

The bus to Las Vegas was a connection through Reno. Felix hoped Edwina, now Bina, would be able to make it to Las Vegas. They had spent the two hours with a bunch of rubber bands, making smaller, more usable bundles of the bills. When Felix suggested hiding some of the bundles in her underwear and bra, she had started to giggle. He realized she didn't own something so frivolous.

They backtracked to the drugstore a few blocks away and bought some underwear and a tight T-shirt-like top. She said it worked. Felix didn't want to know, but she finally looked like she had a female figure—bumps and all.

Felix hugged her when he said goodbye. He felt more like a parent sending a child off to summer camp than getting rid of a witness. Felix never had to kill anyone who wasn't already dying, but he didn't want any loose ends either.

As he drove, he finally let himself get angry. In his soul, he knew Thelma would be looked after better than anything he had ever provided, but it was the taking away from him that made him mad. He knew she was alive, but he would never again touch her arm, hold her hand, or kiss her head goodnight. He would never again be able to tell her how sorry he was for the day at the mine. He would never again just be able to sit in the room and listen to her breathe as she slept.

He went into the garage and brought out the two-gallon can of gas. He shook it. About a gallon and a half... more than enough. He took some rags and the cheap cotton work gloves out of the van. There was a place about a mile away he knew where only kids came, and even then, mostly just on Friday and Saturday nights to drink stolen liquor, smoke stolen cigarettes, and tell stolen stories.

He could see lights ahead. He pulled over to the side. Opening the gas can, he soaked a rag damp and then started wiping every surface he thought Edwina might have ever touched. The doors were open, and yet the car reeked of gasoline. After a few minutes, the car was wiped clean.

Felix drove through the collective of street toughs. He knew what he was looking for. It would be the kid who was the hanger-on. He didn't have enough to be a real player in the club, but he felt if he hung around long enough...

Felix pulled up. The thin, short kid would be perfect. Felix got out, pulling the key from the ignition at the same time. His left hand reached into his pocket and pulled out the two thousand. He walked over to the kid and shielded the kid from the other toughs. He showed the kid the wad of money and then shoved it in the kid's front pants pocket. He grabbed the kid's right hand and turned it palm up. Felix dropped the key in the hand and rolled the fingers closed. "Don't get caught."

Turning, Felix walked off into the night. The crowd behind him was eerily silent as they gathered around the new cool kid. Felix smiled as he walked. He knew a place on the way home that he could get a burrito. It had turned out to be a nice evening for a walk. Tomorrow would be a lot different.

The sun came up in the screened-in porch. Almost all the wood paneling was off the low wall. The amount of money would pose a problem with Felix's travel. No matter how you break it up, six hundred and forty-seven grand was a large package. Felix knew he would have to stash large chunks of the money at places he could have access to at later dates.

He had tried to sleep, but the idea of how *they* had come into *his* home and taken *his* wife from *him* had him back up by two. The wiping down of all surfaces had started with rubbing alcohol and gin. The areas open to the outside, he switched to a mix of acetone and benzene gas. From now on, he would be wearing gloves as he got ready.

Felix stood in the phone booth. "No, Bill, I'm fine... It's my wife who's very ill. No, it doesn't look good for the rest of the week." He looked around at the street while his boss talked.

"Bill... Bill... how much personal time do I have built up? Okay, fine, I'll take the three weeks. Yes, I know how busy we are. I'm one of those idiots out there on the street for ten or twelve hours a day."

A large set of doubles rolled down the road past the gas

station. Felix didn't need to hear his boss to know the man was getting mad. But he wasn't getting his way—not today.

"Bill? Bill... I think maybe you need to go out to the dock, put on one of those itchy stupid-looking shirts, and go drive my truck up your ass."

He held out the phone.

"Bill... whether you like it or not, my wife is dying. I'm not going to let her die alone."

Felix let the man run his mouth in a quieter tone.

"She has spacious parietal encephalitis. It means she got hit in the head, and now she's dying. I've lost my wife and the only friend I ever had. I don't care if I lose my job. You can't compete. All I'm asking is for the three weeks off. I doubt she'll last that long, but you know doctors. As soon as I've buried my wife, I'll be back. Then I won't ever need another day off."

Felix looked at the woman in the car with three kids. She needed gas, but the kids needed a minder. Felix missed the days when gas station attendants helped people—especially people like her.

"Bill... Bill, they're calling me. I've gotta go. We'll talk soon." He hung up.

"Hi, ma'am. What kind of gas y'all need, and how much?" Felix calmed down as he pumped the woman's tank full. She'd asked for only three dollars' worth. She had no idea how far her three dollars were going to go in a twenty-gallon tank. While he watched the pump dial turn, he peeled off five hundred-dollar bills and folded them in his right hand.

"Thank you, ma'am—that will be three dollars even."

As she handed him the bills, he pointed at the little girl

in the passenger seat. "Those sure are pretty curls there, little girl." As the mother turned to look at her daughter, Felix dropped the money and walked away.

He was around the corner of the building before the woman could come to her senses and get out of the car. Felix knew she would be stuck with the kids instead of being able to chase after the stranger. He hopped over the low fence and walked down the hill into the bushes. He had parked the white van on the other side.

Three hours later, he walked into the mining and hardware supply in Mokelumne Hill. The town was tiny, but it had what every dry gulch and hard rocker needed... dynamite or the fixing to make your own explosives.

"Hey, Pete. Long time since you worked on the hole."

Felix slipped into his identity of Peter Farnham. "You know how it is, Steve. I have to put in the time working for the man before I get to come up here and throw my life savings down some money pit."

"You still working the drift over by Shingle Springs?"

"Nah. The ore never came back to pencil out, so I'm working an old straight back just southeast of Grizzly Flats. It's around the face from the old Mailbox mine. I figured they stripped the face of the mountain, but I'd be sneaking out the back door. Who knows... and I've got a month to find out if I'm wasting my time."

"Well, what can we set you up with today?"

"How about three hundred pounds of Royal DX, a twenty can of sebacate, and a ten weight of polyiso to start. I should still have some left up at the cabin, but who knows if it's any good. The raccoons tend to like it once they get a taste of it."

"What kind of primers are you looking for?"

"You know I'm old school. I think I have a roll of det left, but how about throwing say, six rolls in and a case of caps."

"Low knock on the caps?"

"Sure, that's fine."

Felix looked around as if he was either shopping or trying to remember something. The next item on his list was highly controlled. "Hey, Steve. Do you got any of the new cutting det cord?"

"The high mag or the phosphorous?"

"Which works best on metal, and which will work on cutting logs?

"You'd want the phosphorous for the wood, but the magnesium can't be beat for metal. Iron or steel?"

"Mostly old steel, but I also have some trees I want to turn into firewood. You can only imagine what I look like trying to drive a chainsaw. It's your worst nightmare."

The man stopped at the door leading into the back. "How much you want of each?"

"How big are the rolls?"

"Two-fifties."

"Hmm... How about three of each, and I can come down next week when I know how much I'll need total."

"We have you on file, right?"

"You'd better... I've been coming up here for how long?"

The man knocked his knuckles on the door jam. "One of these days, you'll hit some serious gold and never go back to that shit hole in San Diego."

"Hey, I'm going to run over to Mabel's and grab some grub. I'll be back in a few."

The man called back from the storage room. "Sure thing. I'll have it ready on the dock."

By shortly after nightfall, Felix was passing back through Pleasanton and rounding third base headed for home. It was a long drive, but a necessary separation from his real life.

He would begin to cook the explosives in the morning, but there was a lot more items on his list to get. This explosion was a lot different from what he would normally do. This one was for revenge.

22

WORD FROM COLORADO

Sundays were the traditional day for rest, family, friends, and food—or as Manny put it, the Four *F*'s. Only, for him, it was family, friends, food, and fun. Somewhere down deep in the man, he missed the days of standing hip to hip in the kitchen with Stella. The giant brick barbecue on the patio was his to command. As Stella and Dolly would say, it was a testosterone reality. The more men knew about barbecues, the less they knew about the controls on a stove.

There had been parties as intimate as just Manny, Stella, and Hooker. Then again, the house had seen over four hundred people, before the police and fire department showed up for Stella's birthday party with a live band they'd arrested the night before. The drunk and disorderly charges were lost when the band agreed to meet their van at a private party.

The neighbors gave up when the police told them there were no officers available to go settle a noise abatement problem. They were told half of the night force was at a riot in the Almaden Valley. The neighbors knew which riot it was, and finally pulled on their clothes and went to party with the Romero family until dawn. Sunrise was about the time Manny stoked up the barbecue and laid a large steel plate down to become the griddle. Three not-so-drunk firefighters eased Manny aside and told him this was what the fire department was expertly trained for.

They had raided the last of the giant larder, and Stella was Queen Bee for the day. Many at the party had never been there before, which meant they did not know about the larder she had started for them and others for when they were in need. That day, Stella gained hundreds of more volunteers for her giant canning fest, which would run for three months as food became available.

It was also the first time Hooker realized just how big of a family he had fallen into. He just didn't understand he would become the center the family would grow and orbit around.

With Hooker usually waking up around three in the afternoon, Manny and Stella's clock had also shifted. The afternoon meal was usually breakfast for Hooker and some snack or meal for Stella and Manny. The days flowed with whatever was up. What never flowed into the house were phone calls.

With Manny retired from the police force because of his injury years before, the two parents' lives rolled with the punches of Hooker's life on the days or nights he was encamped at the Hacienda Romero. Same as during Manny's career, a phone call was hardly ever a welcome event.

When he worked the streets, and he was home, it would

mean overtime or to come fill in because something had gone horribly wrong. When he was at work, it only meant Stella needed to grab her purse and head for the Valley Medical Center where they'd taken him.

On a Sunday morning at eleven after ten, no good could come of the phone ringing.

Stella's heart clenched.

Manny rolled his head over and looked at the offending piece of plastic and electronics. Even though it was his favorite weapon or tool, it had rung before he wanted to use it.

His right arm flopped out next to the wireless handset resting in its charger. He looked at Stella. Her eyes burned back at him. They both held their breaths as he scooped up the handset and brought it toward his ear. On the way, his thumb pushed the green button.

"Romero."

Stella watched him carefully. He rarely reacted. There were tragic times she almost had to beat him to get him to tell her what was going on.

"Uhum... how bad?"

She watched him talk with his eyes closed. His voice was dull.

"Did he actually use the word critical, or are you...?"

Stella picked up her coffee mug. She looked at the cold dregs left in the bottom half. She hated wasting good coffee—but this may be one of those times when she didn't mind.

"Well, I don't think I would use a siren or lights... it could make things worse..."

Stella started to rise. This conversation had just stepped

back at least fifteen years when Manny worked the streets. Detectives never used lights and sirens. She sat.

"I think it's time to bring in the commander on this. Just a minute, Danny..." Manny laid the phone on his chest. Rolling his head toward Stella as he opened his eyes, he asked. "How are we set for eggs?"

"Manny Romero, I am going to skin you alive." She pointed. "Is that Danny Sweets?"

She rose, and he smiled softly as he held out the phone. She took the phone gently but with pure threat in her eyes.

She put the phone to her ear. "Hello, Danny." She closed her eyes. "Is your mama home, or are you two just latchkey kids?"

Manny could hear the big man on the other end of the line laugh... then obey the silent command.

"Tilly... What in Hades are these men-children trying to cook up? I love you dearly like a sister, but I was lying here making wonderful sweet love to my man when your boy decided it would be just wonderful to call his extra mama..."

The two giggled as she carried the phone into the kitchen. Stella knew she would need more coffee.

"No, I think we're pretty low on almost anything. I was just going to whip up some gruel and slop it onto some trencher boards and call it good."

Manny loved hearing her talk to Sweets' mother, Tilly. They were more alike than Stella was with her blood sister, Dolly.

"You figure the menu and get what we need, and we'll see you three about two or so. Hooker is not going anywhere this evening. I need him and the Squirt down in the barn to move some pallets of canned goods around. I have three care vans showing up at nine tomorrow morning."

She listened, and then again noticed a note she had left yesterday for Hooker. "Honey, I just remembered something. We have a few others coming. Make it four or five more, I think the men are going to do the man thing, but Candy is here, and Willie will bring Hank, so there's plenty of girl stuff. Maddie can choose for herself which room she wants to be in."

Manny pulled himself up. Things just got interesting.

"We'll see you about two-thirty-ish." Stella hung up as she walked back in and placed the phone in the charger. She returned to her place on the long side of the giant couch and sat down. She sipped her coffee as she found where she had left off in the paper.

Manny just sat and stared at the paper she had between them. The silence was enough. Finally, she couldn't stand it and folded down the one corner.

The right eye showed, and Manny started. "Willie, Hank, Maddie... this slipped your mind?"

"And Chet and one of those guys from up at Moffett... I think he's a captain or something."

"Captain John Trask, the explosives expert?"

She moved the corner of the newspaper back up. "See, you're already up to speed. Brunch is at three."

WITH ALL FOUR leaves installed and turned sideways, the table extended out into the vestibule. The thirteen were comfortable around the table, which fully extended, could fit sixteen. When Stella ordered the table to match the size and look of the gigantic front doors, Manny thought she had slipped a gear. In those days, they thought they didn't know fourteen people to invite over. Between his work and Stella taking care of those in need, they never found the time or reason to gather in many people—even though they had designed the house around entertaining large groups. After Hooker had become a fixture and Manny retired with a bullet to the spine, there seemed to be a pent-up bucketful of reasons. This close family was only one reason.

"Now, Stella, you just quit your Jack-in-the-box jumping up and down. I've got the coffee covered." She reached across the table as if to cover Stella's hand with hers. Between the wide table and both women possessing well-endowed chests, it was more of a gesture than a real reach out.

Stella settled back down and watched Tilly. She could see the devil twinkling in those eyes, even if the face was relaxed into an almost sanguine deadpan.

"Now there... doesn't that just feel better?" But Stella pointed behind her at the coffee carafe.

Tilly nodded as she settled even deeper into her seat. "Uh-huh, I've got this." Without breaking eye contact, she continued. "Danny, sweetheart..."

The man jumped up with a smile as if he had been waiting for the request he knew was coming. Tilly smiled and nodded. Stella quietly jiggled with laughter. Sweets hung his head down onto the back of his propped-up hand. He heard it coming for the last twenty years. His mama was Queen Bee. What Sweets could do, he did. Everything else was on Danny. Even with Sweets' blindness, he knew his brother did it with grace, a smile, and looked good doing it—whatever she asked.

Sweets raised his head toward where he knew the Navy captain was. "So the bombs were—"

Dolly cut him off. "Sweets, honey... not at my table. After you men have enjoyed the company of us ladies, you can go into the office and speak of the crudities of this world all you want. Even the swear jar doesn't apply in the man room if the door's shut. But here, at this table—my table—only things of pleasant and kindness are spoken about."

"Yes, ma'am." Even Sweets didn't have to have sight to know she had spoken with a warm yet firm smile. Sweets knew his Queen Bee.

Maddie cleared her throat as she placed her carefully folded napkin on the table. "How do you like the Granny car in the rain, Candy?"

"It's noisy when it rains hard. I can barely hear the radio."

Maddie and Willie both frowned. "But the Dart is radio delete. It doesn't have a radio." Hooker and the Squirt laughed. Candy had delivered the best punch with a completely innocent face. She was definitely learning to fit into the fighting ranks of the family.

Sweets got the joke but wanted to continue the subject. "Don't you have to be sometimes driving after midnight?"

"Yes. Sometimes we shadow the swing shift at the hospitals. They're the most informative about patient care. As we get people ready to sleep for the night, many need drug doses, narcotics for sleep, pain meds, and diaper changes. The difficult ones with dimes in them just need to have their pulse taken and heads examined."

Chet snorted. "Careful there, little nursey. We have you surrounded."

Candy grew big eyes. "Ooo, spoken with five bits of wisdom..." The table laughed. Hooker and the Squirt had each two dimes and some pieces, where Chet only had some pieces still floating around in him.

Candy turned back to Sweets. "To answer the question you were really asking, Hooker got me a little battery radio, so I could listen to my favorite disc jockey after midnight. I think his name is Wolf Man Joe or something."

The table roared at Sweets' expense.

As the noise settled down, Sweets mumbled clearly, "Yeah, I think that's the show Danny listens to back there with the engineer."

The table erupted with laughter as they all rose to clear plates and get ready for the second part of the day. Cooking would be in the kitchen, and bombs would be dropping in the office. Maddie took the easy way out and chose the man-talk. Hank was always up for the kitchen. Everyone knew it was a fair exchange.

Not everyone would fit in the office, so they opted for Candy's front room in the apartment built in the basement just off the three-car garage. Instead of taking Manny out in the heavy rain, Hooker pushed his empty chair down the secret stairs while Manny clung to the large back of Danny. Hooker knew Manny was well under a hundred-twenty-pounds—as the lower half had atrophied.

Hooker started the coffee percolator in the small kitchenette area. Chairs were brought from the storage room across the garage as people found places to settle in.

"Before we get to the explosives, let's cover what we got

from Colorado. Chet, you spoke with the sheriff out there?" Manny rolled forward on his forearms—to adjust his attention.

"Yes, at length, actually—the guy was born and raised in the house he lives in. He is the third generation to the area and the only one who didn't go into the family business of mining." Chet looked at his fingernails and smiled. "He said even as a kid, he liked his fingernails clean."

The CHP captain opened a thin manila folder and looked at his notes. His eyes scanned the pages until he was oriented.

"To understand what we're dealing with today, we need to understand the father—Helmut Lysander." Chet flipped back a few pages. "According to immigrations, he came to America, running away from Hitler in 1936. He was young and knew explosives. He approached the American team at the Olympics and asked for asylum. Later, he worked as a cannon charge expert for the Pacific fleet in Pearl Harbor. After the attack, he moved, along with many others, to Alameda, and then eventually, down to Long Beach in California. He spent the rest of the war shuttling back and forth from Long Beach and San Diego's North Island. After the war, he moved to the mining areas of Colorado and worked as a..." Chet laughed. "This has to be wrong... but it says 'powder monkey.'"

Captain Trask and the Squirt both at the same time, "It's right." They looked at each other. Trask held his palm out to the kid.

The Squirt nodded and offered the explanation. "This really is in the Navy's wheelhouse—as it's an old naval term. Back in the heyday of sail and mass destruction of beautiful sailing ships, the powder monkey—or powder boy—was a small boy who shuttled gunpowder from the hold to the cannons. Later, the term was applied to someone who worked with explosives. They were also known as blasters."

Trask smiled and nodded with a satisfied look on his face. "And you know this why?"

The Squirt nodded the top of his head in Willie's direction.

Willie squirmed a tiny bit. "Well, when we started working with you on the big bang thing, Maddie thought a little research into naval explosives would be in order. So when the Squirt was free to move around in a library, Maddie turned him loose."

The Squirt added in, "It was very interesting to find explosives—well, firebombs at least, dated all the way back to the Phoenicians and the Henweighs." He waited with a deadpan face.

Trask frowned, but he wasn't going to get caught in his lack of knowledge. "And what's a Henweigh?"

Hooker snorted as Willie answered the old gear-head joke. "About two to three pounds."

The room groaned.

Sweets still had his face down in his hand. The thumb and forefinger were pinching the bridge of his nose. New to the workings of these campfire meetings to hash out information and see what everyone is thinking, he wasn't sure if he had a place in the discussion. Danny rested his hand on the younger brother's shoulder and leaned over. "Are you okay, man?"

Sweets shook his head but sat up. "What I'm hearing is this man comes to America with valuable knowledge. Then during the war effort, we give him even more knowledge. This man has a son, whom I assume went into the family business... so he buys explosives and blows things up. Am I up to speed here?"

Trask and Chet both grimaced. Trask took the lead. "Not exactly—but you have the basics. If all he did were to purchase five hundred pounds of dynamite, we'd have a way to track the sale. However, this man has knowledge of not only how explosive materials work, but also how to make them the way he wants them to work. In the pharmacy world, these kinds of people are called compounders. They take a little of this and a touch of that combined with a smidge of other and pretty soon, you have a drug nobody makes commercially. This is what the man can do."

He paused to make sure this sank in before going on. "Let's say you have a case of eighty-percent dynamite. You put it under a Lincoln Towncar..."

Danny rumbled. "Make it a Cadillac."

Manny laughed. "Just don't tell Stella."

Trask massaged his face. He knew he was in a room full of car guys. He looked over at Maddie.

Maddie smiled. "Ford LTD. It's essentially a wannabe and weighs about thirty-seven pounds lighter, but with a crap engine."

Trask laughed. He now knew who was probably the expert in the room... or in this case, the mistress of knowledge. "Okay, we have this puke green old LTD and a case of dynamite." Everyone nods. "We want to make the car blow or be thrown forty feet in the air. The case of dynamite will get it to about thirty-seven, but it isn't forty. This guy knows how to mix chemicals he can buy, semi-unrestricted, to make the green lemon reach forty feet. Not forty-two and not thirty-eight, but forty. Which... is the real reason why this guy is so very scary. He knows what to do.

"We now know he blew the entire guts of the main building at Frontier Village. The glass blew out, but nothing collapsed. Well, until a little shaker a few days later. We also know he wiped the walls of the hardware store clean and didn't break a single window. He retarded the explosion and redirected the concussion. Then there's the floor of the Federal Reserve transfer station. He placed fifty-some charges which cut the floor out from beneath the armored truck. Then he blew the back doors in such a way as to take the doors off but left the sides of the truck in essentially normal condition. They'll only need to weld on new hinges. Oh, and did I mention when the doors blew? They were sucked out of the truck and thrown to the two sides, so they were out of the way for a forklift to take the pallets of money?"

Sweets held up his two hands in surrender. "I get it. I get it..." His voice trailed off.

Hooker knew the look. "What have you got, Sweets?" The look was when the man had tapped into his other sight and didn't know where it fit in.

"There is a truck..."

"Yes, he blew it up."

"That was last week... too small. This one is larger. Delivery van... square..."

Five stomachs in the room churned, knowing the visions Sweets sees—are somehow true.

23

THE DELIVERY VAN

Felix stood at the back end of the delivery van. His trained eye measured the long cavity of the cargo area. The van was rated to carry more than ten thousand pounds of newspapers. He knew the load he would put in the van would only fill the cargo area about six feet deep and weigh much less than a load of newspapers. The only problem was the newspaper's name painted on the sides and back door.

He turned toward the balding man in the cardigan sweater. "Eight-hundred, you said. How does it run? I have to drive all the way to Texas with the load."

The man scratched his head and lied. "Oh, no problem there. They just took her off the line, and she was the main truck down Salinas' way."

Felix looked at the rust edging along the wheel wells and anywhere the metal ended. It was obvious to him this truck had sat idle for a few years. He thought about sticking the liar in the back of the van and burying him in the fertilizer he would have to pick up soon. He handed the bills to the man in exchange for the keys.

"You'll need to twiddle with the gas a bit to get her started. These Detroit engines are kind of fussy that way."

Felix didn't even look at the man. He now knew the man was praying the truck would start. He probably had never seen the truck even run. Rolling his eyes and closing his eyelids, Felix pulled open the door and stepped up into the stand-up driver's area. He pulled down the jump seat and sat. He looked for the keyhole.

"I think it's over there on the right."

Felix found it. He pumped the gas twice and turned the key. The battery had enough power to crank the starter, and in a few heartbeats, the engine caught and coughed into some likeness of life. Felix figured it would live for as many miles as he needed it to.

He waved at the bald man who was counting his money. Felix didn't think about it. The money came from another twisted dealer and another shady deal. The seamy underside of the world wasn't Felix's to clean up. His mind was more biblical—they had taken his wife and his reason for living. The extra money from his explosive work had started as a means to retire. After the accident, it became a means to keep his wife with him and to provide for her care—something Felix felt the system had never done—care.

The large van rattled down the forgotten highway. The faster interstates and freeways produced many such pockets of long-forgotten culture and civilization. As the world went zipping by a mile away, the calmer, quieter old road wound between the mounds of small hills, straightened through the meadows and pastures, and wiggled through the groves of trees. Tucked here and there were former homes—now just so many boards waiting for a strong windstorm to scatter what was left of lives and dreams.

Felix eased the step-van onto the abused gravel approach to the battered Atlantic Richfield gas station. The metal skin was showing signs of a metropolis of rust under the faded paint—cancer under the makeup of an old whore. The three windows remaining stood cracked and sprawled from a former neighborhood kid's BB gun. The surrounding trees stood shriveled from the years of drought. The dry had only been good for the mesquite, which survived more from the humidity in the sea air than anything in the ground. The recent winter rains, sparse as they were, had washed the leaves, adding some darker green.

Felix stepped down from the van and walked to the new lock he had installed a few years before. He cupped his hand under the lock as he lifted it. The penny trapped there by the weight of the lock—dropped into his hand. The old station with its two work bays sat tucked into a pocket, keeping it out of any serious wind. Over the years, the penny never dislodged from any of the powerful storms ravaging the Bay Area. The low hills protected the small valley from the rage of any storms, but also prevented much of the rain from reaching the surrounding trees and ground.

Felix rolled the door up on the second bay. The rough rumble startled a sparrow, which flew out from under the small metal eaves where it had found a rust hole large enough to nest in. Felix smiled knowingly as he watched the bird fly away. The Bay Area was just warm enough that the small birds did not migrate with the winter. They just hunkered into smaller holes and wintered over. Thelma would have said they know where to seek out a place where the love is just closer to them.

As he walked back to the van, he looked up-country. Through a sparse smattering of trees, one could see a small clearing—if there were enough rain, it would be a small meadow.

Felix stopped at the van door. The meadow in his mind was decades before and a thousand miles away. The young girl had been wearing a yellow dress. Her legs churned as she ran through the new high mountain flowers. Tiny blue blooms speckled the low grass of the sloping meadow. Yellow buttercups washed like tiny rivers cutting through the miniature grasses. A single flower would start the meandering stripe of yellow and flood into thousands as they ran like a stream of butter, and then they would peter out to a single flower—and then they were gone.

A seven-year-old Felix stood in the hard-nailed shoes marking him as an immigrant. His shorts were leather lederhosen with integrated braces and a small placard across the chest. Only the white shirt was a nod to being in America. A little girl with long blonde hair glowing in the sunshine spun and ran like one of the angels his grandmother had told him about. He knew they were standing on a very high mountain, so they must be closer to his grandmother's heaven than the adults thought.

The girl spun with her arms outstretched. Her hair floated in a slower arch but nearly touched her outstretched trailing hand. Her circling the meadow finally drew her near to Felix.

"*Vas ist dein name?*" He asked her name.

The little girl spun one more time and stopped. She looked at the funny boy in the shorts. "You talk funny."

"*Wie ist dein name?*" He wanted her to say more. Her voice sounded like the tinkling of the tiny harp hanging on the back of their front door. When the door opened or closed, the little balls on strings played the harp by knocking on the strings.

The girl took another step forward and pointed to the flowers painted on the placard crossing his chest from suspender to suspender.

"Those flowers are pretty."

"*Wer bist du?*" Who are you?

She touched the tiny blue and black flower on his chest. She looked into his eyes. "I know where that flower is." She took his hand. "Come on. I'll show it to you."

He followed her—and never let go.

Until they took her away from him.

His face darkened as he stepped up into the van. Putting it in gear, he eased the Ford step-van into the garage bay. He was aware of the tight clearances the large square shape of the commercial truck created. When the nose of the van was about two feet from the narrow workbench, he stopped. Stepping down, he moved toward the back of the van to check the clearance between the back and the door. Felix knew he would need at least two feet. He eyeballed the distance from the back of the bumper to the metal meet-plate where the door locked down to... the three feet would be more than enough.

He returned to the cab and turned the engine off. Habit had him close the van's door. Walking to the large roll-up entrance, he pulled the chain, drawing it down. He gazed through the trees as the door rumbled down. In a moment, the metal severed his vision of the field and the memory. The memory and the woman had been removed by a system with no heart or compassion. Like his father, Felix never rose to anger. It only seethed in his gut as his mind stepped through the paces of what was needed for revenge.

Felix looked at the large empty metal cylinder in the corner. It would take hours for the tank to reach full pressure. Felix ran his hand over many areas of the van's body. He knew he had at least a day of sanding to do. He could only work in the daylight. Any light at night would draw attention to the old abandoned gas station, as well as to him. He flipped the circuit breaker and heard the compressor start to hum within the insulated box he had built. Under normal conditions, sound suppression is never used. It overheats the compressor, and after a short while, the compressor motor dies, or the compressor cylinders overheat and seize.

Felix rechecked the stacks of sanding disks for the pneumatic sander. The sanding wouldn't have to look professional, but the job did have to have a certain finish to it to pass casual scrutiny. His mental checklist had him kick the new five-gallon can of acetone and tip back the four gallons of paint. The paint was enamel house paint for trim but flawlessly mixed to match the needed look. Felix's eyes passed over the two boxes of other supplies, as well as the valuable roll of white paper containing layout drawings with small holes pricked along the lines.

Felix walked back to the far corner and out the small door. Turning, he locked up. Walking to the second bay door, he picked up the large lock that was painted to look old —snapping it shut in the hasp. Reaching into his left pocket, he drew out the penny and slipped it behind the lock. It stayed.

Straightening up, he glanced back at the trees. The meadow now hid in the freshening gloom. Felix knew in his heart—the important meadow was now gone forever. With a drooped face, he turned back south and walked out to the road. His home was a couple of hours away walking, but the Volkswagen, now painted tan, was only a mile away. He would be back in the morning.

24

WAKE UP THE NEIGHBORS

Hooker had been mildly aware of a moving van across the street sometime during the last few weeks. He wasn't certain if it was about moving stuff out or if there was a new neighbor. Either one would come to surface only when Stella knew she had his attention and would remember what she was saying. Five-forty in the morning after hauling a smashed bobtail down to Salinas was not the time. Because of the emergency work on the 101 around Prunedale, Hooker had taken the long way home by means of Santa Cruz and up over the 17 to Saratoga. At the crest, Dolly had asked him to take a tow for Central Tow going to Daley City. The miles had taken their toll, and he was ready for a fluffy pillow. Even Box was moving slowly at the end of their day. The cat had taken a paused stop on the gas tank before jumping to the ground. At three years old, Hooker knew age hadn't stopped the large cat—it had just been a long day.

Hooker dropped to the ground and turned to close and lock the door. He ran his hand over the new paint. The enamel was smooth, but he knew the clear coats would be even smoother when they were all done. It was just a matter of finding the time to schedule the week or so of paint.

Hooker turned at the sound of Box growling. The mangled cat didn't have a normal voice box of a cat. His growl was more like Hooker missing a shift and the gears clashing in the transmission. It was more of a series of chopped growls instead of one long, drawn out growl. The cat stood stiff as he looked intently at the neighbor's front yard.

Hooker knew the neighbor had recently installed a doggie door for their young yellow Lab named Mike. The dog had the run to relieve himself in the early morning.

"Box... Leave Mike alone."

The sound of two dogs growling ended in yelping and a whine—Box exploded. The orange streak was almost impossible to follow with the eye. Hooker spun and started running—he knew this would not end well and would require his hand in the fight.

The mass of fur was more dark brown and black than the yellow of Mike. Hooker hadn't seen a new German Shepherd in the neighborhood. He glanced over at the dark house across the way as he ran.

The orange missile hit the mass of fur. Even moving in a whirling mass, Box had targeted the interloper. The first hit looked to be only a glancing blow. Hooker was sure what was tossed from Box's mouth was a dark brown and black ear. Box landed, turned, and aimed. A split second, and he sprang for the second hit. This time, he stayed in the mix.

Hooker stopped. He could see Box had his mouth sunk into the large dog's remaining ear. His front paws, the size of fifty-cent pieces each, were on each side of the head with claws anchored into the face just behind the eyes. Box's body was a machine. The hind legs were a blur and working on fur—still connected to chunks of skin. Pieces of the large dog flew out behind Box like a lawnmower throwing grass.

The large dog shifted from attacking the young Labrador to defending itself from the unseen demon. It threw its head from side to side to dislodge the cat. Once free, it could attack. Except the orange demon was Box.

The cat had stripped the entire back and neck of fur. Box bunched at the head. With a raking upward sweep of the front paws, he peeled the face from behind the eyes and into the ear holes. As Box released the ear from his mouth, he continued into a forward flip and landed five feet away from the large dog still straddling Mike. Box crouched and waited. The low growl had turned to a chuffing Hooker had only heard twice before. Box was not going to let this dog live.

The dog hesitated for only a heartbeat and then sprang. As he came in from the top, Box charged from underneath and then did a backflip. The dog tried to respond by arching as it landed. Its face came in and was within its defensive front legs. Box was waiting.

The dog's lower jaw landed in Box's mouth. Hooker could hear the teeth grinding into the jawbone as the large paws reached expertly into the eye sockets. Both eyeballs exploded at the same time. Box's powerful hind legs shredded deep through the soft neck. The sound of the dogs howling seemed to stretch for miles in every direction and then snapped back to a wet boiling as the dog collapsed.

Less than the three racing heartbeats of Hooker's, the

fight was over. The large dog lay heaving. Its last breaths gurgled through the bloody mass that had been its throat. The large mangled dog was incapable of even whimpering. The mass lay heaving on the concrete like so much half-ground hamburger.

Box stood over the mass and then raised a leg and pissed.

Hooker turned back to his truck. He returned with a short pipe, usually only used as a cheater extension for the four-way star lug wrench. It was now a tool of euthanasia. He looked up for Box.

Box was licking and checking his friend and neighbor, Mike. The young dog had suffered only a few bites before the avenging missile had struck. Hooker didn't want to think about what could have happened if they had stopped to get another call or just taken a little longer. He thought about Uncle Willie's favorite saying: *There are no accidents in this universe; things are meant to happen.*

Hooker looked at the large body. He looked around in the growing light of the early morning. There was no evidence of a collar. He felt around what remained of the neck. There was no hollow even suggesting a collar. It was not uncommon. Even Box didn't wear a collar. But then again, Box was Box and not one of the foo-foo cats living down the street in one of the big houses.

Hooker looked Mike over. The young Lab was lying stretched out and enjoying the open administrations of his secret friend. "I'll wake your dad in a few minutes, Mike. I need to handle this first." He pointed to the body of the dog, which was well over a hundred pounds. Hooker knew a dog this size would not go unnoticed in the neighborhood for more than a day. He stood and walked across the street.

Hooker stood at the door and pushed the button again. He could hear the set of obnoxious chimes ringing in probably the hall of the house. He thought about them and chuckled silently, knowing if Stella had ever installed something so ridiculous, Manny would have shot them the second time they chimed. Luckily, they all had the same taste in their door announcement. There was an eight-pound rot-iron knocker on the giant doors of Hacienda Romero.

Hooker saw a face peek out of the tall window next to the door. The man opened the door. Hooker took in the whole picture. The fuzzy pinkish bathrobe, the fuzzy light blue slippers, and the small poodle dyed pink with light blue ears. Hooker didn't have to see to know the tail was also blue to match the ears and blue pom-poms shaped at the tiny feet.

The man's comb-over was standing almost straight up. He blinked, which didn't help the look of the owl-like face. "Yes?"

Hooker coughed the laughter out of his throat and pulled his best deadpan face. "Um, sorry to wake you, but there was a serious dogfight..."

The man was horror-struck. "Oh no... Mr. Puddles is strictly an inside dog."

"Yes, I see it now. It wasn't a dog I recognized—and with you being new to the neighborhood, I thought I'd better check."

The man frowned, which did not help with the look of his face with the large hooked beak of his nose. "And you are...?"

A female voice whined from somewhere back in the house. Hooker figured from a warm bed. "Who is it, Bill, and what do they want at this hour?"

The man's face slumped, and he rolled his eyes. Hooker could see the long-suffering familiarity etched in his features.

He stuck his hand out. "My name is Hooker. I live in the large hacienda across the street with Manny and Stella Romero."

The man offered him a limp, dead fish of a hand. "You must be the owner of the big yellow noisy truck."

Hooker knew down deep he and this couple would not become the best of friends. "Yes, sir. It's my living, and I try to keep things as quiet around here as possible. I work nights and usually gone from late afternoon until the morning."

The man was already closing the door. "Well, just be mindful. You have neighbors now."

Hooker crossed the street steaming.

He knelt next to the young yellow Lab—still being licked by Box. "How are you doing, kid? Can you walk? Want to go back in?" Hooker looked at the area still oozing a little blood near where the neck met the shoulder. "Come on, Mike... Let's go wake your daddy up."

For the second time, Hooker stood pushing a button at a door. This time, thankfully, the bell was the old-fashioned dingdong. Hooker smiled. He thought ya gotta respect a guy who is a dingdong and proud enough to show it.

The door swung open, and Ray stood in the doorway with nothing but his smile.

Hooker laughed. "Well, good morning to you too, sunshine."

Ray snorted and smiled. "You need a jumpstart, Hooker?" The man was one of the coaches at San Jose City College, but he could moonlight as a stand-up comedian or heckler. He had one of the fastest minds and mouths Hooker knew.

"Nah, I'm good, Ray... but Mike here got attacked..."

"Not by Box, those two little fuckers sneak around here and hang out together."

"Nah, it wasn't Box—for once. The body is out here. I've never seen the dog before." He waved his thumb back toward the street.

Ray started to step out into the tiny courtyard running the length of his garage. Hooker put up his hand to stop him. "Um, Ray..." He waved at the man's privates.

"What time is it?"

"Not quite six."

"Nobody will be up for—"

"I woke the new guy. I'm sure he's fully awake now."

Ray frowned. "Yeah, I met the panty-waist and his harridan from Houston. Give me a minute. I'll be right out."

Minutes later, they stood over the carcass. Ray shook his head. "Nope, can't say I've ever seen this one. What did it look like before the freight train hit it?" He looked over where Box was still taking care of the young Lab.

"Like a very large German Sheppard, but with all the parts in the right places."

"Hmmm..." The man thought with his braced arm and hand to his chin. His lips were screwed into a prune. "Looks more like German sausage now."

Ray looked down the street, and Hooker could tell he had just gotten serious. It was like a switch the man threw back and forth.

"Give me a few minutes," he said and took off running in a lazy loping way. Even though it looked almost like he was running in slow motion, Hooker could see he was eating up serious ground. He turned into the pinkish house at the crest of the hill. A few minutes later, he returned with another person in a bathrobe walking along beside him. They were talking animatedly. As they got closer, Hooker could see longer, dark hair in a ponytail.

"Hooker, this is Dalia—like the flower. She's Mike's personal girlfriend."

The woman smiled as she stuck out her hand. "Glad to finally meet the famous son of Manny and Stella. I've seen your truck, and I've heard some wild stories..."

"Don't believe a word of them—they're all true." Hooker smiled and shook her hand.

"Is it true about getting shot up by the killer last year?"

Ray snorted. "If it's change you want, Hooker has... what, about two or three dimes still in you?"

"Two and a half dimes..."

Ray pointed to the dead dog. "What do you think, Doll?"

She knelt down and was not hesitant to push and move the head. "I think he got into it with a mountain lion." She started to look up at the men and then noticed the twenty-plus pounds of Box still working over an almost purring Mike. "Oh."

Ray chuffed. "Doll, meet Box. Just don't try to shake hands with him." He looked at Hooker and pointed at the carcass. "This took how long?"

Hooker thought about how much time. "Three, maybe four seconds—five seconds would be tops."

The vet slowly rose as she pulled her robe tighter. "Alone?"

"Box doesn't need backup. Last year I watched him take down a full-grown man in less than two."

"Killed him?"

"If I had let him..."

She thought for a few heartbeats. "I don't think I want to be his vet."

Hooker smiled. "He's only needed one vet, who is Connie over at South County Services. She saved his life three years ago—and he's never forgotten her. When he walks in and jumps up on the counter, all the others clear the room. Even I wouldn't be allowed to hug him the way she does." He nodded at the carcass. "Have you've seen this dog around?"

"Seen this around? Yes. Dog... no. This is what is known as a Kai-dog. A dog runs away and gets knocked up by a coyote. The litter is a straight cross between those two, but when a pack produces generations, you get all the strong traits of the more powerful dogs." She knelt and rubbed back the fur. "This hair shows the undercoat of some large winter dogs like Newfoundland, Saint Bernard, Husky, Great Pyrenees and a few other breeds which all run well over a hundred pounds. Cross them with other dogs and the small forty or fifty-pound coyote, and you get a powerful wild dog like this. My guess is he left the pack to start his own. I've seen him around for the last few months." She stood back up. "My personal feeling is your cat did the neighborhood a favor."

Ray stared at the large dog. "Thanks, Doll." He looked up at her. "Sorry for waking you at this hour."

She opened her bathrobe to disclose the running shorts

and T-shirt that said UCD Track. "Are you kidding? You almost missed me. I was heading out to run the hill."

The man smiled. "You run the hill? Shoot, give me a few minutes, and I'll go with you."

"I'll call the county and get this picked up while I wait for your slow old butt. I know I can smoke a tweety-bird from Stanford."

Hooker held up his hands. "I'm out of this fight. Dalia, it was nice to meet you, and thank you for taking care of this."

"Please, everyone calls me Doll. My last name is Hause." She smiled.

Hooker chuckled. "Okay, Doll, it is." He turned for the hacienda. "Let's go, Box. Mike is plenty washed." He turned back as he remembered the one wound on the neck. The vet was already looking the pup over. Hooker smiled. He liked this woman's style. Obviously, Ray did too.

25

NEW DEVELOPMENTS

The tapping on the door was light but sufficient. Hooker stirred.

Hooker didn't have to open his eyes. He didn't have to look at the clock. He just instinctively knew it wasn't three in the afternoon yet. Somewhere deep in his body, there was a clock that knew certain times, like, at three in the afternoon, it was time to get up. At midnight, the radio dispatch changed from the auto club to Dolly. Ten after midnight and Sweets took his first break in the music to tell you it was KLIV in San Jose—the world's best place to live. One-forty, Dolly will put her feet up on the desk, close her eyes, and wait for the first drunk wreck. Karen says she's even seen her not move anything but her arm to pick up the lollipop microphone to call Hooker. Three in the morning and the first batch of apple fritters hit the hot oil at the Whole Donut—seven days a week. The two people watching the run of the number-one seller among the night shift cops were Ralph and Mai—the co-owners. Four-fifteen and the blinking red light at Monterey Highway and Alma stops blinking red and turns to blinking yellow for the next thirty-four minutes.

Hooker knew it was before noon.

He swung his legs over the edge of the bed and padded into his bathroom. A small sound announced the arrival of Box. Halfway across the expanse of white onyx tile, the deep rattle of the cat's purr started to echo in the room. Hooker's right hand hung beside the toilet. The large cat turned, sitting so the single ear protruded into the knuckles of Hooker's hand—which automatically started to massage it. Hooker thought about the morning's event. "You did great this morning, Box. Sorry about Mike getting bit, but I think it's for the good your relationship is now out in the open."

Hooker flushed and splashed his face with some water. He would take a shower later.

Walking into his dark bedroom, he moved with the confidence of knowing everything was where it was supposed to be. He stuck his left foot down into the boot and followed with the right. Reaching down on both sides of the boots, he grabbed hold of the belt on his pants and drew them up in one movement. Three deft movements later, and they were zipped, buttoned, and belted. He stepped to the closet and drew a T-shirt from one of the hangers. Slipping it on, he stepped to the door. Time from the quiet knock to his opening the door had been three minutes.

He stepped into the hallway. A movement to his right caught his eye. The Squirt was walking out of his room while reading a thick book. Hooker noticed the slight twitch of the head bobbing up, recognizing Hooker's presence. The Squirt was studying. Hooker turned left, and the two zombies headed for the kitchen area.

Hooker looked at Stella standing by the large stone-topped island. Her right hand was pointing back at the office. Hooker changed course, and the Squirt followed.

Manny was at the desk but turned sideways and backed up to the wall. Hooker looked at the couch just inside the door. Chet sat in full uniform.

"Is this an official visit, or are you here to arrest me for all the times I exceeded the speed limit?" Hooker had never seen the man in his official dress uniform. The man was overwhelming with officialdom.

Chet didn't smile at the playful banter. "There have been some developments."

Hooker took a seat in one of the club chairs, and the Squirt closed his book and sat. "The bomber...?" Chet nodded.

"Four days ago, the Department of Human Services received a request for assistance in a seizer by a peer department in Colorado. The Colorado department had been tracking down Felix Lysander and his wife Thelma for over four years. They tracked them to a location in Milpitas."

The Squirt coughed. "Written or phone?"

Chet frowned. "Written or phone, what?"

"The request—did they make the request officially by sending a conformed notice of intent, or was the request made verbally by phone? How the request is made makes a difference."

"They showed up in person."

The Squirt duck-lipped and nodded his approval. "Qualifies as very official..."

Hooker sat back and leaned on the arm of the chair—still not quite awake. "What happened?"

Chet opened a slim folder on the desk. "They took the wife, Thelma, into protective custody. Evidently, she is in a vegetative state and should be under constant care. Five years ago, Felix removed her from the county hospital in the middle of the night and disappeared into the night with her. They had been looking for them since."

Manny rocked forward on his forearms. "Where is she now?"

"Back in Colorado—in a locked ward."

"So the case is closed." Hooker was still wondering why he was awake at... he looked at the reflection in the glass covering a photo taken of Manny, face down in a dark ally. The reflection was of the clock behind his head. In his mind, Hooker reversed the image and came up with eleven-twenty or so.

"No. Well... yes and no. Thelma is in Colorado—that part is closed. We're still looking for Felix for the bombings."

"And I'm awake because...?"

"The people from Colorado said Felix was not known as a hothead or a violent man—other than being someone who plays with explosives. But to their knowledge, he has never killed anyone before..."

Hooker rolled his hand in the air. "But...?"

"Nobody had ever taken his wife away before. So they don't know how he'll react."

The Squirt frowned. "But she was in a hospital before... in Colorado..."

Chet pulled the file toward him and looked at some notations. "Yes, following an accident at a mine where she was struck in the head by a piece of flying rock. She was taken to a hospital and placed on a respirator in..." He pulled the folder closer and then turned a page. "That was in 1968. A year later was when Felix busted her out, and they fled."

"So she had basically recovered."

Chet read through the notes. "No... according to the medical examiner at the time, she was basal responsive. In other words—one step above a coma. She was off life support and could be spoon-fed. The examiner had recommended transfer to a state care facility. Felix took her and disappeared the night before she was to be transferred."

Hooker's voice was from a long way off, and a long time ago. "If she had transferred, he would have lost her forever."

The four digested the observation. The clock on the wall ticked, echoing the deeper tone of the tick in the tall grandfather clock in the other room.

Manny eased cautiously onto his forearms and then settled back. "I think we can assume we're no longer dealing with a rational person." He looked to Chet.

The officer shook his head. "No telling what he's capable of now. Maybe he never killed before, but I would assume now all limiting factors are wiped from the playing field, as it were."

Hooker shifted. "So, what are we looking out for now?"

The Squirt grumped, "Anything and everything. The guy blew up the whole inside of Frontier Village and only blew out half of the windows. He cut a perfect hole through twenty-two inches of reinforced floor and then blew the hinges off a federal armored truck—while derailing a freight train. Heck, this guy could probably drop all four corner buildings at First and Stevens Creek and still leave the streetlights working."

Chet thought as he listened. "I think he would probably do something a lot more personal than some random buildings."

26

PAINT AND DECEPTION

The whole interior of the bay hung in diffused plastic. There was clearer plastic sheeting, but Felix wanted the obscuring quality as well. By wetting the windows, he had also lined the glass with the same plastic. From the outside, it increased the dirty windows to add to the lack of being able to see in. The side effect was the light inside the old gas station evened into a soft illumination without shadows.

He had attached a makeshift sound absorber to the random orbital sander. He wasn't sure how much the sound would be dampened, but anything would help. The result was enough for him to hear the sandpaper grit grind against the paint. The full-face rebreathe mask also had its own sound of the air pressurizing the mask to his face after filtering out the dust, and eventually, the paint particles.

This was not the first vehicle he had painted. Shortly after the wedding, Thelma had gotten a job as a secretary over in the next town. Because of Felix and his dad's work, the panel truck was sometimes needed to drive long distances for work. They needed a second car. The state highway troopers were having an auction of their old fleet of cars. Felix had secured the winning bid on a 1946 Studebaker sedan.

The car spun out and rolled down a small grassy hill in a high-speed chase reaching speeds of over eighty miles per hour. The smaller deuce coupe had made the curve. The driver had gotten away to run moonshine another day. The patrol car had its police lights removed and put up for auction with one cracked window. Felix and his dad sanded the entire black and white car by hand. They filled all the bolt holes and then painted the body with some barn-red paint they had found. Thelma had called it her Cherry. The Cherry had lasted her for almost six years. Each year, Felix carefully brushed out another coat of red paint. The fact that the car was painted with barn paint—applied with a four-inch brush never bothered Thelma. It was her first car, and Felix not only bought it but also painted it for her in her favorite color. To her, the color and Felix painting were the only points of importance.

Now, as he sanded with a much faster sander, Felix still thought about all the fun the two shared on the roads and highways of Colorado and New Mexico. Sometimes, they would just drive until they were tired and then climb into the large backseat to sleep. The next day, they would look on the map and find a different way home. By the time they sold the car, Felix had replaced the tires three times.

He turned the sander over as he released the switch. The sandpaper was loaded with the old paint. There was no running water in the gas station, so he had to do the sanding dry. Dry meant he would go through many 120-grit paper disks. Felix stared out the window at the light fog as his fingernail found the edge of the paper and peeled it off the sander. His mind was only a few dozen miles away. He was starting to plan. This time, he did not have directions. This time, he did not have schematics. This time, like in the mines, it was all his own show—and he knew what he wanted to do. It was just a matter of figuring out how to do it.

The last disk started to load with paint. Felix stopped and walked around the entire van. It was good enough for what he had planned.

Winding up the air hose, he detached the sander and put it back in the small box. It would not get used again. He placed the box in the backseat of the Volkswagen van. The new license plates on the small car had come off a Datsun pickup lying at the bottom of a small wash. The shape of the engine dented the hood from the underside. The large boulder the truck came to rest on might have had something to do with it. The registration stickers had been courtesy of a Ford parked at a supermarket about eleven the night before.

Felix turned to the large can of acetone. Splashing some out in a can, he began to wash down the entire van—inside and out. From now on, he would be wearing latex gloves or leather gloves any time he touched the van. Fires have a cleansing effect—but explosives leave much, which he did not want to leave.

As he washed, he remembered the trial. He had thought it was a legal job. The man had filled out all the paperwork and even had what Felix thought was the legal permit to blast the mine. As it turned out—the mine did not belong to the man. As best as Felix could find out later, the mine belonged to an ex-partner who had run off with the man's wife.

Because some of the timberings in the mine were steel, and the man had said he wanted all the shafts, drifts, and winzes dropped at the same time, Felix had overcharged the explosive load. The result was the entire mine had all but disappeared inside the mine, but places Felix had touched were still found.

The police pulled fingerprints and matched them to Felix's explosives credentials. They had prints for seven of his fingers.

If Felix had been a party to the criminal side of the job, he would still be in Colorado State Penitentiary, but when they started looking for him, he was easy to find. Everyone in the mining community knew he was at the hospital, sitting, waiting for his Thelma to wake up. The Grand Jury held a meeting and found he had no knowledge of the duplicitous nature of the crime. He was an innocent dupe.

The now not-so-innocent man took the small can of acetone-drenched rags covered with paint dust out the back door and into the small forest. In the clearing, he laid them out on the patch of ground he had cleared the day before. There was three feet of raw earth cleared around all the rags laid out flat. Felix lightly dusted dirt over the rags—just enough to cover them. From experience, he knew the acetone would wick up through the thin blanket of earth and evaporate by the next morning. The last thing Felix wanted was a small forest fire, a bunch of fire trucks, and people crawling all over the area.

Felix went back into the station and began cleaning up everything. The few noisy pieces of equipment he could not afford to ignore were the exhaust fans he had mounted in the ceiling with ducting out through areas disguised in the eaves. He had not planned on painting anything, but when he mixed up his C-4, he had to vent the fumes with an explosion-proof fan.

The fan had been running all during the washing stage. With his walk out to the clearing, he had cleared the smell from his nostrils and could now smell if there were any residual fumes. There didn't seem to be, so he shut down the fans.

Felix checked the supplies for the paint one more time. He didn't want to have to go get more supplies in the middle of the day.

With everything in place, he sat down in what had been the office at one time and waited for the night to become dark. Only then, would he open the back door and push the Volkswagen out and leave. He knew the police would be watching his home by now, but they would never think about him camping out.

Two long days of driving had seen Felix through stashing money and reserves in preparation for his final departure. He had come to feel fondly toward the bay and the scenery. However, for Felix, people come and go. Now with them stealing Thelma from him, he was willing to go. But, first, there was his complaint he needed to file. It would have his signature on it.

In three days, he would start bringing the fertilizer to the gas station.

WHERE DID HE GO?

The roll-over had only started the mess on the 101. The early morning commute got out of hand as people got great jobs in what some people were calling the Silicon Valley. With the larger income, those people wanted larger houses than their neighbors had or at least larger than the house they grew up in. With most of the land already developed decades before, the orchards and farmlands to the south never stood a chance. The 'Hill of Stupid' Hooker drove up to get to Manny and Stella's was a great example—but it was only the start.

The farther south, the cheaper the land, and the more house you could buy. Who cared if the only difference between your pink house and their tan house was your garage was on the left, and theirs was on the right: next two houses—the same. Next two, same again, and so it went until you found yourself two hundred homes later, back on the same street at the beginning home.

The news of some poor, working stiff at the end of a lot of days of overtime would come home and get shot coming through what he thought was his front door—but was actually three blocks over and two streets south—was only a matter of time. When it did happen, everyone would just nod and say, *yup…it was bound to happen.*

The hard pounding rain never made it easier. When the computer worker usually left their house at five in the morning, they would leave at four-thirty and drive aggressively as they prayed they would make it to work before their boss. Hooker was always amazed he never found steering wheels twisted out of shape from people grabbing them in a death grip.

Through the rain, he watched another slow line of cars crawling by the wreck, single-file, in the breakdown lane. The faces were lost in the pre-five o'clock in the morning dark, but the white knuckles always stood out at the top of the steering wheels. Their color drained and now replaced by the jaundiced yellow of his flashers and the white of his work lights. The color flowed yellow, white, yellow, white… their wipers keeping a backbeat while their blood pressure and heart took the beating.

Hooker looked down the long jumble of the wreck. It looked like a yard sale gone horribly wrong. He counted five auto club trucks and three commercial. Without asking Dolly, he already knew they had drained the entire towing fleet of the South Bay.

The evidence would eventually be stacked in a long line of cars parked parallel with large yellow oil cake markings as to which car belonged to which towing company. One of the trucks was marked for Tri-County, who was rushing to get back from a haul out to Lodi. Hooker smirked and hummed the tune, *Stuck in Lodi Again.* If the driver didn't get back when CHP cleared the scene, they would throw it to Hooker.

It was going to be a great day for Hooker. He had already stashed two small bobtail trucks, and this tracker guaranteed the trailers were his as well. He would come back for the rolled over bobtail with its nose still slammed into the back of the Pacer, which died suddenly from driving through a large lake of a puddle. He could see Don dragging the other two box vans into the center, which would keep the scene working while Hooker grabbed what he could.

Hooker pulled the levers, and the rear end of the smaller truck rose until there were about six inches of clearance. Rushing back around the nose, he checked the steering rope secured in the driver's door. The rope, looped in and around the steering wheel, would hold the front wheels running semi-straight. A slight cock on a car of a box van was no more than a foot or so running out of the straight, but okay. On a larger truck, Hooker had a special rig that could freeze the steering in perfect alignment. On a thirty-six-foot-long truck, the slight cock could put the frontend running in half of the next lane.

Hooker had only seen it happen once. He had vowed in his second month of towing it would never happen with any of his tows. Eleven years in, concerted watching every detail and no jokes about towing wrong had ever been made at Hooker's expense.

On the other hand, other disgruntled tow drivers who lost tows to the quicker kid started calling him a whore by the moniker of mockery—Southside Hooker. Hooker took to the name and painted it on his rig's tow cranes. The subtext told it all. *When you need a quickie.* The following year at the Tow Truck Rodeo, he proved five times over, he was the fastest, and he had the fastest truck.

As Hooker scrambled into the cab of Mae West, he whistled between his teeth. The CHP wound his finger over his head and stopped the traffic.

Mae nosed out into the lanes and shot down the one mile to the next off-ramp. Hooker watched the bobtail as it tracked behind. There was going to be no problem parking it in the Safeway parking lot overlooking the freeway.

As he pulled into the large lot, Hooker could see his other three trucks lined up as if they had been parked there overnight. He drew in and unhooked number four and headed back for number five of seven or eight—if he could beat Tri-County's driver to the last bone.

Much later in the day, Hooker was unhooking the last of the eight vehicles lined up in the Fly's back lot. He would get all the tows, Fly would get any storage, and if she converted any or all into bodywork, Hooker would get a thin slice of the residuals. Very likely, this long day would make his month—if nothing bad happened.

Hooker didn't have to look to know the footstep he was hearing. The walk of only one leg and a mass of aluminum and titanium on the other side was distinct. "Who let the dog out in the yard on a beautiful day like today?"

"Well, at least the rain has lightened…"

Hooker dragged the chains out from under the box van and poured them into the back of the working bed of Mae. "It was pig ugly this morning on the wreck. Forget cats and dogs—it was Chips and taxicabs." Hooker wiped his hand and stuck out his fist. The man bounced his on top of Hooker's hand. Hooker felt the sluggishness in the man's hit and studied his face. "Gee, sunshine... you look radiantly like shit."

"Jeez, Hooker, I don't know whether to thank you or just take you out and shoot you. That Mai is a shooter. She shoot her eye at you, and you are dead. Dead at the wall, dead in the shower... Do you have any idea how hard it is to take a shower with only one leg as it is? Then the crazy woman gets that look in her eyes and starts talking sexy baby talk... and do you think she would let me lie down or something? Noooo... she wants to do it standing up. And then she hooks one leg straight up and over my shoulder—"

Hooker closed his eyes and held out his two hands with index fingers making the sign of a cross. "Hang on, super stud... you are talking to a man here with virgin ears. Last week, Candy and I moved up to holding hands for more than ten minutes, and then she kissed me on the ear. Dog, I'm telling you—I almost passed out from the excitement."

He opened his eyes. The man had a confused look on his face.

"Dog, what you and Mai do is none—and I do mean none—of my business. You have been around the world a good bunch, but I'm still at home. I am still trying to figure out the simple stuff—do not be telling me the college stuff. I might want to take it home and take it out for a spin—which might just freak Candy and me both out. I don't want to lose her."

The man raised his shoulders and took a deep breath, held it as if he needed to say something, and then let it out slowly. "I'm sorry, dude. I didn't mean to lay that all on you. You're right. It's my stuff..."

"Dog, talk to her. Just talk. Tell her what's going on. I

think she's just so excited to get a guy who doesn't treat her like crap. You're a stand-up guy. You just don't want to. She hasn't been around a gimp and doesn't know your boundaries." Hooker thought about the small wooden stool in his shower. "Maybe what you also need is a small wooden shower stool. Ask her or the Fly—it's a Japanese thing. They might know where to get one, along with a soap bucket and sea sponges and brushes. If Mai likes being in the shower with you, get a bigger shower and put her to good use washing your back."

The man studied Hooker. "You know, for a cocky kid, you make a lot of sense. I'll talk to her tonight—hopefully before she attacks me at the door."

Hooker closed his eyes and hung his head. He wasn't going to win this one. "What did you come out here for, Dog? I know it wasn't to stand in the rain and talk about your sex life."

The man smiled his big toothy smile. "Nah... it was to tell you there is a CHP officer waiting for you in the office." The man turned on the metal leg and wobbled off.

"Thanks, Dog." Hooker closed the side door on the toolboxes. Turning, he smiled evilly. "Hey, Dog?"

The man turned around.

"So doing it in the shower is a nice thing?"

The man laughed from the bottom of his last foot. "For me, it's either going to be a heart attack... or just fall and bust my ass. For you... try it. You may just find you like swimming upstream." He waved and continued into the building he ruled.

Hooker climbed into the truck as he thought about the effect of the six large showerheads pumping five hundred gallons a minute, and what it would feel like at the right moment. He ground his head around and felt the stiffness in his neck. It had been a long night.

Hooker slid out the door of Mae and looked at the CHP cruiser. He didn't recognize the tail number painted on the back bumper panel. It wouldn't be either of his friends Micha or the captain, Chet. He leaned forward in the rain and headed for the office.

Stepping into the office, he fanned his rain jacket. He didn't mind the rain, but the nonstop fire hose of the last ten hours was too much. The two large storms the radio had been talking about for days had decided to have a convention in San Jose.

"Hooker." The nasal tone of the Japanese woman was distinctive. By the echo, Hooker could tell she was in her office—a place she avoided more than bill collectors. Hooker swung through the low gate and headed down the short hall.

"Hooker, this is Officer Pool, I'll leave you two. Whatever CHP track Hooker down for, the Fly no want to know." Hooker could hear her giggling as she walked down the hall. He knew her ears would be tuned to the finest of noises coming from this office.

Hooker sat on the corner of the almost unused desk. "What can I do for you, officer?"

The man looked back around to see if it was okay to talk.

Hooker snorted. "She isn't standing anywhere you'll see her. Besides, she had this office bugged—don't you, Spider-Woman?" His voice had never risen.

"You leave me out of your mess, Hooker." The voice had come from the other end of the main office. Hooker just deadpanned the officer as if to say, *see, I told you so.* "So, what are you here for? Are you here to arrest me?"

"No." The man thought a second about how it all looked, clandestine and all. "Oh, heavens no... It's not like that at all." He was flustered and out of his element.

"Okay, I didn't get caught—again. So what do you need? And by the way, I need another couple boxes of thirty-minute flares. The guys last night used every one, and so did I."

"I've got three fresh boxes in the..." The officer realized he had just been roped into giving up flares. Flares were the universal bargaining chip in the world of towing, and the thirty-minute CHP flares were the gold standard. His shoulders slumped. "Sure, I'll get you some flares. The captain should have warned me about you."

"What does Chet want?"

The man fished a piece of paper out of his shirt pocket and handed it to Hooker. "He asked me to track you down on the QT and have you meet him there. He said to go ninety-seven and then silence."

Hooker looked at the address. It looked like a residential area in Milpitas. He looked at the large map the Fly had as a back wall. It covered the area from Fremont down to Gilroy and across to the coast range. He stepped to the list of streets and found the one he was looking for. Cross-referencing it to the vertical and horizontal of the map, he found the small street. It was only four blocks long. From what he could tell, the address would be near the end. From the street number, he figured it looked north to nothing but the San Francisco Bay.

Hooker muttered, "Nice view—but a lousy neighborhood." Turning to the officer, he held up the note. "Thanks, Pool. Now let's go shopping in your trunk." He smiled. The patrol knew most of the drivers were fast to pop flares to keep accidents safe to work in. If it looked like it was going to be a long hard wreck, they would build Vs and Ws out of the flares so the one would light the next as it burned down. CHP offices stocked thousands of boxes of flares, and their trunks held at least one unused box. If a driver asked nicely, the officers would dig out a couple of handfuls. If the driver was known as there to help with the larger accidents… they were usually rewarded with more. Hooker usually found a box or two on the working bed of Mae. However, the morning's wreck had stripped every cruiser and tow truck of flares.

The officer softly groaned as he opened his trunk. Hooker smiled down on the glory of a full back trunk. He patted the young officer on the shoulder. "You just made my day. Are you at the beginning or end of your shift?"

"End. I'm off at one."

"I'll leave you two boxes just in case." He leaned in and embraced four of the unopened boxes and walked off to store them in Mae. Thinking, he turned as he laid the boxes on the bed. "Did you load up before you saw Captain Davis or after?"

"After. He said you would strip anything I had."

Hooker laughed and waved. "Thanks, Pool. I owe you a donut at the Whole Donut." The officer waved and slid into his cruiser.

Hooker stowed the flares and locked the side box. He knew the same positioned box on the other side was still empty, but he had another CHP officer to see.

He pulled out the Thomas book and found the same street. He figured out the route in and put the book on the dashboard. It was rare he had to check for addresses because he had almost been everywhere he towed—to, or from. However, with the twists and turns of a town laid out by drunks and roads made by crazy people, Milpitas would require the map book.

Some of the twists and turns had even Hooker backing up and taking a second run at the turn. The streets were never the problem. It was how people parked or simply left a vehicle. Some were nothing more than a hulk—gutted long ago by some gang and now just a shade stop for cats and dogs roaming freely about the neighborhood.

Finally, he was at a point where he was looking at the bay, which started no more than a hundred yards in front of him. He looked right and saw a lone CHP cruiser sitting in front of a house. Hooker thought about the position, and then jockeyed a three-point turn, which had him backing Mae down the street to the cul-de-sac. He parked ten yards in front of the cruiser.

He knocked on the screen door. "Chet?"

"In the back, Hooker."

Hooker walked through a sterile house. There was only a rocking chair facing a small black and white television on a couple of milk cartons in the front room. The kitchen had a small dining table with only two chairs. None of them matched. He stepped through to a screened porch. He could tell the crime scene boys had been here. The black fingerprint dust was everywhere.

"Luuucy, you forgot to dust..." Hooker looked up at his friend, who was sitting on a bed. "Anything?"

The man shook his head and duck-lipped just short of a raspberry. "Our boy was interesting. From rent receipts, they lived here for about five years. He always paid a month in advance and always cash. The property management company said he was paying two hundred dollars, but I'm guessing he might have paid four hundred so the property owner would never come around.

"Neighbors we interviewed said they rarely saw the guy, but during the day, there was always a yellow VW bug here. They described a woman as about five-two and maybe a hundred pounds. It was hard to know as she was always wearing a down coat—winter and summer. The sketch artist was out, and the three gave close descriptions, so they're canvassing the area. The plate numbers matched a Volkswagen stolen about six years ago. We don't hold out much hope in finding the car or the woman."

"I see there're some prints near the outside door..."

"We're guessing they're not our guy. We think he trained himself to touch only in certain areas. It means less cleaning up after yourself, and you don't have to remember everywhere you might have touched. We figured this is where he slept and worked. The entire table and the walls in this area match the area around the keyed doorknob—wiped clean with acetone. Notice the lamps are pull string, not the original chain."

Chet got up and pulled a knife from his pocket. He opened it and leaned toward the wall. "This is an extremely interesting wall."

Hooker glanced around the room. "Looks like it was built maybe as an addition to the screened in the porch."

"Hmm, we'll get to the screen in a moment." He started

prying the boards off and revealing the cavities behind. When he was finished, half the wallboards were stacked on the table. Hooker studied the series of shelves.

"What the heck? Why is there a stud missing there by the table, but—" He stopped as he was about to touch the four strange shelves. Chet nodded that it was okay.

"They're all dished. What would you put on a dished shelf?"

Chet reached over onto the bed. His hand returned holding a wire. Hooker looked at the spliced wire. Each piece of copper was only about two inches long—soldered to the next and the next until it made a wire about twenty inches long.

Chet raised his one eyebrow. "Remember at Frontier Village, the inspector had asked if they had some electrical work done recently? It was because he kept finding tiny pieces of wire with solder on the end." Chet pointed at the pieced wire in his hand. "He must have made hundreds of them and stacked them in there. The bomb guys were impressed. They said if he had gone with long conventional runs of wire, they would have spotted it and figured out things from there. There's a coding labeled on the wire every so often they can trace where it came from and finally figure out where it was sold and maybe who to. But with this guy, he used stripped wire, and took the time to splice together something the bomb would blow apart and become just background debris lost in the rubble."

"All of this for what?"

Chet held up his right index finger. "Ah, and that is the sixty thousand dollar question. Or maybe should I say the eighty-five thousand..." He sat back down on the bed. "As I waited here over the last hour, I got to thinking about him living out here, and his wife, an invalid, in the bedroom. The man was making a living wage at De Salvo driving a local delivery truck—"

"Pick up or dropping?"

Chet frowned. "Why?"

"It makes a huge difference. Delivery trucks work a certain area—say the southwest quarter of downtown. However, the trucks doing pickups would cover all of downtown. It's a much larger area, but you still get to know everything about the area."

"I'll check." He laid back and stuck the knife in the wall between two boards. "I figured if he had rigged all of those boards with magnets, why would he stop there?" The lower board popped off the wall as Chet moved to the next one down. "I figure this is the original stash hole, but he stopped going to it and maybe in his hurry forgot about it."

Hooker stared at the stacks of money still in the bank wrappers. "How much did you..."

"Eighty-five grand—all in fifties and twenties and not in sequential numbers—they were rewrapped by a bank. Rewrapped by hand... by a bank in Texas." He sat back up. "I'll bet we find some interesting explosions in Texas too."

Hooker sat on the desk table. His eyes were dancing all around the room, looking for answers. Chet had seen this with Hooker before.

"So the bills are not fresh, crisp, and clean."

"No. They're old and used."

"It's his running money." Hooker focused and looked at Chet. "He still might have to come back for it. He hasn't flown the coup."

Chet pointed to the three-feet-tall wall, running nearly fifteen feet. "That's a lot of room for money."

Hooker frowned—his mouth drew to one side. Waving Chet out of the way, Hooker laid face down across the bed.

"Just don't touch..." Chet regretted saying it as he did.

Hooker shot him a disgusted look. Both knew he had been around enough crime scenes to know what to do.

Hooker reached in his pants pocket and slid out his new commando knife. He held the safety and slid the button. The blade slicked out the end—six inches of thin double-edged death. Hooker carefully slid the blade between the top two stacks and the third. Lifting the money, he slid it out and carefully set it on the bed as if it were a bomb. He looked in the cavity. "Do you have the little pocket flashlight you carry in your jacket?"

The officer handed him the light. Hooker turned it on and illuminated the back wall of the cavity. He studied the smoothness and thought about it. Getting up, he went over and examined the other cavities in the long wall. He looked at the exposed money and then about half of the cavities on the long wall.

He stood. "I was wrong. He won't need to come back. In fact, I think he may have just forgotten about this wall stash."

Chet sat back and smiled. He loved watching Hooker and the Squirt figure problems out. The Squirt had the freaky memory, but Hooker had an uncanny way of seeing details most people don't. "So what makes you think he's going to walk away from eighty-five thousand dollars?"

"He doesn't need it."

"Who doesn't need eighty-five grand when they're on the run?"

"Someone who needs to run light." Hooker pointed at the money. "Look at it. There's at least a briefcase worth of money there. Maybe even a small suitcase... like an overnight bag."

"Okay, so why is it a problem?"

"It's not. It's the other eight hundred grand he has with him now. It's a lot to carry."

Chet started to say something smart, but then stopped and tried to figure out what Hooker had figured out in minutes—but he had missed. "Okay, you got me. Explain how you figure this."

Hooker smiled. He only wished Manny was here, but he figured word would get back to him and Dolly both.

"We know he's storing his parts for the bombs here." He waved his hands along an area near and over the table. Chet nodded.

"We know what he makes—he plants only C-4, which is like plastic." He waits for the nod. "And the other parts are the wires and some kind of trigger. My guess is the trigger is as susceptible to moisture as the wire." He looked at Chet and waited for the nod.

"So, what does he store in the wall that would be sensitive to the moisture coming off the bay?"

"The money."

"And we know he stored it in the wall for years. Long enough, unless protected, for mold and mildew to set in and destroy his stash." He climbed back over the bed and showed Chet the walls of the cavity.

"What is the coating?"

"My guess is sandwich bags."

"It's what?" The man's face folded up in a scowl.

"Plastic sandwich bags..." Hooker sat up, went over to the other wall, and directed the flashlight along the much larger areas. "See, he sealed these as well. All told, I think the holding capacity here is close enough to ten times the little hole over there. But I also think he has much larger bills. My guess is more than half of what he has is in hundreds. With Benjamins, you can stick twenty grand in your front pocket. So maybe he even has a million to do with what he needs to do."

"Okay, but get back to the sandwich bags..."

"Have you ever left a sandwich in a bag on your dashboard during the summer? It melts the bag, and the bag welds itself to the dashboard."

"Okay, I can see that. But lining the wall...?"

"Easy. I'm assuming he probably knows his way around some kind of torch. After all, we know he can solder." Chet nodded at the wire.

"So you hold a single layer of the bag against the area you want it to bond with and run the torch near it until the bag melts just enough to bond, but not burn up. He probably pushed on it with a block of wood—maybe wrapped with aluminum foil or something so it wouldn't stick to the block he was using as an iron. Because remember, he wants the whole compartment sealed."

Chet stared at the man that he kept mistaking for *the kid*. "What?"

The older man just shook his head and laughed. "Being around you this last year gives me mixed feelings."

Hooker leaned back with dramatic horror on his face. "Is this an Uncle Willie talk?"

The two busted up laughing. "No. Oh, God, no. I've

known about you from almost the day you started pulling wrecks for Don. I just actually met you this last year with the shotgun whacko. I'm not far from retirement age..." He looked down at his hands picking at each other.

Hooker could tell the man was deep in a serious emotional state. He asked softly, "So what's the problem?"

The man lifted his head and looked the other way out the screen toward the bay. "I don't know what I would want most—a do-over of the last ten years to watch you grow into the man you've become or just an extra ten years in this job to see where you go from here."

He turned back, and Hooker could see the wet in his eyes. The man was at peace with finally understanding where he stood in his world... but there was still a haunting.

Hooker almost whispered as he said softly, "It's okay, Chet. Neither one of us is going anywhere. We have as much time as you want. Heck, look at Manny—he never stopped. But I don't think this is all about doing this stuff or about me... I think you're missing Carol." The man nodded and wiped at his eyes. "It's called companionship. It's been almost four years since she passed away. I think even she would tell you it's okay to move on. You aren't a solitary guy. You do better when you have someone to do things with."

Chet looked where the bedroom was in the house. He thought about the man who slept out here with his wife in there. He had her possessively, but if the reports were right, he had lost her years before they moved here. The man had already lived in a prison of his own making for almost a decade... and now, they were working to stick him in a different prison.

He turned back to Hooker. "You really think Carol would approve?"

"I'll let Dolly kick your ass tomorrow over dinner."

"I wasn't invited."

"I'll make room."

Chet studied the young man's eyes and realized just what kind of man he had become. He was a long way from the snot-nosed run-away kid hauling garbage and jumping batteries with a bogus driver's license. He now fully understood where Manny and Willie stood on Hooker.

Hooker surveyed the room and then looked out the screen toward the bay. He thought about the choice to live here. The bay stretched to the hazy, thin line horizon of Marin County. The house and neighborhood were hard-beaten old houses built before the Great War to End All Wars. They were worker housing then, and marginal now. It was a great place to hide, where there were no nosey neighbors—and hell, everyone had something to hide. When people are beaten up by life, they look for other outlets, and not many of those are legal. Hooker guessed it was a little moonshine here, a pot plant or two there, and maybe someone was cooking up drugs. LSD was all but out of favor now. Hooker guessed the neighborhood probably had a meth cook stamping out powder for druggies and little white pills for waitresses working two jobs, truck drivers running double logs, and cops working as much overtime as they could stay awake for. Hooker knew cops were no angels. They were just working stiffs with a badge and gun who were willing to run toward trouble instead of away.

He frowned and realized what he had just watched. A

small bug landed on the screen and vaporized with a sizzling snap. He turned with wide eyes.

Chet smiled and wiggled his eyebrows. "Impressive, isn't it? But don't touch it. He wired it to the 220 instead of the 110." He pointed out to the small dock with a tiny rowboat tied to it. "I don't know if he had to or not, but he had a ready-made body dump out in the marsh. If anyone lays their whole hand on the copper screening, they either get thrown a few long yards on their ass, or it will just stop their heart where they stand. Lucky for the investigators, the first one had barely set foot in here when a fly landed on the screen. Word got passed quickly to watch for any booby-traps. There weren't any others, so I figured this was his form of security. Although, looking in here, there's nothing but the bed, desk, chair, and the two lamps. He hired some woman to watch his wife while he was at work, so someone was here most of the time. I don't know why he went to the trouble and expense to screen the porch in copper and then paint it to look like regular screening. We haven't found the switch to turn it off yet."

Hooker thought. "Hmm, did you check the front door to see if it's also wired?"

"Damn." The man got up and went to the front door.

Hooker pointed at the striker plate after a few minutes. "Right there. It only works when the door is closed. I'll bet we'll find a hidden switch outside. It'll be where he normally walks when he comes home." They went outside, and Hooker went through the movements a few times, reen-acting coming home and parking, and then walking to the front door. Finally, he thought about the panel truck.

He shifted his thinking and started from the far side of

the driveway. He walked around the imaginary truck backed into the drive, right up to the house. The ruts in the gravel were deepest and were formed by habit. The gravel leading to the beaten-down garage was smooth but disturbed as if a light car had parked there, albeit randomly.

The house had the cheapest form of siding—batten over a wide board. There was a batten every foot with a count of twenty. The switch was just above Hooker's hanging hand. The man was taller than he was. It was a simple rocker switch buried into the batten. Hooker followed the batten up with his eye and along the header board. The painted over wires peeked out here and there, but not so it would draw any attention. He showed the setup to Chet.

"Think there is a switch to find in the screened porch?"

"I doubt it. I think he wired it straight into the fuse... so it was always on."

They both turned as a loud motorcycle roared down the street. Slowing at the end of the cul-de-sac, it turned. The rider sat on the chopper studying the CHP car and the large tow truck. The rhythmic thumping of the large engine pulsed in the neighborhood.

Chet looked at Hooker. "I think my presence is making the natives restless."

Hooker was studying the way the rider held their arms. One draped—at rest while the other was cocked out stiff. Hooker knew the set of arms. He turned slightly and quietly nodded, "Give me a minute."

Hooker walked to the street and stood at the back end of Mae. He leaned against the corner of the working deck and crossed his legs, relaxed and watchful.

Carefully, the biker drew in the clutch and heel-kicked

into first gear. Easing down the street, the biker tossed their head, and a large thick braid pulled up out of the front to fly around to the back. Hooker smiled. Not *his* head...*her* head. His memory hadn't failed him.

The bike chuffed to a coasting stop in front of Hooker.

"Afternoon, Max... It is Max, isn't it?"

The woman smiled, "Only if you're the towing whore who works the south side of San Joe." She pulled her glove off the right hand. Hooker knew she wouldn't take the glove off the injured left. He had seen what had become of it when he pulled it from the wreck a few years before.

They shook. "You're a long way from your territory, Hooker." She reached over and turned off the bike. It chuffed in protest and settled into silence.

"I'm a whore, Max. I go where the money is."

She turned and looked at the cruiser and officer. "The house was crawling with cops yesterday, and I thought they'd left this morning."

Hooker could sense the unease. He didn't know what she was into, but it probably wasn't printing names on pencils to sell on the corner downtown. "You can relax, Max. This investigation only has to do with this house and the person who lived here."

"The guy was pretty much a ghost. Stuck to his own business."

Hooker looked around. "Seems like that pretty much sums up the entire neighborhood." He looked back at the large woman as she pulled the braid that looked more like a lethal weapon than hair back around to hang down her front. "Is this where you call home, Max?"

The woman weighed the man she hardly knew.

"Jeez, Max, you can trust me. You trusted me to save your clutch hand from the wreck..."

She seemed to settle. "Yeah, you're right." She looked around. "It ain't pretty... but it's home."

"See... that wasn't so hard. We're not here sniffing around the neighborhood. Chet couldn't care less what you're doing in the privacy of your own home. His only concern would be if you were pushing this hog down his highway at twenty over."

"Why would I be going so slow? The engine would over-heat." She smiled.

Hooker laughed. "Now there's the Max, who gave the nurses conniption fits and liked the moonshine I snuck into the hospital." He gently reminded her she might owe him some grace.

She smiled at the memories. "There was one little redhead. She had the nicest little..." She looked back at Chet and then up at Hooker. She moved the wrap-around dark glasses up onto the top of her head. "I don't know much about the guy. Like I said, Dan kept to himself."

"What do you know?"

She rubbed her lower lip and jaw. "He drove an old panel truck. The plates were from Colorado. The paint wasn't car paint. It looked like he just used what he had to paint over some old signage. It was something about mines or mining. His wife must have worked nights or something. Her yellow Volkswagen was always here during the day. It was the screwiest thing. His panel had Colorado plates, and the tabs were up-to-date, but the VW, those plates were years out-of-date. She was a squirrel. I saw her a few times.

Same as Dan—kept to herself. Kind of hunched over, and she looked like she could have been his mother."

Hooker thought about the power of sharing information. "Thanks, Max. It doesn't add really to what we know, but it does confirm a few things. First off, the guy's name was Felix—Dan was the name he'd taken. They were hiding out in plain sight. The woman you saw was looking after Felix's wife, who was invalid while he was at work. The rest we'd pieced together." Hooker stuck his hand out. "It was good seeing you again." He nodded at the left hand that never left the handlebar. "How's the hand and arm?"

She screwed her face into a shrug. "Eh, it's stiff like the doctors said it would be, but I can still pull the clutch... so I get by."

"I wasn't sure who you were until you whipped the big-ass braid around." He smiled.

She lowered her glasses and smiled with a nod at the truck. "Some big-assed things are sometimes our signature trademark. I see you around now and then. You don't see me, though, because I'm most times in my car."

"What do you drive?"

"A '70 Roadrunner—black primer, shaker hood with a six-pack."

Hooker snorted. "Got a skull and crossbones on the back right bumper?"

She raised her glasses and looked at him.

"Oh, beans and wieners, Max...It is Mopar, after all. Of course, I'm going to notice. It sits down at a bar just off Willow Glen most nights."

"Stop in some night. I'll buy you coffee. Just ignore the

girls. The Balls & Sticks is only about the pool tables. The others aren't allowed. You, I'll make an exception for."

"What about my partner?"

"You don't have a partner."

Hooker smiled and walked to the door. He opened it as he watched Max. "Box. Grass."

The orange streak was on the street and only paused for a second to look at the motorcycle. As he stood stiff-legged on the grass, he watched the woman laughing.

"Now I don't know why, but it is the perfect partner for you. It looks like he's good in a scrap too."

"More than just good. I watched him drop a full-grown man in under three seconds last year. Just the other day, he took on a hundred-pound Kai-dog."

"How did he do?"

"Didn't even breathe hard... it was all over in about five or six seconds."

"Hurt the dog?"

"Nope... killed the dog. Tore up its back before ripping out its throat."

Max whipped her braid around through the air as she looked back at Box. "You're shittin' me."

Hooker just stared and then, with a deadpan look, slowly ground his head back and forth.

"Why would he take on, much less kill a dog the size of a man?"

"The dog was wild and was attacking our neighbor's young yellow Lab. I think Box is sweet on the kid."

The woman pursed her lips and nodded. She watched the large cat walk back over and sit down next to Hooker's leg. "I think I can understand that."

28

RIGGING

Felix fingered the switch. The light turned on.

The step-van was all painted and just needed a day before putting on the decals. The brown was not a color most people would paint a house, and Felix had to get it custom mixed. The man had been a little nosey for Felix's taste, but then he was in the tiny town of Sebastopol, and the man did not know him. Felix pled being new to the area.

The paint shot on better than he thought it would. Having a matching primer had certainly helped. He only half chuckled about how much easier it was to spray on paint than painting a car with a four-inch house painting brush, but times were always tough, and you did with what you had. His chest ached about his Thelma having never seen the good days.

His hand felt along the bottom of the rail for the roll-down door. He felt the roller button depress—a small green light lit. He moved his finger back up, as the door would do if opening—the green light winked out, and the small red light went on.

Eventually, when everything was ready, there would be a series of nine green lights set in a box pattern glowing like a monochromatic tic-tac-toe board. The board was set high on the back of the one side. This time, Felix didn't worry about leaving only tiny debris to be scattered among the rubble. This time, he was leaving a statement. Everything would be straight out of the box perfect.

When all nine of the green lights in the box were on, he started preparing the rest of the van. The whole job would take two days, even though it was just about placing all the parts. The construction adhesive was the hard part.

He picked up the yardstick and started laying out the six-inch grid on one wall. In the sequence, the explosives forming the grid on this side would be the second thing to happen. The first trigger would ignite four runs of the fast detonation cord. These four lines ran in layers of the sodium nitrite fertilizer. The fertilizer burned slower or exploded and expanded slower than the detonation cord. As the one-ton of mass slowly reached its critical mass, the cord burned ahead at the speed of sound. The four lines crossed each other on the way to their final destination. This was a fail-safe in case one of the lines had not burned its way to the crossover.

Once the burn was past the crossover, it split into forty lines racing up the center of the wall and then flashing out across the grid. Meanwhile, another four lines ran under all the fertilizer to ignite a series of other detonation lines. These triggered the shaped forms of C-4 to push the entire mass out of the now-opened wall of the van. The result was in the form of two hundred tiny bombs of C-4 connected directly to their own miniature compression triggers. These tiny bombs would speed up the mass of the now flying fertilizer and cause a double-tone concussion within the one explosion.

The high brisance of the C-4 would crack concrete and shatter windows, and the slower bass explosion of the fertilizer would deliver the mass concussion driving the shattered face of the building into and through the rest of the building, in effect—destroying the building. It would just have to wait for the demolition crews to finish the job.

Felix ran a bead of the construction adhesive down the pencil line. Putting down the tube gun, he picked up the end of the detonation cord and pushed it into the adhesive. It stuck perfectly. Only detonation would knock it loose. He repeated the process with the rest of the lines and then did the horizontal lines. The tails of the horizontal draped over the hook he had suspended until the adhesive dried. The tails of the odd lines hung on the left and the evens on the right.

Every other one of the tails on each side gathered to its own detonation point. In theory, the four sets of runs would start burning within a hundredth of a second of the others, cutting an identical pattern of metal squares.

Felix thought back to his childhood. His father had sat him on his knee and showed him a hand grenade. His father had slowly taken it apart and showed the young Felix how it all worked. He had explained how the cuts in the shell were the weak parts, and therefore, the grenade would turn into little square pieces of metal shrapnel when it exploded. Later Felix understood the true power and theory—only close concussion resulted in death by a grenade—it was the shrapnel doing all the widespread destruction.

In the mines, there were many pieces of machinery they used, much like a grenade to wreak havoc on the mine walls. Much as the bomb in the van would do, the shrapnel and high-energy explosives did the setup, and the mass explosives did the deep trauma, which would bring the mine walls down—closing the cavern or shaft.

A geologist had once explained to Felix what he was replicating in the mine was the same devastation happening with an earthquake. The first shockwave to hit is the high-frequency wave, which races to the surface and then radiates out from the surface epicenter. Because it's high frequency, it's much faster. It's called the 'S' wave for sound or snap. It is the first to hit a building, and it jars the foundation away from the center, causing micro cracking in foundations and stiff walls.

The second wave travels through the rock strata and is called the 'P' wave for pulse or power. It is coming directly from the fault slip and has all the mass of the earthquake behind it. It is what pushes back and forth, and up and down as wave after wave hits. This is what causes the weakened building to fall.

Felix looked at the wall and ran his eyes over every inch of every run of the detonation cord. He reached over and started separating the tails out to the end of where they would start. There would be four start points for the wall. From those points, all the remaining action would flow.

He braided the many cords together into one. He remembered how she had taught him how to braid her thick, long hair with the multiple strands instead of the usual three.

The result was a braid hanging flatter down the back of her head. His hands hung helplessly in the air. So much was no longer his.

Sluggishly, he started moving again and bound each of the braided ends to a low exploding blasting cap with electrical tape. He then slid a thick piece of pipe over each of the caps and braids and taped them in place. This would restrict the small explosion inside the pipe and ignite only the braid.

Backing out of the van, he visualized the next step. He had done the process thousands of times. You take the explosion you want, walk it backward into the components you need, and how and where they need to be laid out.

He walked around the van to a small roll-around table. He picked up the mug and drank some of the tepid coffee. He thought about using the torch to warm it up, but he now had the bags of fertilizer in the building. What he did, what he used, and what he created were now restricted. No sparks, no flames... nothing that could ignite the explosive nature of the fertilizer. The fumes hung threatening in the air.

His left hand felt in the paper wrapping and found the second half of the sub sandwich he had bought this morning. He bit off a small bite and chewed mindlessly. His eyes were wandering awash across the many components left to place, but his mind was in a meadow of small mountain flowers. All the smells of the explosives drove his memories of those flowers, the girl, the day, and all the days after. All the years that had followed. All of his life—now gone.

He laid the last part of the sandwich down in the paper. He glanced in the mug—one last swallow of the now cold coffee. He swallowed and turned back toward the one wall.

He picked up the rough leather work gloves. Pulling them on, he looked at two piles of steel plates. The quarter-inch mild steel would lie across the floor of the van. The three-eighths armor plate would stand up the wall. The flooring was in one-foot squares. There was also a series of plate-only six-inch wide and twenty inches long—those would start the second layer.

Carrying the squares two at a time, Felix layered the floor of the van. The next layer he glued with dots of the construction adhesive. This made a half-inch thick, dull cushion for the explosive. It would uniformly push down, resulting in the axles and wheels collapsing as they all worked together in directing the force. The van would be one giant shape charge like a stand-up claymore mine. The force of the explosion is directed toward the enemy—the ones who took the only person who made his life worth living.

With the floor in place, he started with the long narrow strips. The strips were only four inches wide but stood almost the entire height of the inside of the van. He glued each of the plates to the wall of the van. A few dots of glue between each plate held them as a single unit. Running over the wheel well, he had ordered the plates cut first at an angle, and then just eleven inches short.

The second and third layers would overlap the seams of the previous by one and a half inches to build as close to a solid hard wall as possible without welding. The layered wall would also defuse any backfire explosion so as not to injure innocent people or structures. Felix's target was not random, and therefore, his weapon was just as targeted.

Once the wall was up and all glued in place, he layered

the eight blankets he had made from lead cold shot for reloading shotgun shells. The birdshot made a compact heavy blanket and would do more absorbing of the backblast than directing the forward destruction. They formed easily over the wheel well of thin metal.

The standing seams of the wall reminded him of the first house Thelma, and he had moved into when they got married. The wind of the Colorado plains came like a flood out of the plains of Canada and straight through the pasteboard walls of the shack. Felix had bought a roll of tarpaper and glued it to the outside wall. It helped, but it wasn't enough. There were some old boards used for cribbing the walls of mines. They were thicker than regular boards, but they were free. The two had spent a long weekend between nailing up two layers of boards and snuggling under the pile of quilts to get warm. Being naked under the covers helped, but trying to nail up boards naked didn't. Thelma had made him put his pants on when he got a splinter in his privates. He caught himself smiling at the memory and came back to where he was. The smile bled into the cold and mixed with the coming night.

As Felix took off his gloves, he looked at the gathering gloom through the windows. He brought nine of the bags of fertilizer over arranging their contents and decided because he was having trouble seeing in the dark; it would be dark enough to leave. The small Volkswagen was now parked a mile away in a clearing popular as a parking spot for day hikers. He would be the last to get back from his hike. He shouldered an old daypack as he closed and locked the door.

He looked about and then hiked in long loping strides out through the trees to the small meadow behind. His route would take him around and back to one of the longer trails people used for hiking.

He thought about the arrangement of the small tiny bombs. He would have to drive to San Jose and look at exactly where he would be parking and the building. The placement of the bombs in the six feet of fertilizer was as critical as conducting a symphony—a little too much brass could drown out the clarinets. Too many violins and cello would make the tympani drums sound wrong. Everything must be played just right to make the music sound the way it should, and everything must explode at the right time—and way—to direct the destruction of the place and people who had taken his Thelma.

Monday would be a day to remember.

29

WHAT TO DO WITH A 3-DAY WEEKEND

Saturday nights were usually hit-and-miss with a touch of weird mixed in. Throw in a three-day weekend with a constant drizzle, and you can count on it being a definite hit and no miss. It was just a matter of waiting for the alcohol to set in.

Unlike the Fourth of July, and its heat to drive the start-drinking time to somewhere before lunch, the winter has its own schedule. Usually, the colder the wind, the sooner the drunks hit the bars. A nice day and the bars load up later. This drizzle was not the cold out of the Alaskan Gulf or a sub-Artic creeper mixed with something up out of Mexico— this drizzle was all San Francisco Bay born and bled.

The onshore breezes push against the downhill fall of the air off the Sierra Nevada Mountains. The blend could go two ways. The famous February 'summer' with every sail-boat out on the water, or the cold convinces the moisture-rich sea air to drop its load. Unfortunately, for the holiday, the load had lasted for five days and was looking the same for the next five days.

Hooker did not care either way. With holidays and alcohol—he got tows and made money. The money was great and paid the bills, but sometimes, it was about keeping busy too. The Squirt was on a break with the academy, and for once, had no studying, so the two men were hanging out in the dark confines of dispatch.

The two had stopped in, and Dolly had strong-armed them to stay for dinner. With still no calls, the two settled into the office. They processed paperwork, which had gotten away from Hooker the previous month. Dolly was also shuffling through her never-ending river of paperwork. Almost every company or department using a radio in the South Bay —flowed through dispatch. This created a mountain of billing. Even some of the law enforcement communication went through her switchboard and radios—creating a small molehill.

Dina had brought the new baby to work, and with the calm of the radios and phone calls, she had the little one in her lap for a feeding. Karen was cooing and making the noises most aunts without children made. They were random baby talk words but were also the same silly talking she made when she got home and snuggled with the husky.

"Hooker?"

"Yeah?"

"How much is it to haul a... just a minute." She ducked back down to the board and wrote what the guy said.

"How much to tow a four-ton trailer up to eighty miles northwest of Portland...? He says it's a cogeneration plant—if it makes a difference."

"Does it have wheels and registered to be on the highways?"

"He says it does and has its co-rate registration and plates."

Hooker looked at the numbers guy. "How far to Portland?"

"Roughly nine-hundred-forty miles—depending on how you go. With the extra eighty, you're right at one-thousand-fifty. You'll have Interstate carriage fees at the border. Last I saw, they would run one hundred-eighty."

Hooker blinked. He did not want the tow. It was too long. He watched the Squirt while he answered Karen. "If it's under eleven-foot, nine-inches, I'll move it for twenty-eight hundred. The site must be accessible for a flatbed."

They listened to the conversation from their perspective, low mumbling. Hooker could see the Squirt trying to work out how Hooker was going to move it when the height would be taller than regulation for a standard travel-all trailer.

"When can you pick it up?"

Hooker smiled. "Where is it?"

"Gilroy... across from the Shilling plant."

"Get his number, and I'll call him in about thirty minutes. But... probably tonight."

Hooker leaned back with his hands laced behind his head and a wider smile on his face. Quietly, he asked the kid, "Have you figured it out yet?"

"Tri-County has a Land-All, but with those numbers, he wouldn't fit the fifteen-foot of clearance. He'd be dodging all over the place, and the over height is the same as a wide load... they want some heavy fees."

Hooker's trained ears could tell the conversation was over in the other room. "Karen?"

"He said its eleven-foot four-inches."

Hooker kept watching the kid. Watching his face as the gears churned the mountains of information was a truly amazing thing to watch. Finally, he was ready to spill the beans. "Dina?"

"Holding on line three..." Hooker had seen the button light up, but the desk phone was turned where he knew the Squirt could not see it.

Hooker's hand hovered over the phone as he watched the kid. "Five... Four... Three..."

The Squirt's face lit up. "Jose."

Hooker smiled, pushed the button for line three, and pushed the button for the speakerphone. "Hola, jefe. Thanks for holding."

The big man on the other line laughed. "Chew want something, Hooker? I know chew. You no call for maybe at least a month. Now you have you white ass in a penche vey, and you needs the magnifico Garcia to come rescue chew."

"Oh, heck no, Jose... I just wanted to know if my chorizo is ready to pick up. I've run out of good things to feed my cat, and I figured when your skank sister comes up to work First Street—she could drop it off." They both laughed at their standard, 'take no prisoners' approach to humor—even if it was at the expense of the man's sister, who was second in line to be the next District Attorney in Santa Clara County.

"Give it a week more on the sausage, Hooker. I just let the flies in, and they no have finished making the taste perfect yet. So how you been?"

"A little busy but not too much. You...?"

"I no have accidents like you, but we be doing okay."

"So, let me ask you this... how low is the new lowboy of yours?"

"Sixteen inches and bridged for eighty-K."

Hooker rolled his head to face the Squirt. The young man was nodding.

Hooker raised his one finger for the Squirt to wait. His smile turned mischievous and evil. "How lazy is that new partner of yours?"

The man rattled off a line or two of pure Mexican swearing. He and his brother were fifth-generation Mexican-Americans, but their language sounded more like they just swam the Rio Grande last year. Finally, the swearing stopped when the laughing got in the way. Hooker and the Squirt could hear the younger brother protesting in the background. "I try to wake him up at decent time each morning, but you know how lazy he is. He go see a girl in San Martin, and he be weak knees *por tres* days until I force him to eat good meat."

"So, it sounds like maybe a few days away from the Chica would be good for the boy?"

"Whatz chew got?"

"Four-ton trailer going from Gilroy to Portland, Oregon area."

"Dat a beeg area, jefe..."

"About eighty miles northwest up the river is my guess."

"How much chew leave por the starving Mexican?"

"Sixteen plus two hundred to cover the Interstate Carriage fees."

"When?"

"How soon can your bambino have the trailer across from the Shilling plant and be ready to roll out to the new interstate?"

Hooker could hear the conversation between the two

brothers. Hooker knew the money would cover the fuel, rubber, and food and still leave the month's payment on the trailer. It was a good deal to cover the payment in the front of the month.

"Hooker?"

"*Si, jefe.*"

"He says he no go for less than two grand. But for two, he can be there in an hour."

"You have a smart partner, Jose. You take care of him. Is he okay to pull it all tonight?"

"No, no jefe. He already have a four-hour tow on his log, so he make Medford den shut down for a nap. He be on site midnight tomorrow."

"Okay, let me get you the information, and I'll get back to you before he rolls. Does he need travel money?"

"No, he has a new Bank AmeriCard, and we have four fuel cards. But thank chew for the offer."

"I wasn't offering—I was going to tell him where a few liquor stores were to hold up."

They laughed and hung up.

The light on two was lit. Hooker picked up the handheld and took down all the information. The man would meet the driver and give him all the maps he would need, as well as the information to cross the state lines.

As he hung up from relaying the information to the older Garcia, he looked at the now smiling Squirt.

"What?"

The Squirt laughed. "You worked your hind-end off to earn just six hundred. I'm proud of you."

Dolly snorted as she stood in the doorway. She had a small catalog in her hand. "He just spent it too. The new cables for Mae will run you just under eight-hundred—each. But they are a business expense and will go under schedule C on your taxes."

Hooker leaned back with a sigh and looked at the kid. "What the big letters giveth, the fine print taketh away."

Dolly leaned against the doorframe. "Amen."

Karen interjected, "Hooker, roll-over, big rig, set of tandems under the Alters—southbound 101. Micha is on-site, and fire is on the way. Looks like a car hit and torched."

The two men exploded into action. Dolly hugged Box but knew the large cat was itching to be out in the air.

Dolly checked the security monitor viewing the parking lot. She nodded, and the three men in her life strolled out the heavy steel door. Two kissed their fingers and touched the 701 badge as they moved past the door. The door thudded shut, and the silence descended like a blanket.

Dolly sat for a moment and then leaned forward to her paperwork. "And so the weekend begins."

30

DIRT AND BOMBS

Felix was damp but not from the rain. The rain had dried out shortly after he arrived at the old gas station. The rain was still to the south, but the last half-mile of the morning's hike had been under gray clouds but no rain.

The still air had reminded him of the fall days in Colorado when he and Thelma had taken short walks because they never knew when an overcast sky would become rain or snow. Some people said they could smell the rain or snow coming hours in advance, but Felix couldn't smell anything in advance except an explosion in a mine. As the years had gone on, Thelma teased she had to go from rubbing the bottle of perfume on her breasts to spritzing herself down like a Nevada whore at a rodeo. Felix wasn't sure if it was true or not, but he could still remember the way she smelled. She had never changed her brand of perfume.

They were in high school, and the Spring Ball was coming up. Felix and his dad had to go into Bolder to get some spare parts. His mother had decided to tag along and to go shopping at one of the department stores. She had invited Thelma. With a smile, Felix's father had grumbled to Felix out in the garage about the girls being up to something—but it was a man's duty to never ask what. Asking was the road to denial and a spoiled dinner. The easiest and most peaceful way was just to ignore them and wait for the surprise.

The surprise was worth the wait. The dress they bought was as summery as a spring alpine meadow. Thelma simply floated in the soft fabric. The petticoats had rustled like a soft breeze through the Aspen trees on a summer afternoon. As she had walked close, Felix lost a friend and fallen in love. It was the moment he smelled her perfume as she stood on her tiptoes to kiss him lightly on the cheek. It was the first kiss he ever remembered. He knew his mother probably kissed him on the head, but he didn't remember. His mother was caring but was not demonstrative in her affections. Even his father only got a called out cautionary to take care as he left for a mine. Thelma's soft lips hovered at his cheek like a butterfly—and then like a butterfly, they were gone. And so was his heart.

The same month, he had bought a new pair of boots. As he put them on, he told the man he needed them one size larger so he could stuff some paper in the toe and grow into them. He had sworn he would not buy another pair until he married Thelma. It was a promise he kept to himself, even when the cobbler in town told him he couldn't fix them again... that when the soles wore out, they would be finished. Felix was twenty, sixteen days shy of his twenty-first birthday.

A few days later, Thelma met him at a mine he and his father were working on. She brought them lunch—something they hardly ever ate. They sat on a large flat rock outcropping and looked out over the large valley containing Boulder and Denver. The day was light with a breeze, which hinted at a coming fall. Thelma asked him what he wanted for his twenty-first birthday. He thought about it as he chewed the sandwich. Finally, he took a drink of water, and as he put the sandwich back toward his mouth, he said, *'For you to marry me.'*

Thelma stopped taking a bite of her sandwich. She replayed the words in her head. He had not stumbled, mumbled, nor stuttered. She took a bite and slowly chewed. Finally, she took a sip of water. Two can play this game. As she put her sandwich up to her mouth, she answered, *'I guess I need to go to town and buy a dress.'* She then took a bite and quietly chewed.

After a moment, she leaned into his arm. He put his arm around her, and she moved closer. Their love and life were like that—easy and matter of fact. When the justice of the peace started to ask the question, *do you...* they had answered in unison—yes. It was all they needed to say.

When she had gotten the job down in the city, she told Felix she needed a car. She was standing at the sink, washing dishes. He was drying. There was no discussion. It was just a fact. He asked what kind. She had told him red. Red it was —barn red.

Felix wiped at his brow and picked up another bag of fertilizer. He dragged it over to the back of the step-van. It was the last layer of fertilizer. Carefully crawling along the wall with the detonation cord attached, he carried the large scoop of fertilizer. The points at both ends were packed down firmer and formed higher. This built more of the nitrate into the overall shaping of the charge.

Of the five parking places he knew he could park the fake delivery van in, the shape of the charge would be the same. At the two extreme ends, the building would only sustain damage to half of the building, but because of the age of the building, it would probably collapse entirely. The three spaces in the middle would be the most effective and were usually the last to be used on any given workday. The commercial deliveries to the county building came and went all day. Usually, they were little more than couriers making a single drop or pick up from only one office. The turnover was rapid and allowed Felix to wait for a space.

The result of the explosion at the center of the building would be catastrophic and probably drop the face of the structure within seconds. Felix almost wished he could wait around and watch. Every single explosion of his had been contained in a mine or a building. The only explosion he had ever watched in its entirety was the planning that went on in his head. Those were silent, nondestructive, and always moved in reverse—explosion to placement to parts. The only one to happen where he could watch would happen when he was already miles away. The same as when the people in the county building took his love and life away from him—he would again be miles away.

Felix sat in the step-van. Everything was ready for Monday—the next day.

31

———

BOOM

Hooker swung the rope over his head and gently let the loop follow his hand as he threw and let go. The lasso caught the Squirt as he walked by. The two laughed. They had been watching some old western movie the night before, and Hank had shown them how to make a lasso. The rope was wrong, but the idea was fun.

"Are you two cowboys just going to horse around today, or are you up for some pancakes?" Uncle Willie stood in the doorway to the house part of the structure.

"Let me at least hog-tie this steer, or he will eat us out of feed in the barn." Hooker laughed and quickly looped a few turns around the Squirts head and neck, who was doing his best to scurry after Willie.

The door was automatically closing on Willie's voice. "Hank slaved long and hard on this..." The fire door closed as the Squirt reached for the knob.

Shrugging his way out of the loops, he let the rope fall to the ground. The Squirt opened the door and bowed his hips forward as he quickly stepped out of the reach of the boot headed for his butt. The two burst into the kitchen dining room, laughing at the ill-fated kick and the abandoned horseplay.

The Squirt draped his arm over Hank's shoulder as the man served up the homemade pancakes. "You are an evil man, Hank."

"Why? Because I like to feed you kids or because I put chocolate chips in my pancakes?" The man smiled with wild eyes at the young man.

"No. Because you taught Hooker how to use the dumb rope—now he's going to keep playing spaghetti western for weeks." Giggling, he kissed him on the neck. The man froze —then started laughing and shied away.

"I told you... I'm Greek, not Roman. There's a big difference."

The kid held up his two index fingers crudely four inches apart with a questioning look on his face.

"No, that would be Sicilian." The two laughed as the Squirt reached over, grabbed the coffee carafe, and felt it was already full. Hank picked up the large plate of pancakes, and the two turned to the table and the other two. Morning had broken.

Later, as Hooker finished the last pancake, Willie sipped his coffee and then put the mug down. Leaning back, he relaxed. Life had taken its time but had turned out good. "Can you be in the north end today?"

Hooker swallowed and wiped his mouth with the napkin. "Why, do you need some Sicilian sausage from Chiaramontes?" He glared at Hank and the Squirt, who were chuckling about something he was sure he didn't want to know.

Willie glared at his partner out of the side of his eyes. "No, I'm fine in the sausage department." He cleared his throat—which set off the other two again. "Ben has my new cutting torch, and I'd like for you to pick it up, please."

"What's wrong with the old one? I mean, you can only burn up so many dresses..."

"It has a double head." This set off Hank and the Squirt even worse. Willie just folded his arms and glared at the both of them. "Can we have an adult breakfast, please?"

Hank just waved his two hands, got up, and headed for the bedroom. The Squirt figured it was the only safe refuge and headed for his room, also. The other two men just watched them go.

Hooker finally turned around and looked at his uncle. "Really...? Double head...?"

The man was turning red. "Oh, hush, and you owe the swear jar a dollar for even thinking like Hank."

The two stared at each other until the giggles set in. Then Hooker couldn't stand it any longer, "Sicilian sausage?" They both broke into laughter.

Finally, with a sense of decorum returning, Willie explained. "It had two full sets of valves and hoses, so you can have a cutting head on one and brazing on the other, instead of having to swap out everything back and forth."

"Slick. Sure, we can head up there."

An hour later found them at the back of Mae West, stowing the tanks and carrier with the new valves already rigged. The streets were all but empty as offices were closed for the holiday.

Hooker always felt a little creepy when the traffic was down. For years, he thought it was because he knew he wouldn't be getting any tows, but then one late night, he was waiting out a slow night over at Ace's house, and they were watching old movies. Vincent Price's movie *The Last Man on Earth* came on, and Hooker knew why he hated holidays—there was no traffic. He had gotten up and driven over to Dolly's and slept on the couch until he got a flat tire at four in the morning.

As he finished cinching down the ropes on the tanks, he grabbed the lead hammer from out of his permanent hole. He started toward the rear tires to check the air pressure when he noticed the kid just standing and staring down the street. He slowly walked around the working bed of the tow truck.

Hooker looked down the street where the Squirt was looking. "What's up?" he asked quietly.

"What day is this?"

"Monday...?" Hooker frowned as he watched the Squirt scan the empty street.

"What is the day about?"

"It's President's Day... why?" Both were still looking down the street.

"What offices would be open?"

"None..." Hooker's eyes started scanning rapidly. Something was really wrong, and he didn't see it.

"Then who would the UPS truck be delivering to on this block?"

"Maybe he just—"

The Squirt started walking. "It was parked there when we got here. They're on a very tight schedule."

Hooker followed. The truck was definitely wrong... even if UPS delivered on holidays. "What are you thinking?"

The Squirt started walking faster. "Radio for a bomb squad. It's a Ford van—UPS only uses Chevy vans made by Grumman. That is *not* a real UPS truck."

Hooker changed course. Running to the cab, he climbed into Mae and grabbed the microphone from behind his seat.

"Dolly, we're at the old county building just off Guadalupe Parkway. We have a bogus UPS truck, and it may be a bomb. We need to get the area blocked off, and the bomb squad rolled."

"10-4, Hooker. We're on it. You get out of there. I don't want to lose you to something stupid. Let the police do their job."

"One of them is here right now."

"Crap. You tell the kid to stop playing cowboy and get out of there."

Hooker looked in the mirror and could see the kid standing on the front bumper of the truck. He was pumping his fist in the air—it was their private code for *danger and hurry.*

Hooker slammed Mae into reverse and dumped the clutch as he hit the air brake release. Mae spun both sets of rear tires as she slewed backward into the street. Hooker could smell the burned rubber as he closed on the scene in the rearview mirrors. He backed and then slowed as he lined up with the front of the step-van.

As he stopped, he saw the Squirt hit the side box holding the hand tools. Hooker slid out and ran toward the back.

"What...?"

"It's full of fertilizer. One wall is laced with cord to blow. There's a box with nine green lights. I can only imagine the doors are booby-trapped." The kid fell on the ground and rolled under the truck. Hooker could hear him continue. "There's a digital clock on the dashboard with wires running back into the cargo area. It is counting down—there're only twelve minutes left."

Hooker could hear the kid working the ratchet wrench on something. "What are you...?"

"Dropping the driveline..."

Hooker looked down the street the way Mae was pointed. The map scrolled out in his mind. Even though this wasn't his territory, he was nonetheless very familiar with where things were and where they led. He spun around and opened the door to the levers controlling the booms and towing equipment. He lowered the sling in preparation for the tow. The kid was right—they could not leave the van there, and the bomb squad would never make it in time.

Hooker ran to the cab and swung up into his seat. He backed the sling up under the front end gently. He saw the kid roll out.

The Squirt threw the wrench in the toolbox and slammed the door shut with a kick of his boot. He raced back to the sling and Hooker.

"We set the J-hooks like usual but only run the chains under the roller bar. Don't lock them on the tie-off hooks. We cross the chains over the front and set them on the opposing boom cable. When we get up to the run-out area of the airport, we can kick them loose and leave it in the middle of the runway and let it blow."

Hooker looked at him as they started setting the hooks

on the front steering. "How are we going to let them run out? I'm not stopping and then get blown to Texas."

The kid hesitated and returned to setting the chain. "I'm thinking."

They tied off the chain, and Hooker started bringing the front end off the ground. Neither one stopped to think the van or the frontend might be booby-trapped.

The van rose and did not blow.

The Squirt suddenly jumped in the back of the working bed. He scrambled up to where the welding rig sat secured. He looked at the cutting torch and then pawed around in the box. He found another cutting head and screwed it into place. "I need duct tape."

Hooker opened the side box and grabbed a roll. "Here."

The Squirt caught the roll and taped the handles of the cutting torch heads to the uprights guiding the cables coming off the two large spools. The torch tips were now pointed directly at the cables two inches away. "I need some cord—about ten or twelve feet lengths—two of them if you have it."

Hooker reached in another box and drew out lengths of half-inch nylon cord. He did a fast shuffle of his arms and cut the lengths. He now knew what the Squirt was doing.

"Time?"

Hooker ran to the back and jumped up on Mae's bed so he could see the clock. "Five minutes and thirty seconds on my mark... four, three, two, mark." He could hear the Squirt start the torches. The flames sounded angry.

As Hooker jumped down and ran for the cab, he saw the kid pull the two cords and test the loops taped to the handles of the cutting torches. The flames constricted to pencils of blue super-hot flames. They hit the cables direct. He released the cords, and the gentle flames wafted in the morning air. As Hooker clambered in the cab, the Squirt swung around the heat shield of the exhaust stack.

"Damn."

"What?"

"Go! I just burned my hand on the exhaust stack." He never thought about the heat on a half-inch nylon cord.

As they pulled away, the driveline of the step-van came loose and lay were the bomb van had been. The bomb squad was two minutes away.

———

TEN BLOCKS AWAY, Felix was looking down the street and then at his watch. The sign on the post said the bus should have been there seven minutes before. He was worried.

"Holiday," the woman said.

Felix spun. "Did you say something?"

The woman looked up from her knitting. "I said, the bus don't run on that schedule. It's a holiday. The number foteen done come but every hour on holidays. It won't be here none for at least another half hour. We be lucky if it come then." She went back to her knitting and ignored the man who was dancing around the bus-stop sign. She had seen her share of antsy kids, and this one had never grown up.

Felix knew if he started to run, she would remember him. If he stayed, he ran the risk of getting caught when the bomb blew. Then the weight of what the woman had said hit him.

"Which holiday?"

The heavyset dark woman took a couple of more stitches. Then her hands lowered to her lap. "Hmm... I think they call it just President's day now. Used to be Washington and Lincoln's birthdays, but you know them politicians out there in Washington. They just love to have long weekends and vacations. So they done take away the fine men's birthdays and just made them share a single day." She shook her head as her knitting resumed. "Just a terrible shame if you asked me. But do they ask poor Laretta Walters, no sir, they do not. Just a cryin' shame."

Holiday. A Federal Holiday. Offices would be closed. Nobody would be working. It was all a waste. Felix sagged onto the other end of the bench. He had lost.

Laretta Walters looked at the man at the other end of the bench. "You okay, young man? You don't look so good. It's only a bus, for gosh sakes."

Felix slowly looked up at the woman. He blinked and thought about what she had said. Dejected, he rose and wandered off. He had become adrift.

32

END OF THE LINE

Mae West roared down the street, slowly building speed. Hooker was highly aware of the nature of the bomb tied to the end of his truck. He had turned on all the lights, rotators, and flashers. He considered using the siren but was afraid the bomb might be booby-trapped for sirens.

"Mama, the bomb is on the move. I'm hauling it down the Guadalupe to the north end of the airport. Call the airport and tell them a bomb will be going off at the end in less than four minutes. This is not a threat—this is a promise."

"Hooker, damn it all. I told you to wait for the police. They are almost there."

"Dolly, this time, the boom is happening on its clock, not yours."

The Squirt chimed in as he counted. "Two-fourteen."

"The Squirt says about two minutes. Gotta go."

The gate at the end of the runway where the parkway curved did not have a chance. The front bumper the size of a

Volkswagen and backed by eleven tons of angry woman blew the gate nearly forty feet in the air and threw it for at least forty yards. Mae never quivered.

Hooker made a giant slow loop to line up with the runway.

"Starting the burn now." The Squirt pulled on the two cords. In back, the two cutting torch pencils of blue death raced out. The stretched cables turned red and then started to melt.

The nylon cords were pulled tight around the exhaust stacks heat shield. The shield did what it was designed to do. It had absorbed heat and was slowly giving it off into the air —but not before it had started to melt the cord caught under the other one. The lower cord went to the cutting torch on the passenger side. The cord stretched, and the nylon loop loosened. The hard blue flame fluttered with some yellow.

The service road looped around so a large airplane could use it as an emergency taxi, and they occasionally did. Hooker guided Mae around the large loop.

The cutting flames melted through the cables as, strand by strand, they began to pop. Stretching, pulling, straining, melting...

The nylon cord stretched thinner. The blue flame fluttered into yellow as the hard force of oxygen was shut off.

Mae took the last turn left and began to line up with the runway.

The Squirt started counting down. "Ten, nine..."

The blue cutting flame leaped through what was left of the cable. The weight of the overloaded van did the rest. The one cable snapped. The cable whipped through the pulleys in the boom. The chain slid down and around the roller bar and bounced on the tarmac as the van—still tied to the passenger side of the towing arm—slewed. The left front tire with the fresh breaks touched down.

With the last left turn, the weight of the van pushed hard against the turn. The front tire touching in a locked position forced the van to push harder.

Eleven tons of Mae West and Hooker felt the backend being pushed sideways for the first time. With all the towing of heavy trucks, he had never felt this. He thought to straighten the truck out, but in forcing the new turn, the rear tires broke traction on the smooth landing strips numbers. Mae slewed, and the step-van's rear tires howled as it was whipped around on the overloaded tires. The leading tire pinched as the weight transferred. The single-chain—still wrapped around the cables suspending the roller bar pulled the front corner. The van tipped toward where it was pulled and slammed into the back of Mae West.

Five of the nine green lights turned red. The clock still had four seconds left to count down. Twelve volts raced through wires to sixteen small blasting caps.

To the naked eye, Mae West disappeared into a fireball the size of Candlestick Park. The entire end of the airport became a boiling mass of red, orange, yellow, and black.

An explosion only takes less than a second to happen, but the expansion can take up to a few seconds to reach the entire area of the expanding gasses. Then, as the now vaporized air becomes a void, everything rushes back in, and the secondary concussion occurs.

In the first hundredth of a second, the side of the van was cut and opened up into shrapnel. The load of fertilizer split into two bombs. The upper freeload pushed its way out of the canister of the van and took most of the paint, rigging, and small items off the working bed as it passed at the eighteen-hundred miles per hour mark. The tiny bombs within the fertilizer exploded and ignited the larger mass. Unrestrained, the larger mass snapped the towing booms from their mounts and threw them back past the Guadalupe Parkway—three hundred yards away. Windows rattled as far away as the east side and downtown. Windows facing the airport became shard of glass buried in living-room walls and office cubicles as far away as a mile in any direction.

The lower half of the fertilizer had been compressed when the van snapped around and slammed into the working bed of Mae. Seemingly taking retribution, the small bombs within the larger bomb built up a static explosion. Once released, the rear half of the working bed, as well as the top of the van and armored wall, became flying shrapnel.

The armored wall became lances—turned the old DC-3 sitting out near the end of the runway for years—into a sieve. The holes punched through instantaneously, showing daylight as the two main landing gears were hit, and the whole plane flattened like a pancake to the ground.

Mae's tandem rear axles almost stayed together as they passed through a large control box across from the taxiway. The landing lights would have to wait while the whole was replaced. The new combined mass of metal, switches, gears, axles, and what was left of wheels and tires came to rest in the middle of the southbound parkway.

The tempered glass of the control tower did not stay inside the tower. The leading crystals hit the four men and knocked them against the far bank of desks. One died instantly when his head struck the edge of the desk and snapped his neck as the body passed under. The other made it through the explosion only to suffer the insult that comes at the end of a career of sitting and eating. The heart raced against the blood clot stopping the flow to the brain. The heart pushed harder against the clot, and the arteries exploded.

Everyone exposed on the airfield was knocked about and deafened.

In the silence—the music of tin and steel parts finally falling to the ground prevailed. It would take almost twelve seconds for everything to return to earth.

Four miles away, the trained ear knew the explosion had not occurred where he had left it. Felix kept walking. The train station was at least a thirty-minute walk away. He would stop for the bag in Sacramento. Seattle was two days away.

33

WHAT TO DO ABOUT MAE

Willie stood in the mud. He had been there before. If he closed his right eye and held his head just right—everything would look almost all right. *Almost.*

The back of Mae's sleeper had taken the brunt of the concussion. The custom ribbing to make the sleeper sound-proof had held the crushing box away from the cab. The spools of coiled cable had become ovals of heat-welded cable. Effectively, the cab and forward were salvageable—everything else was gone or soon to be.

"What you think, Mr. Knight... time to get a new truck? I have nice five-year-old Peterbilt. It has long frame. I make into max-weight tow truck for when doctors through with Hooker—again... this time."

Willie looked into the mangled and misaligned eyes of Mae West. If he had been dreaming, he knew she would be giving him a wink. There was no other machine like Mae. It may be true about it being what's up front that counts, but Willie had just had an idea of how to make it also about the rest of the machine. He turned with a shy smile and looked down at the Japanese woman with the false eyelashes.

"No new truck, but throwing her onto a new frame for a max-weight rig sounds good, and while we're stretching her, let's add some inches to the sleeper. Sometimes Hooker doesn't travel alone—thirty inches of sleeping space is a little tight."

The Fly looked at him with one of her more evil smiles. "That cat not that big."

Willie snorted. "You haven't tried to share a bed with him."

The Fly snorted. "Hooker or cat?"

———

TWO MILES AWAY, Hooker laid in one bed and the Squirt in the other. They were both sleeping thanks to large doses of painkillers and sedatives.

The nurse turned to the two students shadowing her. Her long braid whipped up and over her shoulder. Bobby Sue smiled at Candy and Holly. "At least, this time, they didn't end up with more metal shoved into them."

Holly blushed. "There're already enough scars."

Candy harrumphed. "Which one?"

The three chorused, "Both."

The blonde civilian adjusted her tight sweater. Beth smiled... she found the scars to be sexy.

SNEAK PEEK

A SOUTHSIDE HOOKER NOVEL

ONE DAY UNDER THE GRASS

CHAPTER ONE

If the girls had been a little younger, a little classier, a little prettier, and a little smarter, even as streetwalkers, they would work San Francisco or Los Angeles. But everyone has to be somewhere. Even in the night in downtown San Jose, there was a little something for almost any taste or preference.

The johns circled in their seven-year-old family cars—some too lazy to remove the child's booster seat from the backseat, others not caring. The color of their money and how fast they finished was everything to the girls.

The sidewalks were barely clean during the day. By night, the gutters collected fortified wine-laced puke, urine, feces, used condoms, and broken syringes, each a gemstone, jewelry of the broken dreams decorating the lives of those at the bottom, who only had lower to look forward to with each passing day.

The girls all knew each other, at least in passing. They knew who did what and who was really what or not. They all knew which block was theirs to walk. They also knew what was semi-clean to wear—and got the best responses—both in stops and spurts. They knew each other's names... most by their street names, some even by their real names. Some even shared cheap hotel rooms together—as the years, drugs, alcohol, and trade all took their toll.

The one female there night after night was the one who seemed least affected by it all. Pete, short for Petunia, worked but not in the sex trade.

The dirty blonde ponytail hung to her shoulders. The gray-blue uniform jumpsuit matched her one blue eye. The red-brown of the thread on her nametag—Pete—matched her other eye. The uniform was loose and baggy—even on the woman her size. Her large pendulous breasts swayed unrestrained in the suit — her work-battered hands raw, callused, and with ropey muscle. The muscles played like piano strings as her hands moved, guiding the three-wheeled West-coaster scooter, a dump bed on the back.

The mail carriers had the same scooter, but a shell protected them from the winter weather. Pete also knew, during the summer, the heat made the shells almost unbearable to drive in. The fiberglass shell also made them loud inside. Pete hated noise.

When she had originally gotten the job, she worked during the day. The noise and smell of the traffic made her almost quit. But, when a night shift came open, she begged for the job. By ten o'clock, downtown San Jose mostly slept—except the ten-block area where the girls walked.

Pete pulled the cart over to the curb in front of Original Joe's. Her eyes continuously moved. She took in everything around her. She once spotted a sparkle on the sidewalk, forty feet away. The streetlight had refracted through the stone—the diamond almost three and a half carats. The pawnshop traded it straight across for an eighteen-foot aluminum canoe someone had painted black.

The new concrete trash cans lining the streets of downtown had beauty tops. Pete found them to be an added annoyance. Every single can, she had to take the lid off, pull the liner up from between the concrete shell and the metal trash can, tie the bag off, and then lift and throw it into the back of her scooter. Then she had to lift the can out to put the new plastic bag liner on, stick it back in the concrete shell, and put the beauty top back on.

If anything was broken, she had to fill out a form to request the day unit come and replace the broken piece. Some nights she wanted to take the short pipe she carried for protection to the beauty top of every single one of the one hundred and fourteen trashcans.

The city-smart guys had mapped out her area and figured she could process one can every five minutes. This gave her plenty of time in her ten-hour shift to handle even the forms. It had not taken her long to figure out which cans were full, which cans were always only half-full, and even better—those which required changing once a week. Pete hated nosy people and hated worse those people who told her how to run her life or do her job.

The only manager who worked the night shift was under a truck or car in the garage. Pete knew him. Most of the night, he was asleep on the creeper. If he processed more than two or three vehicles in a shift, he had consumed too much coffee and needed to work it off. The paperwork was also pushed off onto the day shift. Pete had seen him rearrange the vehicles in the lot to make it seem like a lot was done—but mostly, it had been sleep.

With a boss like him, she didn't feel bad about how she did her job of collecting the city's trash.

Can after can, she moved methodically through the city. By ten o'clock, she was in the busy section with the working girls. This block was a quieter part on the north end. Pete knew the six girls who worked the block from Monday night to Saturday night. Her night off during the week had floated up and down from Tuesday to Friday. The one thing a woman in the city could never get was two days off in a row. Her boss never worked on Saturday or Sunday. One was sports night, and the other was the Sabbath. She was never sure what religion he claimed to be, so she didn't know or care which day was his religious day. Her lack of religion didn't matter—she got Sunday off because there wasn't enough garbage to collect.

Pete pulled the scooter to the curb. She turned the engine off and just sat looking down the street. Her eyes scanned the street, but a part of her mind was twelve hours and twelve miles away. The car pulled up at the end of the block—a 1960 Buick, four-door, a family man who should be using his money to buy better food instead of a blowjob on a Friday night. Pete could see the head of hair in the passenger seat.

Pete turned and opened the small utility box. Pulling her Roy Rogers lunch pail out, she got off the scooter and sat on the bus stop bench. The last bus was at nine-fifty. The next one would come just before dawn.

Her right hand reached into the back pocket of her overalls and withdrew the latex gloves. On the street, it was easier to put on clean gloves instead of finding somewhere to wash her hands. The leather work gloves lay on the seat of the scooter.

She opened the lunch pail and withdrew the thermos. She removed the top and set the cup down. Reaching into the lunch pail, she removed the sandwich and then the still cool can of cola. Prying off the pop-top, she dropped it into the can. Aside from the bubbles, the cola looked just like coffee when she poured it into the cup. Chugging the last of the can, she pitched it into the back of the scooter.

Pete pulled the sandwich out of its baggie and leaned back. Taking a bite of the sandwich, she chewed slowly and waited.

The footsteps were light, but the sound of how the heels thudded on the sidewalk disclosed the exhaustion. Pete knew the woman was only a little over five feet tall and wore a size four dress. The extra padding and breasts helped her fill out the stretchy dresses she liked. From the back, she was alluring, but her face showed her age and drug abuse. The woman was well past her street prime—but had nowhere else to go.

"Hi, Pete..." The voice was a little girl but was husky from age and alcohol.

Pete looked up at her. "Oh, oh, hi... um... Star. How are you?"

The woman came around and plopped mid-bench. Her sigh deep and mournful, she replied, "You know... same old same old."

Pete took a bite of her sandwich and slowly chewed as

she leaned back on the bench and nodded. She nudged her chin at the scooter half full of bags of garbage. "Picking up for me... how about you?" She looked over at the woman. Again, she thought about how the body package was great, but the face was just a hole in the package where someone had scribbled crayon over the face, drawing Groucho Marx eyebrows and the hint of a mustache. Even the eyes were slightly crooked.

"Two so far..."

Pete took another bite. *Hope springs eternal.* Ten o'clock—the woman's chances of one more blowjob tonight were between slim and never going to happen. Two or three ten-dollar blowjobs a night was what the woman averaged and lived on. She shared an eight-dollar room with another whore who used it until midnight. The services she offered didn't work well in the front seat of a car.

"I don't know, Pete..." The woman sighed deeper as she looked up and down the almost empty street. "Sometimes, I just want to lie down and just never wake up."

"That's kind of a depressing thing to say..."

The whore looked at Pete. "It just doesn't matter anymore—my prince is never going to come and sweep me off my feet. Watch..." She saw a few cars coming. She hooked both thumbs in the stretchy top of her dress and pulled it down and under her teats. She sat back with both hanging out with no bra.

The three cars passed without so much as a head turned. The two women watched as the taillights flashed bright red for half a second when they got to the end of the block where two hookers with long legs and not much else but a smile stood.

Pete looked back at Star. The whore was pulling herself back in her top. "See... nothing."

Pete thought a moment and then pulled the flipper on the rubber stopper of the thermos. She pulled the stopper out and passed it over to the woman. "Here, you can have the rest of my coffee. I'm not going to finish it." She held up her red lid-cup.

Star took a sip. "It's a little old, but it tastes good after the last guy. I swear... I don't know what the hell people eat these days. His sperm tasted like a bad poop in a goat barn."

Pete continued to eat. She didn't want to know how the woman knew about goats—much less the taste of the animal's poop.

The occasional car drove past. Pete sipped on her soda and finished her sandwich. She reached over and carefully picked up the thermos where it had fallen on the bench. She poured out the remaining warm coffee and cyanide. She packed it in the lunch pail with the baggie.

Pete put the pail back in the utility compartment. Turning, she took the beauty lid off the concrete trash bin and pulled up the plastic bag. She tied off the half-full bag, pulled it out, and placed it on the end of the bench. She pulled the metal can out, inserted the new bag, and then put the can back into the concrete shell. Replacing the beauty top, Pete pressed her hands against her back and bent backward, stretching her sore back—as she looked around. The street was empty.

Bending, she pushed her shoulder into the dead woman's gut. She was lighter than Pete thought. She stood, took two steps, and tossed her into the area between the carefully arranged bags of trash. She reached and grabbed the other bag and tossed it on top.

Sliding down onto the seat of the scooter, she glanced at the large watch on her wrist. It had taken almost twenty minutes less than she had planned on. She turned the key and pushed the silver button. The scooter chugged and shuddered to life. Pete put the scooter in gear and eased from the curb. Looking in the rearview mirror, she hung a U-turn in the middle of the empty block. At the corner, the traffic lights had just started to flash red. Moonrise was still an hour away. The temperature sign on the Woolworth's building read eighty-one degrees.

The tiny red taillights of the scooter disappeared up Stevens Creek Boulevard. The whore on the second corner thought it was strange for Pete to be heading north when Pete was usually working south at this time of night. The end of the cigarette swelled hot red as she took another drag. By the time she breathed the smoke out toward the street, a car was coming, and everything else forgotten.

THE MORNING SUN was only half up as the heat of the day started to rise. The barrel-chested man stood in the black aluminum canoe as he pushed on the long pole. The sea of tan grass slid quietly past him. He stood steady in the boat— he had been standing in canoes and pirogues all of his life. The Everglades in Florida, the bayous of southern Louisiana, the sea of grass in the South San Francisco bay, all of them to Lane were the same—grass above, water, and mud below.

Lane saw the world as night and day. The sky, grass, and

areas he moved in were day. The surface of the water was the demarcation border leading into the night. Lane remembered his mother telling him as a boy—when a body slides into the water, they are sliding into night. All the water in his life had been dark. His momma never lied.

He tugged at the binding bandage around his chest. He hated his chest. As a man, it betrayed him. The bandage helped flatten the shape, but at times, he felt like he couldn't breathe. He pulled the long-billed hat closer to his eyes. The shadow was dark, but in the early sunlight on the water, the reflection played in the blue and brown eyes. In school, he was teased about how he must be from Australia. Rarely did those mean children ever tease him again.

The canoe flowed on the freshwater river, which ran between the two saltwater marshes and grew full of salt grass and bulrushes. He knew what he was looking for, the area where the most crabs and ghost shrimp were—under the trestle. He tossed his head, and the short ponytail flipped off his shoulder and hung down the back of his neck to his shoulders.

He switched sides with the pole and started to turn the canoe into the grass. He looked up at the timbers of the trestle. He hadn't been to this spot since just after the New Year. He could name what was under the sea of grass—they had all been friends. Now they slept in the night of the water.

The back of his hands was ropey with muscle. He pulled back the trap. The woman quietly lay as if she were asleep.

Lane reached down and lifted the slightly built body to the edge of the canoe. Placing his left hand in the middle of the crossbeam, he lightly jumped the gunwale and stood in the shallow water and mud to just above his waist. The water wasn't cold, but it wasn't warm. He reached in for the body. Lifting, he turned and then slowly pushed the body under the grass and into the night of the dark water.

He watched the last of the legs and feet slip into the shadows and night. He whispered, "Sleep... Sleep well, Star."

ALSO BY BAER CHARLTON

Novels

The Very Littlest Dragon: NEW 2019 Editions
(Newly edited editions available: an all-new full-color ebook, a paperback with coloring pages, and a full-color Collector's Edition hardback)

Stoneheart
(Pulitzer Nominee 2015)

Angel Flights
What About Marsha?
Pirate's Patch
Dry Bridge of Vengeance

—

Southside Hooker Series

Death on a Dime – Book One
Night Vision – Book Two
Unbidden Garden – Book Three
Boomtown – Book Four
One Day Under the Grass – Book Five

Southside Hooker Series: Books 1–5 Box Set
(Collector's Edition hardback & ebook available)

—

Thorny Wallace Series

Death in the Valley – Book One
Light to Light – Book Two

BAER CHARLTON

ABOUT THE AUTHOR

BAER CHARLTON

Baer Charlton graduated from UC Irvine with a degree in Social Anthropology, monkeyed around for a while, and then proceeded onward with a life of global travel, multi-disciplinary adventure, and meeting the memorable array of characters he would come to describe in his writing. He has ridden things with gears, engines, and sails, and made things with wood, leather, and metal. He has been stitched back together more times than the average hockey team; his long-suffering wife and an assortment of cats and dogs have nursed him back to health after each surgery.

Baer knows a lot about many things in this world. History flows through his veins and pours out of him at the slightest provocation. Do not ask him what you may think is a simple question unless you have the time to hear a fasci-nating story.

You can find more about Baer at his website.
www.baercharlton.com

9 781949 316315